THE LAST DEMON

Dark Covenant Series Book 3

DEAN RASMUSSEN

DARK VENTURE PRESS

The Last Demon: Dark Covenant Series Book 3

Dean Rasmussen

For more information about this book, visit:

www.deanrasmussen.com
dean@deanrasmussen.com

The Last Demon: Dark Covenant Series Book 3

Published by: Dark Venture Press

Cover Art: MiblArt

Formatted with Vellum

❧   I   ❧

Tess spotted the pit through the trees and gasped. The moon's light reflected off the water's glassy black surface at the far edge of the quarry. It was there, just like everyone had said, like a gaping mouth ready to swallow them up if they dared to step too close.

It might try. The pit had claimed the lives of eight miners, their bodies never recovered after a catastrophic collapse decades earlier. Authorities had sealed up the quarry, and there were signs posted at every entrance warning trespassers of the dangers. It made no difference. They had found a compromised section of the fence and had crawled through easily. Nothing would stop them from getting a glimpse of the notorious pit. And they planned to do more than just get a look at it. They planned to descend into its bowels.

They were close now. Their flashlights lit up the area and reflected off the pit's surface. The moonlight peeking through the passing clouds provided a little light, but the overgrown trees blocked most of it. Summer was only weeks away, but the air was cool and jackets were necessary.

Jonah had volunteered to make the dive, despite the chilly temperature. He was one of those polar bear divers, the kind that plunged into the freezing water of a Minnesota lake in the middle of winter, wearing nothing but trunks and goggles. He was wearing a wet suit now, with his mask dangling around his neck and a flashlight in his hand. The look on his face showed he was ready to go—nothing but confidence behind those eyes. He lived for that sort of extreme stunt. As a top swimmer on the University's swim team, he thrived on it. Tess wasn't going to argue. She needed someone brave and strong enough to make the dive.

Stepping out across the quarry, Tess headed toward the incinerator first. She just wanted to get a look at the historic tower that had caught her imagination years earlier. Reaching it, she lit up the rusted metal mouth. The walls inside were still covered in soot, garbage, and the rotting carcass of a bird, but there was room to build a small fire.

She pulled out some crumpled newspaper and kindling from her backpack and added some dried twigs before trying to light it. Glancing at the others before striking the match, she shielded the flame from the breeze with her hand.

"If we can get this lit," she said, "it will help with our ritual later."

For a moment, the fire started. Then it died. A bit of smoke drifted into the air, some of it blowing back into her face. She coughed and swore under her breath, then struck another match and tried again. The kindling finally caught after a few minutes of working it, and the flames grew higher.

Through it all, Marcy kept glancing back toward the pit.

"You feeling okay?" Tess asked her.

"Yeah," she said. "I'm just a little sad, I guess."

"About your grandfather?" Tess asked.

She nodded. "It's just so strange to think that his body is still down there somewhere."

"Just think of this place as where he was laid to rest."

"I suppose."

After it was clear the fire wouldn't go out, they walked to the edge of the quarry and stopped. The pit loomed in front of them like a giant black mirror. Surrounded by shrubs and saplings, it was covered by a heavy, steel grate, but a section of it had partially collapsed, either through corrosion or vandalism or both. It was roughly twelve feet across, with an irregular oval shape, and sharp breaks along the edges mixed with rounded erosion.

Staring down into the water's infinite blackness, Tess couldn't help but be reminded of its tragic history. Nearly fifty years had passed since the collapse had shut down the mine for good. Eight miners, including Marcy's grandfather, had gotten trapped down there in the collapse, buried beneath tons of rubble. The shaft had filled with water before the crews could reach any of them, and eventually, the efforts to retrieve their bodies were abandoned. The pit became their grave, sealing them far below the surface.

The quarry had sat abandoned and neglected since then. A simple granite marker stood beside the pit's opening:

Here lie the souls of eight miners who died tragically on April 8th, 1927.

It listed the names in alphabetical order.

"We should start," Tess said.

Marcy nodded solemnly.

Derek paused. "Why is it flooded now? I mean... if it's a system of caves down there. What's keeping the water from draining away?"

"It does," Tess answered, "over years, even decades. It cycles between filling up and draining. Karst geology, runoff, and the cave system beneath us leave the area quite unstable."

Derek opened his mouth again but then closed it.

She turned to face Jonah. "Are you ready?"

"Always." He nodded once and set down the beer cooler they'd brought along. There was no beer in it now, but it would work perfectly to lift out the rocks from the pit. Opening it, he removed two fifty-foot coils of rope inside. Without a word, he looped one around the cooler's handle and tied it, then wrapped the other rope around his waist. He tugged on both when he was done.

"When you get down there," Tess said, "ignore the rocks on the bottom. That's all the debris from the collapse. Look for the opening. Remember the one I showed you in the pictures earlier. When you find it, go through there."

"The one that looked like teeth," he said.

She nodded. "That's it. Go in as far as you can and grab anything that looks interesting. And... don't get stuck."

He laughed. "I'll try not to."

"That's where they last saw the miners. The stones in that vein are the ones we're looking for."

"Got it."

Claire stood beside Tess with her arms crossed over her chest. She didn't go to college, but her parents ran a psychic parlor in Minneapolis. They'd met years earlier at the local library when they were teenagers, both of them fascinated with all things occult, and it hadn't taken any effort to convince her to come along. Claire just wanted to know if the stories were true about what was really at the bottom of the pit, just like the rest of them. And if everything went well, they would find out soon.

Derek was the first to dip his hand into the water. He leaned down and touched the blackness that rippled when his fingers broke the surface. He laughed and glanced at Jonah. "It's freezing, man. Are you sure you want to do this?"

Jonah dropped beside him, tested the water, then scoffed. "No problem. This is like a sauna compared to a frozen Minnesota lake."

"Well then, what are you waiting for?" Derek asked him.

Jonah didn't wait. He kicked away his sandals, slipped on his mask, and a moment later, he was ready to go. He wasn't shivering or complaining despite the temperature, and he turned back to Derek with a stoic stare. "After I'm in the water, hand me the cooler."

Derek double-checked the rope around Jonah's waist, making sure it was secure.

Jonah turned to them. "Let me be clear," he said. "Two tugs on the rope with the cooler mean to start reeling it in. Two tugs on *my* rope mean to start bringing me up, but if I keep tugging, it means to get me the hell out of there. Got it?"

"Got it," Derek said.

Jonah dipped his toes into the black water, switched on the flashlight, and glanced back at Tess. "How many rocks do you *absolutely* need?"

"As many as you can get," she said.

"Well, consider yourself lucky if I can get one. I just hope I don't find anything *else* down there." He glanced at Marcy, then looked away. "No disrespect to your grandfather."

"It's fine," Marcy said.

Jonah sat along the edge of the pit and sank his lower legs into the water. "So much trouble for a few rocks."

"They're not just rocks," she said.

"Demon rocks then," he said sarcastically.

"You're not going to back out now, are you?" Tess asked.

"Nah, this will be easy."

"I know you don't believe it, but after we're finished, you'll see that all this trouble is worthwhile."

Jonah nodded once. "Then I hope they're down there."

"They're down there." Her gaze narrowed.

"If you say so, but no matter what happens, you're buying the beer... even if I come up empty-handed."

"You won't come up empty-handed."

"We'll see." Jonah lowered himself slowly into the water up to his neck and then turned to Derek. "Just remember that I can hold my breath for a little over a minute easily, but if I'm down there for over two minutes, then you should start pulling up my rope, even if I haven't tugged on it yet."

"Got it," Derek said.

Jonah laughed and looked at each of them. "You're all crazy. You know that, right?"

"You won't think we're crazy before we leave," Tess said.

Derek dropped the cooler into the water. Jonah took it and pushed it down until the water spilled over the edges and filled it. A moment later, it sank into the depths, disappearing within the water's darkness. Tess held the other end of the rope, but Derek had tied both ropes around a massive stone nearby, just in case. Tess tugged on it, testing it for strength.

Jonah glanced down into the water. "I hope we go home with something more than just a worthless pile of rocks and a few laughs."

"Just go to the spot I showed you in the picture."

"Got it." Jonah adjusted his mask.

"Be careful," Marcy said to him.

He met her gaze. "It's only like thirty feet down. Easy peasy."

Tess checked the time on her wristwatch. At the same time, Jonah took a deep breath and then plunged beneath the surface.

The rope followed him. Derek let it out quickly at first as he descended until it slowed a few seconds later. Waves splashed and rippled against the pit walls, until the black water swallowed the light of Jonah's flashlight.

They waited in silence like that for what seemed like an hour, anticipating any sign that he'd made it or was at least on his way back up. Claire and Marcy joined Derek in holding Jonah's rope, with Tess alone holding the other.

Checking her watch again, a full minute had passed.

Nothing. No tugs. No movement.

Tess even flexed the rope to make sure it hadn't gone limp. Still nothing.

"Should we start pulling up?" Derek asked.

"Not yet," Tess insisted.

Claire touched her stomach. "I don't feel so good."

Marcy stepped forward and leaned over the water, staring down into it with a panicked expression. "Jonah? Oh my God, I don't see anything moving down there. I think we should pull him up now."

Derek tugged on it. "It's caught on something."

"Yes," Tess said. "There's a weight to it now."

Tess pulled, and Derek joined in.

"Has it been two minutes yet?" Marcy asked in a shaky voice.

"One minute," Tess said. "The cooler seems heavier now. He's got something."

"Pull him up!" Marcy called out. She was already pulling on Jonah's rope. "He's been down there long enough."

"Give him some time," Tess said. The rope jerked twice. "There it is! Give me a hand with the cooler."

It took all four of them to lift whatever was weighing down the rope. They reeled it in hand-over-hand until the top edge of the cooler finally broke the surface.

Not Jonah.

Just the cooler stuffed with stones. It scraped over the edge of the pit and crashed against the ground, splashing a bit of water with it.

Marcy draped herself over the edge of the pit with her face inches from the water. "Where is he? He's still down there!"

"He'll be up in a minute." Tess dropped beside the cooler and started inspecting the stones one by one. "Be patient."

Claire, Marcy, and Derek ignored her and pulled on Jonah's rope anyway. It was taut, but Jonah hadn't given the signal yet to bring him up.

"Pull!" Marcy cried.

They did. There was weight on the rope, but no movement.

Claire let the rope go and moved up beside the pit. Before anyone could object, she started to undress. She'd completely unbuttoned her shirt when the water broke open and Jonah's gasping face appeared.

He clutched at the edge of the pit. Marcy grabbed him first, balancing herself to keep from falling in with him. Tess joined her, grabbing one of his arms. They pulled him out of the water, and dragged him over the edge. A moment later he collapsed on the ground in front of them still clutching the flashlight in his hand. He was limp and shivering now but laughing.

"You all owe me a beer," he said.

"You'll get more than a beer," Marcy said, wrapping her arm around him.

Claire grabbed the towels they'd brought along and wrapped him in them. As he continued to gasp for breath, they helped him over to the fire from the incinerator and gathered around him.

"I'm fine." He shivered without releasing any of the towels and glanced back toward the stones he'd brought up in the cooler. "I got as many as I could grab. The light... didn't go far, and those suckers wouldn't budge at first. They were nearly impossible to break free."

Tess lifted one from the cooler and shook her head. "No, this isn't it." She couldn't see them well in that light, so she enlisted Derek's help in carrying the cooler over near the incinerator and placing it on the stone table they'd spotted earlier. She inspected another one, then another. Grabbing one of the larger ones, she scrutinized it closer. It had a sickly cream color with a coarse surface and lines like veins beneath a thin layer of skin. "Yes, *this* is it! It's amazing you found one. A miracle."

"It wasn't easy," Jonah said.

"I'm sure it wasn't," she said.

With Jonah leaning against the stone table near the incinerator, Tess moved on to the other rocks. Of the twenty-two rocks Jonah had retrieved, only five of them had the signature veins.

"Do you see what I mean?" Tess pointed to the veined patterns in the stone. They looked like twisted, screaming faces.

"That's weird," Derek said.

"Do you believe me now?" Tess asked.

"They *are* like little faces." Jonah flipped over one of the stones in his hands.

"That's just the natural rock patterns," Derek said.

"Not like anything I've ever seen," Claire added.

"And we should test them out," Tess said. "Let's do it here. Right now."

Marcy touched Jonah's arm. "Shouldn't we let him warm up first?"

"I'm fine," Jonah said. "I've been waiting all day to see Tess do her thing."

"Did you see anything else down there?" Marcy glanced back toward the water.

Jonah followed her gaze. "Like... bones? No, nothing like that. I'm sure the miners who died are buried beneath tons of rock. But... there *was* more down there. The opening went a lot deeper, but I ran out of air."

"You did well." Tess grabbed her backpack and unpacked her supplies. She'd brought along candles, matches, an old book of invocations that she'd stolen from the University's library, bookmarked for just that moment, and a small pocket knife.

Flipping open the knife, she placed it on the stone table with the blade pointing toward Jonah.

Derek frowned. "What's that for?"

"The ritual requires blood," Tess said.

"Wait. Do you mean *our* blood?" Jonah frowned.

"Is that really necessary?" Marcy asked.

"Definitely," Tess said. "We all agreed we would make this happen, right? This is the only way."

"You didn't say anything about blood," Derek said.

"How much blood?" Claire asked.

"Just a few drops," Tess answered.

"That's all?"

"That's it."

Jonah shivered and tightened the towel around his chest. "I'll pass. I did my part."

Tess stared at him for a long moment. "You're backing out? It's the whole reason we came here."

He shook his head. "You said you wanted my help to retrieve the rocks. That's all. Now it's your turn."

Tess turned to face Marcy. "You'll do this with me, right?"

Marcy glanced at Jonah and then back to Tess. "Can I just watch?"

Tess scowled. "I thought we were all in agreement on this." She turned to Derek. "What about you?"

He shook his head. "I'm not cutting myself on purpose for anyone, much less a demon. Of course, I'd love to see *you* conjure the demon."

She turned to Claire, glancing down at her friend's swollen belly. "Are you ready? This is everything you wanted, right? This is the only way."

Claire didn't hesitate, grabbing the knife and staring at it with a fiery determination. "I won't back down."

Tess grinned. "Good girl."

"Where do you want the blood?" Claire held out her upturned palm.

Tess grabbed the largest stone and slid it across the stone table in front of Claire. "Anywhere on this. As long as it lands somewhere on its surface, that's all that matters. Just one drop."

Claire slashed the knife across her finger a little too hard, and blood immediately oozed from the wound. Several drops dripped across the side of the stone.

"Perfect." Tess grabbed her book and recited the first line of Latin text in a loud voice. This was the invocation to get the demon's attention. She stared into Claire's eyes before continuing. "I need you to repeat after me."

Claire nodded.

Tess spoke the words with authority toward the stone.

Claire repeated them slowly, enunciating each syllable carefully.

There were only a few lines, but each one held a unique importance. When Tess finished, she nodded. "That's it. We're bound to it now."

Claire glanced around. "Bound to what?"

Before Tess could answer, the fire in the incinerator surged higher. The black water in the pit began to boil, and steam rose off its surface.

Thick black smoke, heavier than mist, rose into the air. The wispy shadow moved across the ground toward them like dark tendrils. It broke into two parts, one heading toward Tess, and the other toward Claire.

Marcy glanced back. "Holy shit."

Everyone watched it approach with wide eyes. Derek backed away, while Marcy and Jonah retreated to the other side of the table.

The smoky forms climbed Claire's body first. It engulfed her face, sweeping across her eyes, ears, and mouth. It was searching for something. A way in. It slid into her mouth, sweeping over her tongue with a freezing bite before forcing its way down her throat. The bitter stench made her gag. The cold flooded her lungs and stole her breath for a moment. She let out a cough, but nothing came out.

At the same time, the sound of cracking branches came from the darkness near the edge of the quarry.

Derek glanced around, and his eyes widened. "Someone's watching us."

"It's nothing." Tess turned her attention back to the smoke form that had started to move up her body next. She gasped when it reached her mouth, but she inhaled the darkness just like Claire. It was impossible to fight it.

"Are you okay?" Marcy rushed up beside Tess.

Tess nodded, but she couldn't speak. Not yet. The smoke still filled her lungs.

Glancing over at Claire, her friend's eyes were bloodshot, and her face was pale. Tess reached out and squeezed her hand. Claire squeezed back.

They each coughed a few more times before the fire in the

incinerator calmed down. The water went smooth again. Everything returned to normal.

Tess straightened. Something had shifted deep inside of her. She smiled at Claire.

Her friend smiled back and nodded. "Do you feel it?"

"It feels wonderful," Tess answered.

"No, I mean, Derek's right. Someone *is* watching us."

A moment later, a flurry of branches cracked behind them. Turning toward the sound, a dark figure burst through the trees. He had one arm raised and shouted at them in a commanding voice.

"Stop this! For God's sake, stop!"

❧ 2 ❧

Nora was preparing spaghetti for her family in the kitchen, but she kept glancing over at the brochure a local college sent at her request. She hadn't opened it yet. No time.

The idea of going back to college had always hovered at the back of her mind, but heading in that direction wouldn't be easy. Yes, they had a little money left from her father's inheritance, but after that she would need to take out loans. That was another problem. She'd heard all the horror stories of college students buried in debt after graduation. On top of that, she needed to help Ally with the family business. The parlor was doing better now after the renovations. It was providing enough income to keep them all afloat, along with Daniel's income.

For the first time in her life, things were finally stable.

Still, she couldn't shake the disturbing images of what had happened to Lucy in the quarry earlier that summer. The event still haunted her mind, day and night. She'd had enough of death and darkness and demons. She needed to head in a different direction. Somehow, she needed to escape her past.

Daniel had been gone all day. The school had called him in again to make some last-minute repairs, even though it was

Sunday. The overtime was great, but it was only temporary. Nora didn't complain.

She'd chosen to make spaghetti because it was fast and easy, but mostly because Lucy had requested it. The girl liked to dangle a noodle in front of Blanco occasionally and watch him swat it away with his paws. Watching her face light up and listening to her laugh at Blanco made it all worthwhile despite the mess.

Ally had spent the day with them. She was in the living room, sitting cross-legged on the floor beside Lucy. Just having Ally around took away the edge of the daily grind.

They were digging through a stack of boxes now. They'd pulled them from a closet near the back door.

Ally leaned into Lucy and gave her a little hug at the same time. "Are you excited for tomorrow?"

Lucy shrugged. "I guess."

"At least you'll get to see all your friends again. I'm sure you're tired of sitting around all day doing nothing."

"I wasn't doing nothing," Lucy said. "I helped Mom and Dad a lot at the parlor, and I made a lot of drawings. Remember?"

Ally laughed. "I remember. You're a regular Picasso. So, what grade are you in this year?"

"Fourth," Lucy answered with a straight face.

"Nine years old now and in the fourth grade. That's a big deal," Ally said. "Are you scared?"

"No." Lucy leaned toward one of the boxes. "I just hope they let me keep drawing stuff."

"I'm sure they will." Ally pulled the box a little closer and started sifting through more items.

They pulled out a pile of old papers and notebooks. These were all the things Nora had removed from Lucy's backpack the previous school year. How could she throw any of it away? The artwork, the doodles, the graded papers. It was nothing to cheer about, but somehow it was priceless.

Nora stirred the pot of spaghetti sauce and let it simmer on the stove while she set out the plates at the table. When every-thing was ready, she walked over to Ally and Lucy and stood beside them. Blanco was curled up beside Lucy, flopping his tail against her leg.

"What did you find?" Nora asked.

"Hidden treasure, of course," Ally said. "We're rich."

"I wish," Nora said.

Ally grabbed a small velvet pouch and opened it in front of Nora. Inside was a bracelet. It was made of silver but simple, with a soft, flowery design around the edge. "Well, look at this."

Lucy reached for it but stopped short of grabbing it from Ally's hands. "Can I see?"

Ally handed it to her.

Lucy slipped it on her wrist and moved her arm up and down, so it slid loosely back and forth.

"It's pretty," Lucy said.

"That used to be your grandma's," Ally said.

"That was Mom's?" Nora cut in.

Ally glanced back at her. "I let Lucy play with it a while back. Looks like it slipped into the box."

Lucy lifted her arm higher and examined it from all sides. "I forgot I had this."

Ally turned back to Lucy. "Do you remember your grandma at all?"

Lucy scrunched her face. "I remember she used to sing me songs at night and read me stories."

"What kind of stories?" Nora asked. "Anything scary?"

"Nothing scary. I don't remember the titles."

"That's okay." Ally dug deeper into the box and pulled out an old photo album. Flipping through the pages, the photos were taken in the months just after Lucy was born. Plenty of images showing Lucy in her stroller and Ally holding Lucy in her arms.

Ally pointed to Lucy in one picture. "You were so tiny. Do you remember that?"

Lucy giggled. "Of course not. I was just a baby."

"A little older than a baby." Ally stared into Lucy's eyes. "You know you've got your grandma's eyes, right?"

Lucy squeezed her eyes shut and glanced away. "I didn't take her eyes."

Ally laughed gently. "I don't mean you've *actually* got her eyes. It's just a figure of speech. I mean, you look like her."

Lucy cringed. "Just don't say that."

Ally tilted her head. "Why not?"

"Because Grandma's dead."

Ally reached out and touched Lucy's back. "Sorry, I didn't mean it in a bad way. I just mean you carry a little piece of her with you. It's our genetics. That's normal."

"I don't want to look like her," Lucy said. "I want to look like *me*."

Ally laughed softly. "I know what you mean. You look exactly like you, but you just happen to look a little like Grandma too. It's alright."

Lucy seemed to consider that while staring at the photos in the photo album. She pointed to a photo of Ally. "You kind of look like Mommy, too."

Ally glanced up and met Nora's gaze. "I suppose we do."

Lucy leaned into Ally. "I wish Grandma were here."

Ally kissed the top of her head. "Me too, kiddo."

Nora reached down and picked up the album. She flipped through the pages in silence, staring at the photos of her mother.

"She lived for her job," Nora said.

"She was committed to it," Ally said.

"I always wondered why she didn't choose to do something else. She was so smart—something you inherited." Nora grinned at her sister. "She could have done anything she wanted."

"We're not so different," Ally said. "For Mom, I guess she was happy."

Nora shook her head and handed the album back to Ally. "I'm not sure she was ever happy with her job. I think she was happy with *us*, yes, because that's all she knew."

"I miss her," Lucy said.

Nora forced a smile. "I miss her too, but let's not go too far down this road tonight, okay? We'll put these away for now. Aren't you hungry?"

Lucy nodded and then touched the bracelet. "Can I keep this?"

Nora nodded. "You can keep it, Lucy. Now, go wash your hands."

Lucy stood, and Blanco jumped away. Twisting the bracelet around her wrist, she slid it up and down her arm. "Can I take this with me to school tomorrow?"

"Definitely not," Nora said. "You might lose it."

Lucy frowned. "I won't."

"You can play with it at home... for now."

With a bitter nod, she turned away and charged upstairs to the bathroom. Blanco followed her.

"Sorry," Ally said. "I wasn't trying to stir things up."

"I know," Nora said.

Ally stared at the closed photo album. "Mom would be so proud of you."

Nora shrugged. "For what?"

"For everything you've survived, and now you're going back to college—"

"*If* I can afford it."

"You can't afford *not* to go. I know Mom would be thrilled with that decision."

"I suppose I have to," she said. "Things can't continue the way they are. Eventually, I think you should take over the family business. You can run everything. I'll step away as soon as I get my life on a different track. I'm not sure how proud Mom would be at seeing me abandon the family business."

"Maybe," Ally said. "Just give it some time. We were all traumatized by what happened at the quarry, and... poor Lucy. But she's doing great."

"I just..." Nora pushed back the emotional pain welling up in her chest. "I just think it's better that Lucy doesn't idolize Mom. She was far from perfect."

Headlights appeared through the window in the driveway. Daniel was home.

As she turned away and headed back toward the kitchen, Ally took her hand and squeezed it. "I won't pressure her to get into the business, if that's what you're suggesting."

Nora nodded. "I'm sure you won't."

"I just want Lucy to remember the good times," Ally said.

"Then let's give her some good times to remember."

$\text{❧} \quad 3 \quad \text{❧}$

Nora found herself standing outside in the quarry. It was dark, and the fire raged in the incinerator. Smoke was pouring from the top of the tower and gathering in the sky like a rain cloud.

She was alone except for one other person. Someone was standing ahead of her near the stone table where Tess had tried to sacrifice Lucy months earlier.

Her mother.

She was dressed in a black robe, expressionless, with her arms extended toward Nora. Instead of rushing toward her, Nora stood still and faced her. This wasn't right. Wasn't her mom... dead?

Before Nora could speak, her mother turned and walked the short distance toward the pit at the edge of the quarry. Nora followed her and stopped beside her when they'd reached the edge. Below them, the pit's darkness seemed to stretch forever into the earth. She could see all the way to the bottom.

Something down there in the darkness caught her attention. A section of the pit had collapsed. From that angle, the fractured rocks along the bottom looked like jagged teeth.

A form emerged from its mouth. Something twisting like a

trail of black smoke crawled out of it and moved out into the open. It hovered through the darkness until it shifted toward her. It had no eyes, or face, or body. Somehow, she knew it was watching her.

Its shape transformed into something almost human, even extending two shadowy limbs toward her, just like her mom had done earlier. It wanted to embrace her like a mother welcoming her child home.

At the same time, Nora's mother turned toward her and smiled. But something was off. The smile didn't reach her eyes.

Nora stepped back. Glancing back down into the pit, the thing had already made its way up the side. The shifting mass of shadows peeked over the edge and let out a guttural cry like a thousand screaming souls all at once.

Nora's mother leaned down and seemed to bow in front of it as it came up over the edge. She even reached out as if offering it her help.

"No, Mom!" Nora threw out her arm to stop her mother. "Don't!"

Her mother continued toward it without a pause and gripped its form. She strained to pull it forward.

It advanced and coalesced into something almost solid in front of her, but its form wavered like a smoldering ash-cloud trying to find its identity. The smell of decaying flesh hung in the air. Was this the demon she'd seen months earlier in front of the incinerator? No. It was different. This one was larger and stronger. She could tell that just by the way it moved. Unlike the other one, this one had been born from the pit, but it was still a newborn, and it would find its full potential...

With a little help.

Nora pulled at her mother's hands. "No! Mom, let it go! Don't let it out!"

Her mother ignored her, even resisted her, helping the beast as it stumbled forward into the firelight.

The thing held a dark and heavy energy. It hadn't yet developed the ability to move on its own in this world, but it would...

With a little help.

Nora fought to pull her mother away, to let the thing drop back into the pit. But her mother wouldn't let go. Instead, she grabbed one of its tendrils and extended it toward her.

Nora shook her head and stepped back further. "No. Never."

Her mother met her gaze, still embracing the tendril. It had wrapped itself around her chest, around her throat.

"Nora," she said, her voice full of sorrow.

And then Nora awoke with a gasp.

WHILE DRIVING LUCY TO SCHOOL THAT MORNING, NORA couldn't stop thinking about her dream. It was Lucy's first day of fourth grade, but the vision still haunted her mind. She hadn't spoken about it to anyone yet, not even Daniel. It had rattled her in a way that he might not understand.

Lucy was in the back seat with Blanco in his carrier. They were both staring out the window, Lucy with a worried look on her face and wide eyes.

"Are you nervous?" Nora asked.

Lucy nodded.

"You'll be fine."

Lucy had brushed her hair for nearly twenty minutes that morning and then had also brushed Blanco's hair. They'd been inseparable all summer, and now the two of them looked like the best of friends in the back seat.

But the dream.

It came back in waves and flooded her mind at odd moments. Sometimes, it took all of her strength to focus on staying present in the moment. The dream had done more than just rattle her—it had shaken her to the core. It had seemed too real.

The images were coming back again now. Her mother and that thing rising from the pit. Pushing her eyes closed for a moment, Nora forced herself to push away the images. It was just a dream, she reminded herself.

The line of cars turning into the school parking lot was longer than she remembered. The sidewalks were filled with parents walking their children to school. A police officer was even directing the traffic at the intersection where they turned up ahead. That was something new. More families *had* moved into the area.

When she finally arrived at the corner to turn into the school's parking lot, the police officer held up his hand, and she stopped. A steady flow of children and parents passed in front of her car heading toward the school. At the same time, something else caught her attention. Someone was waving at her from the other corner. A familiar woman gesturing for her to come forward.

Her mother.

She was dressed in the same black robe from the dream. There was no mistaking that it was her. Despite the glass and the car's engine, she could even hear her mother's voice calling to her in a gentle tone. "Nora..."

The police officer's whistle snapped her out of it. He stepped toward her car, glaring at her while waving her forward frantically. All the pedestrians had passed. She had the green light. She was holding up traffic.

Nora pushed the gas a little too hard while going around the corner, nearly hitting the car in front of her. Taking a deep breath, she clutched the steering wheel and glanced back at Lucy in the rearview mirror. Her daughter was staring at her from the back seat. Nora smiled, but Lucy didn't smile back. Her little face showed a bit of fear and... pain?

"Mom?" Lucy said.

Nora met her gaze in the mirror again. "Yes, honey?"

"I don't feel so good."

Nora studied her daughter's face for a moment. "What's wrong?"

"My stomach hurts."

The pained look on Lucy's face stabbed at Nora's heart. Had she upset her daughter with her reckless driving? She forced a smile. "I'm sure you're just anxious about your first day back. It's normal."

Lucy glanced down. "It doesn't feel normal."

Nora considered the other possibilities. Lucy had eaten breakfast that morning, so she couldn't be hungry already. Was Lucy getting sick?

"Feel your forehead," Nora said.

Lucy put her hand up to her forehead.

"Is your forehead hot?"

Lucy shook her head. "My head isn't sick. It's my stomach."

"I understand, honey," Nora said. "Listen, you'll feel better after you get into your classroom and see all your friends again."

"None of my friends are in my class this year."

Another stab to the heart. "You'll meet new friends."

"I don't want new friends," she said.

"You'll be just fine, honey," Nora said. "Your friends are there, even if you don't see them all the time, and you might even see Daddy. He's working at the school again this year."

Lucy didn't answer.

Nora circled the parking lot with the other cars and finally came to a stop in the drop-off zone out front. A student aide came over, opened the door, and helped Lucy out of the car.

"Everything will be okay, honey," Nora said.

Lucy nodded and then glanced at Blanco before shutting the door.

Nora had no time to watch her daughter walk all the way to the school's entrance before the teachers standing on the corner started urging her to keep moving.

"Move forward," they said over and over while making wide gestures. "Don't stop."

Nora followed their directions and found herself back out on the street moments later. Glancing at Blanco in the rearview mirror, he was looking at her.

～

NORA ARRIVED AT THE PARLOR A SHORT TIME LATER AND PUT Blanco in the break room that had become his home away from home recently. She found Ally near the front desk, talking with someone on the phone. Her sister had already flipped over the "OPEN" sign on the door and switched on the lights. Everything was ready to go.

A moment later, the first customer of the day stepped through the door. She was a silver-haired old woman in a lavender dress. A new customer, but something about her looked... familiar. Maybe it was the way she parted her hair on the side and... her smile. She had a sweet, vulnerable smile... like Nora's mother.

And then it all came flooding back. The dream flashed through Nora's mind. All of it—the sounds, the smells, the horrifying vision of that shadow thing coming toward her—came rushing back.

"*Nora.*" Her mother's voice filled her mind.

It was so clear.

For a moment, Nora couldn't focus on the old woman, couldn't hear what she'd said or even see her face. It was her mother standing in front of her now, wearing the same black robe she'd worn to the pit in her dream.

Ally was staring at her while talking on the phone. She looked nervous.

The vision faded a moment later, leaving Nora's mind blank. What was she supposed to say to customers again? She couldn't think straight.

"Nora?" Ally's voice broke her out of it.

Nora shuddered. "I... I'm sorry."

"I'm here for my reading," the old woman said with a nervous smile.

Nora's mom was gone. It was just the old woman in front of her now. A sweet old lady with a curious stare. Nora glanced back at her sister.

Ally ended the call abruptly and rushed over. "How can I help you?"

The woman looked at each of them before answering. "My name is Amber Johnson. I'm here for my nine o'clock reading."

"Yes." Ally nodded. "We're ready for you. I can take you back now."

The woman stepped confidently toward the back room. After she passed, Ally leaned into Nora and whispered, "Are you okay?"

Nora rubbed her forehead. "I had a nightmare last night."

"Do you need some... time?"

Nora understood what her sister meant. Did she need some time away from the parlor to calm down?

Nora shook her head. "I'm just... a little frazzled. I'll be fine."

Ally met her gaze for a moment and then grabbed an item off the front desk—something she needed for her psychic reading— her glasses. She touched Nora's shoulder before leaving.

After they were gone, Nora took her place behind the front desk and tried to focus on the computer screen. She had to work through the invoices and inventory, but the words seemed meaningless at the moment. Something had clouded her mind like the smoke that had crept out of the pit in her dream. She wanted a long break, but there wasn't time. If she didn't stay on top of things, they'd fall even further behind.

Forcing herself to focus on the information in front of her, she continued her work.

You're going to be just fine. It's just because you had the dream with... Mom. It wasn't real. None of it was real.

She took another breath and continued typing.

And then the phone rang.

She shuddered at the sound and glanced at her phone's screen. The school.

Daniel sometimes called from there, using the school's phone instead of his own, but most likely it was an automated message reminding parents of some upcoming event.

She answered it. "Hello?"

Instead of Daniel or a recording, a woman spoke in a solemn tone. "This is Principal Ashford from Maple Valley Elementary. We have your daughter Lucy here in my office."

Nora's focus instantly snapped back, and her heart beat faster. "Is she okay?"

"Well, she's okay... but you'll need to come to the school right away and pick her up, I'm afraid."

"Why? What happened?"

"I'm afraid... she bit another student."

❦ 4 ❧

Lucy clutched her pencil. Her stomach churned. She couldn't remember ever having been this nervous at school. Not like this. At least no one was staring at her.

"Good afternoon," the teacher said from the front of the room. "I'm Mrs. Anderson. I'd like each of you to introduce themselves. Please stand, say your name, and tell us one interesting thing about yourself."

Mrs. Anderson had a warm smile, but that did little to calm Lucy's racing heart. Lucy shrank into her seat. The thought of talking about herself in front of everybody terrified her. They would laugh if she made any mistakes. And she *would* make mistakes.

The boy on the left side of the room stood first. He was just a few chairs in front of where Lucy was sitting. Her turn was coming soon.

How could she get out of this?

There was no way out.

A tall boy with bushy blonde hair and a puffy black shirt helped to block her from the rest of the class, but she couldn't hide forever. Shrinking further into her chair, Lucy avoided the teacher's gaze.

The first student finished.

Another student stood and spoke.

Lucy's heart raced, and her chest ached. The student sitting beside her in the next row glanced over with a curious expression. Another boy with blonde hair. He had a mean face.

She frowned. *What are you looking at?*

Staring forward again, she could see him staring at her from the corner of her eye.

Go away! Just go away!

The students in front of Lucy stood and spoke in turn. Each time, she turned her gaze toward the window. She didn't want to think about it. Talking in front of others was worse than any nightmare. Outside, the line of trees near the edge of the property swayed in the breeze. The leaves were still green, but some of them were starting to turn brown. Soon, they'd all dry up and fall to the ground, and it would be too cold to play outside.

She just wanted to run outside and play. Run and run and run some more until she was gone.

Thinking about going outside slowed her heart a bit until the tall boy in front of her finally stood and spoke. He had a loud voice and made everyone laugh.

Her heart pounded.

She would be next.

She glanced around at the other students. None of the faces were familiar. None of her friends from last year were in her class. She was alone. They'd all been assigned to other classes.

This sucks.

Nobody to talk to. The thought of starting over was only making things worse.

The boy in front of her kept talking. He wouldn't stop. It didn't matter though, because she wasn't listening. Her stomach hurt too much to focus. He was saying something about the Mall of America, and then he made another joke. Everyone laughed again.

Everyone except Lucy.

The boy's voice made a strange, crackling sound when he spoke. The words were distorted and drawn out like crunching through dried leaves.

Couldn't anyone else hear it? It was getting louder, but they just kept laughing. Why were they laughing?

The noise intensified, and Lucy gripped her pencil tighter.

It snapped in half.

The pieces dropped onto her desk. She grabbed one of them and cracked that one in half.

She wanted to cry. She wanted to scream or throw up. If she could, she would.

More than anything, she wanted to go home.

And then, silence.

She was next.

The boy in the next row glanced over at her again. He grinned.

He stared directly at her, and he didn't look away.

Stop it! She screamed at him in her mind. *Why are you staring at me?*

He was looking down at her broken pencil and her trembling hands.

But then his grin faded. His smile vanished. His eyes widened.

At the same time, something inside her chest exploded. She couldn't breathe. Darkness filled the edges of her vision. It crept in from the sides as if someone were closing a curtain.

Her arms were suddenly warm and wet, and they itched. Glancing down, everything was red. She was still clutching the broken end of her pencil in one hand, but now she was scraping it down the length of her arm from her elbow to just below her wrist.

She did it again.

And again.

Blood seeped from the gashes, and a satisfying chill swept through her. The rich color seemed to shimmer in the light coming in through the window. The way it flowed across her skin and dripped onto her desk in front of her seemed almost... beautiful.

Mesmerizing.

The boy in front of her turned around to face her. He gasped. At least he'd shut up.

After the boy had stopped speaking, some of the other students had started clapping. Lucy clapped too—hard—even though her hands stung.

Hallelujah, he was done.

The room went silent. Even the teacher stopped talking.

Thank God.

Silence.

And then someone cried, "Oh my God! What... what are you doing?"

It was the creepy boy sitting next to her. He'd shoved his chair back and had nearly fallen over.

Yes. Get away from me.

She watched him scramble away from her. He was staring at her in a different way now. His eyes were full of horror.

The boy in front of her was staring at her with... pity? Ridicule? Had he made a joke about her?

"Stop staring at me!" Lucy finally screamed.

But he didn't look away.

Before she could stop herself, she jumped out of her seat and leapt onto his back.

"Stop staring!" she screamed again.

Her nails scraped across his shirt and dug into his shoulders. Lurching toward his head, she opened her jaws as wide as they would go and bit down. Her teeth landed in his hair and scraped across his skull.

It drew blood. The warm fluid filled her mouth. It tasted like iron and salt.

He let out a panicked cry and tried to shake her off, but she held on.

The class erupted in screams. A flurry of chairs rattled and scraped across the floor. Her classmates scattered toward the door.

Lucy held on as long as she could, but the boy finally threw her off. She landed on the floor on her back, staring up at the ceiling. Her head ached, but she laughed.

Mrs. Anderson rushed over and held her down. She was shouting to the other students in a panic, but most of them were already gone.

Lucy continued to thrash and kick under the weight of the teacher's body. She couldn't help it. They were playing a game. A fun game, and she'd won. She smeared some of the blood from her chin across the teacher's white blouse. She did it on purpose, just to see it soak into the woman's fabric.

"Lucy, stop!" Mrs. Anderson cried. "What's gotten into you? Oh, my God!"

The sound of wild animals rumbled through her chest and throat. Terrifying screams. All of them came up and out in deafening waves.

And someone was crying. The boy she'd attacked was still in the room. He was watching everything while clutching his bloody scalp. The blood dripped through his fingers and across his face.

The screams echoed across the room, rising to a piercing climax, and then stopped.

The darkness faded at the same time as waves of pain surged through Lucy's body.

"What..." Lucy groaned and winced within the pain. "What happened?"

When she finally lifted her head and glanced around, the classroom was empty. The other students were gone. Mrs. Anderson had pinned her to the floor. The woman's eyes were wide, and her face was full of terror. She was crying. The tears dripped onto Lucy's face.

A tear pooled at the corner of Lucy's mouth, mixing with the blood.

Lucy smiled... and licked her lips.

$$\text{❦} \quad 5 \quad \text{❦}$$

When Nora walked into the principal's office, her chest tightened. The room was full. Daniel was sitting in a chair next to Lucy. A police officer was leaning against the wall in the corner, a nurse in scrubs stood beside Lucy, and a middle-aged woman smiled sympathetically with her arms folded over her chest.

An older blonde woman in a navy-blue blazer was standing in front of the desk. She stepped forward when Nora arrived and greeted her with a firm handshake. "Mrs. Vale? Thank you for coming so quickly. I'm Principal Hatrick."

Daniel turned his gaze to Nora, but he wasn't smiling. His eyes were full of concern, but also a bit of anger.

Lucy was staring at the floor. Her right arm was covered in bandages. Nora rushed to her daughter's side and dropped in front of her. "Oh, my God! What happened?"

"We're trying to figure that out," the principal said. "Lucy had some sort of disagreement with one of her classmates, and she... bit him."

"*Bit* him?" Nora tried to look into Lucy's eyes, but the girl wouldn't look up. "Lucy, what happened? Who did this to you?"

"According to the witnesses," the principal said, "she did it to herself... with a pencil. Then she proceeded to bite the other student."

None of it seemed real. The conversation, the bandages. How could something like that have happened? Touching the bandages with her fingertips, Nora couldn't help but imagine what lay beneath them. Lucy flinched but stayed quiet.

"I've cleaned up the wound, but the cuts are deep," the nurse said. "She may need stitches. I was about to call an ambulance, but since Daniel was already here at the school, he offered to take her."

Nora nodded slowly. "Can I... see?"

"Of course." The nurse stepped forward and bent down in front of Lucy while pulling back one side of the bandages.

Nora leaned closer. Several marks ran down Lucy's arm. The larger gashes were parallel and even. Had something clawed at the girl? But then there were smaller cuts too. Some of them curled into loops.

The nurse covered the wounds again. "The other student was taken to urgent care, as a precaution, but he'll be okay. Fortunately, the child's thick hair prevented more serious injuries to his head."

"His... head?" Nora glanced at Daniel and turned back to Lucy. "I don't understand. What's going on here?"

"We're trying to figure that out," the principal said. "This is completely beyond anything Lucy's done before. That's why we suggest she undergo a psychological evaluation to see if there are any underlying issues."

"She doesn't need a psychological evaluation." Daniel's jaw tightened. "She's not crazy."

"It's just a recommendation at this point," the principal said. "I just want to be clear about her future at the school. This can never happen again. We can't allow students to behave like this."

"Well, we certainly don't encourage this type of thing." Nora raised her voice, maybe a little too much. "Is that what you're insinuating?"

"I'm not insinuating anything." The principal held up a hand. "But somehow, you need to take steps to make sure that nothing like this ever happens again."

"She's never done anything like this before. Never." Daniel shook his head. "You're acting like she's some sort of criminal."

The police officer stayed silent, still leaning against the principal's desk.

"I'm not suggesting any such thing," she said, "but she'll need to stay home for the rest of the week. This is a serious matter."

"She's suspended?" Daniel asked. "What did the other student do to provoke her? They must have done something really messed up for her to act like this."

The principal nodded, but in a way that suggested she was just trying to calm him down. "We'll be collecting information from the other student after he returns from the hospital. In any case, this is unacceptable behavior. According to one witness, they were sitting a few feet apart, and Lucy suddenly lunged at the other child without provocation."

"The other boy," the teacher finally spoke up. Her voice wavered. "He was standing in front of Lucy, answering my questions when she lunged at him while his back was turned."

Daniel turned back to face Lucy. "Is that true?"

Lucy looked up for the first time, her eyes full of tears. "I... I don't remember."

"What *do* you remember?" Nora asked.

Lucy shook her head, her face full of genuine sorrow. "Nothing."

Nora stared at her daughter for a long moment. "You must remember something."

Lucy shook her head again. "I don't remember, Mommy. I was waiting for my turn to talk. I was scared to stand up in front of everyone... and then I woke up on the floor with Mrs. Anderson on top of me."

Mrs. Anderson spoke up. "I was forced to restrain her."

Lucy extended her bandaged arm. "It hurts, Mommy."

"We'll get you to a doctor now," Daniel said.

Nora shook her head. "I can't believe any of this."

"Nor can we," the principal added. "But you'll need to take her now. We'll need to record the incident and suspend her. We'll also require her to talk with the school counselor on a weekly basis after she returns, just to evaluate her."

"Someone must have provoked her." Nora shook her head again. "She's never acted like this. Someone must have done *something*. Someone bullied or teased her?"

The nurse shook her head too. "By all accounts, Lucy lunged at the boy without provocation."

"Still," the principal said, "we'll look further into the matter."

The police officer finally stood with a sigh. "It's important to take steps now, while she's young, before things get out of control."

Daniel stared at him incredulously. "What are you saying? That she's some sort of monster?"

"No, sir." The officer straightened. "But it's important to get her some help to address this sort of behavior."

"This sort of behavior..." Nora shook her head. "None of this adds up."

The nurse stood and held out a tube of cream, turning it so Nora could see the front label. "I put some of this on her cuts to help with healing. The doctor will almost certainly provide a prescription, but you should add some every few hours to keep the wounds from scarring. It will also help with the itching."

Nora's face warmed. How was any of this possible? It all felt like a horrible dream.

She accepted the bottle of cream from the nurse and stepped toward the door. Daniel nudged Lucy to stand. She did, then leaned into his side while clutching her wounded arm.

"I'll take her to the doctor," Daniel said to Nora.

"I'll do it," Nora said. "I know you have to get back to work."

Daniel hesitated but then nodded and gave Lucy a hug. "You'll be okay."

Lucy stepped over to Nora, a fresh wave of tears filling her eyes. "I'm sorry, Mommy."

Nora embraced her. "We'll talk about it later."

"On the way out," the principal said, "you'll need to sign something. There's an envelope. It'll be at the front desk. Let me know if you have questions. She can come back next Monday, assuming there are no more concerns."

Nora turned away and headed back toward the front desk. Lucy clutched her waist all the way. They didn't speak a word, not even after Nora signed the papers and received copies.

After they were outside, Nora finally spoke on their way to the car. "You really don't remember anything?"

"I'm sorry," Lucy said again.

"It's not your fault," she said. "I'm sure... it's not your fault."

Lucy went quiet again until after they climbed into the car. With the doors shut, she spoke in a soft voice from the back seat while staring down at her arm. "I remember one thing, Mommy. I remember... I liked it."

⚜   6   ⚜

Ally had just finished cleaning up after the last client when Nora and Lucy arrived at the parlor. Her sister wasn't smiling. Not a good sign. As soon as they came inside, Lucy picked up Blanco and bolted past them without a word toward the break room.

After she was gone, Ally turned back to Nora. "How'd it go at the school?"

Nora placed her purse on the front desk and glanced back toward the hallway before speaking in a whisper. "They told me she bit someone."

It took Ally a moment to process what her sister had just said. "*Bit* someone?"

"I didn't believe them, at first," Nora said. "But after we had a talk in the car on the way home, I know she did it. I just can't imagine what could have caused her to do such a thing."

Ally glanced back toward the break room. "I can't either."

Nora shrugged. "I'm sure she'll talk about it more when she's ready. Maybe someone was teasing her? Who knows?"

"That's... weird."

"I know. And the worst part is that she bit the boy in the *head*."

Ally's eyes widened. "Oh, my God."

"It's hard to believe, especially for her. Something must have really set her off. You know she's never acted like this before. The school suspended her, of course, for the rest of the week. At least, they didn't escalate it."

"She's only nine."

Nora squeezed her forehead while closing her eyes for a moment. "I don't know what to do. Should we get her a psychologist?"

Ally struggled to answer. The idea that her sweet, harmless niece had done such a thing still seemed surreal. It was impossible. "Sure, if you think that's what's best for her."

Nora took her place behind the desk and stared at the computer screen with a blank expression. "It doesn't make sense, Ally. None of this makes any sense."

Ally nodded beside her sister and then stepped away. "I'll talk with her."

"Sure."

The sound of Lucy's infectious giggles echoed through the hallway. Ally headed toward the laughter and stepped into the break room a moment later, closing the door behind her. Lucy was sitting on the floor with Blanco in her lap. The girl glanced up when Ally came in, smiled, and then continued playing with Blanco as if nothing unusual had happened that morning.

Standing by the door for a moment, Ally finally sat at the break table and watched them play. There was no sign of Lucy's aberrant behavior anywhere within that gentle innocence. Lucy caressed Blanco's paws, and he didn't seem to mind. They were like two best friends now, and the bond between them had grown strong.

Maybe Lucy just needed more time to adjust to school again —with the new schedule, the new grade, the new faces.

Only a moment later, Blanco let out a low growl and pulled away. He jumped out of her arms and headed across the room without looking back.

Lucy's smile faded, and she glanced down.

The mood in the room had suddenly shifted, so Ally went over to Lucy and dropped beside her on the floor. "Had a rough time at school today, huh, kiddo?"

"Yeah," Lucy said without looking up.

"You'll get through it. Whatever you did, I'm sure you had a good reason for it. Was the other kid teasing you?"

Lucy shrugged.

"It doesn't matter," Ally said. "We all get angry sometimes. It's just part of the learning process. If you feel you want to talk about it, or anything, just go ahead and speak your mind."

Lucy glanced up with watering eyes. "Am I evil?"

Ally swept her arm around Lucy's shoulders and pulled her closer. "Definitely not. Is that what you think? That you're bad?"

Lucy nodded.

"You're not," Ally said. "I've seen bad, let me tell you. But if you want to tell me anything—"

"Not right now."

"Sure," Ally said. "Maybe later. Anytime you want to talk, I'm here."

Blanco moved to a spot near the door and sat watching them.

Lucy got up from her seat and crawled toward him with a precocious grin.

"What are you doing?" Ally asked.

Lucy narrowed her eyes at Blanco. "We're just playing."

"He doesn't look too happy about it."

Lucy showed a coy expression. "He knows I'm just kidding."

"Maybe give him a break for a little while." Ally tapped the break table and gestured to it at the same time. "We'll find something else for you to do. Have a seat. I'll get you something."

Lucy groaned but stood and sat at the table across from Ally.

Ally found a few sheets of paper and some crayons nearby. As soon as she placed everything on the table, Lucy picked up one of the crayons and stared at it.

"Don't you trust me?" Lucy asked.

"Excuse me?" Ally asked.

"This is a crayon."

"Yes..." Ally stared at it curiously for a long moment.

"You think I'm going to hurt you, don't you?"

"No." Ally met Lucy's gaze. The girl's eyes held something she'd never seen before. Hate?

"I'd like a pencil, please."

Glancing away for a moment, Ally found one and handed it to her. "I just thought you'd like to draw something with color."

"Black is a color. I like black."

Ally held back her thoughts. Instead, she leaned forward and stared into Lucy's eyes. Was there something different about her now? Something that hadn't been there yesterday? "Are you feeling okay?"

"Why?" Lucy started drawing without looking up.

"It's just..."

"You're scared of me."

Ally's breath paused a moment. "That's silly. I'm not scared."

"You are," Lucy said. "You're scared I'm going to do something crazy with my pencil."

Ally leaned back. "No. Don't say things like that."

"It's true. I can see it in your eyes."

Ally glanced back down at Blanco, who still hadn't come away from the door. Instead, he pressed his nose against it, then stared back at them with wide eyes.

Turning back to Lucy, Ally focused on the bandages on the girl's arm. They were still fresh, and what Nora had said about Lucy biting another student—in the head—was too horrifying to think about. "Did someone at school hurt you?"

"Nobody hurt me." Lucy continued drawing circles that filled the paper, swirling loops that grew darker near the center. "I hurt myself. Didn't Mommy tell you that?"

"She did," Ally said. "I'm just concerned about what happened to your arm."

"I cut it."

"Why would you do something like that?"

"I wanted to."

"Why would you want to?"

Lucy shrugged.

Ally leaned forward again to get a better look at what Lucy was drawing. "It's dangerous to cut yourself."

Lucy laughed. "No more dangerous than sitting across from a girl who bit someone's head."

The comment sent a chill through Ally. This was wrong. Disturbed. Either something unthinkable had happened to Lucy at school or the trauma of the past had finally caught up with her.

"When did you start to feel like this?" Ally asked her.

"Feel like what?" Lucy said.

"Feel like hurting people."

"I don't want to hurt anyone, Aunt Ally." She spoke in a soft, sweet voice, but her eyes betrayed something darker behind them. She gestured toward the bandages. "It hurts, you know."

"I'm sure it does."

Ally waited for Lucy to say something else, but silence hung between them instead. She wanted to reach out and pull Lucy into her arms, to rescue the girl from whatever had polluted her mind, but she hesitated. She stared at the pencil's tip as it scratched across the paper.

You're right, Lucy. I am afraid of you. Afraid for you.

The pencil's tip cracked and broke off. Lucy glanced around the table, picked up one of the crayons—a black one—and continued drawing as if she'd forgotten everything she'd just said. Her smile—her *true* smile—came back slowly.

The sound of someone entering the parlor filled the air. Ally's next client had arrived early. She pushed through her fears and brushed the hair away from Lucy's eyes. "Are you going to be okay back here alone? I have to leave. I have a client."

Lucy nodded enthusiastically and finally looked up. The darkness in the girl's eyes was gone. "I love you, Aunt Ally."

"I love you too, kiddo."

When Ally stood, Blanco nudged his nose against the edge of the door. As soon as the door opened, he raced away toward the front of the parlor.

"He'll come back." Ally smiled sympathetically.

Lucy shook her head. "No, he won't."

Ally wanted to ask what she meant by that, but there wasn't time. She had work to do. Leaving with a strange tension in her chest, she greeted the client a moment later beside the front counter. Nora had already checked the woman in.

The woman's name was Tammy. A tall, thin Asian woman, with black hair obscuring one side of her face. A large hoop earring and thick makeup dominated the other side. She smiled during their greeting, but her gaze kept drifting toward the back room.

Ally didn't keep her waiting. "Follow me, Tammy."

Leading her back to the seance room to begin, Ally started her routine, and within a few minutes she had already gone through the process of connecting with the spirit world. It came easily now, but Lucy's words kept drifting back into her mind.

You think I'm going to hurt you, don't you?

Ally pushed the thoughts away. It was difficult enough to focus on Tammy's session. The woman had paid for a tarot card reading—nothing too difficult—but it was the client's first visit, and she wanted it to go well. Ally went through the cards one by one, revealing the woman's fortune based on which cards came up.

At one point, the Death card came up. It seemed to rattle Tammy, but Ally downplayed its significance, even brushing it off with a little laugh.

"It doesn't mean you're going to literally die," Ally said. "It can mean a multitude of things. The end of a toxic relationship, a transformation, or just letting go of an old habit."

Tammy seemed to accept her explanation, and Ally continued.

The reading took longer than expected, but she made it through to the end without a hitch. Only after she'd finished did someone interrupt them with a knock at the door. It had to be Nora, coming to remind her the session had finished—sometimes she went over the time without realizing it. But instead, a soft voice came from the other side.

"Aunt Ally?"

Lucy's voice.

Ally smiled apologetically to Tammy. "I'm sorry. My niece is home sick from school today."

"That's okay," Tammy said. "I've learned so much from you already. Thank you so much."

Ally stood, then Tammy, and they stepped toward the door. When Ally opened it, Lucy's beaming face stared up at them. Instead of moving aside, Lucy stood in the way, blocking the woman's exit.

Lucy seemed to study Tammy's face for a moment, then she burst out laughing. "My aunt is wrong. You're going to die soon."

❧ 7 ❧

Ally was helpless to stop the look of horror that spread across Tammy's face. The woman stared down at Lucy with bulging eyes. "What did you say?"

Lucy grinned. "You're going to die soon... in a most horrible way."

The woman started to tremble, and her face drained of color. She turned toward Ally with her mouth gaping. "What is going on here?"

Ally had no answer. "I'm... I'm so sorry."

Tammy didn't respond. Instead, she shoved past Lucy, clearly going out of her way to avoid touching the girl, and hurried down the hall toward the front door. Ally went after her.

"I'm so sorry," Ally called out. "She's just a child. She must have overheard us talking. Maybe she was trying to make a joke—"

"Do you see me laughing?" Tammy slowed near the front desk. "How could anyone say something like that?"

"I'm sure it's just a misunderstanding." Ally offered an apologetic smile, but it didn't seem to help.

Lucy had followed them but stopped at the end of the hallway. She watched everything with an expression of fear and confusion.

Tammy turned back and glared at her. "That's a terrible thing to say."

Lucy's gaze dropped to the floor, and she whispered, "I'm sorry."

"I'll talk to her." Ally stepped between them. "And I'll refund your money, of course."

"Keep it," Tammy snapped. She backed away, casting one last uneasy look at Lucy. "I don't want to spend another minute in this place."

Before Ally could say anything else, Tammy hurried outside toward the parking lot. Moments later, her orange car pulled out onto the street. It passed briefly in front of their parlor window before speeding away.

Nora looked at Ally and then turned to Lucy. "What just happened?"

"Lucy scared her away," Ally said.

"Seriously?" Nora asked. "Lucy, what did you do?"

Lucy stared up at them nervously. "I didn't do anything. Why are you looking at me like that? Why does everyone look at me like that?"

"Lucy, you just told that woman she was going to die," Ally said. "Why would you say something like that?"

"I didn't."

"You didn't mean it?" Ally asked.

"I didn't say it."

Ally studied Lucy's face for a moment. "You said it to her in the doorway just a minute ago. Don't you remember?"

Lucy shook her head. She was holding one of her drawings, but it was facing away from them.

Nora crouched in front of her daughter and grabbed her gently by the shoulders. "Oh, my God, Lucy. Did you really say that?"

"No, Mommy."

"But Ally heard you say something to that woman," Nora said. "What did you say?"

"I don't think I said anything."

"You did," Ally said softly. "Even if you don't remember it."

"You don't remember *any* of it?" Nora asked her.

Lucy shook her head again. "I was drawing in the back room, and I wanted to show you what I drew. And then everyone started yelling at me."

Ally stared into Lucy's eyes. Was her strange behavior somehow connected to what had happened at school? "Did you black out?"

Lucy shrugged. "What's a black out?"

"It's when someone doesn't remember what happened for a period of time. Everything's blacked out in their memory."

Lucy tilted her head. "I suppose..."

Ally and Nora looked at each other, but neither of them seemed to have an answer.

"You don't believe me?" Lucy's eyes watered.

When Ally hesitated, Nora spoke up instead. "We do believe you, honey. It's just hard to understand how a thing like that happened."

Lucy frowned. "Is there something wrong with me?"

"No," Nora said. "Nothing's wrong with you. But I think we might need to have someone else look at you."

"I don't want to go back to the doctor." Lucy covered her injured arm with the drawing.

"Not the same one as before, honey," Nora said. "We don't have to do that again. We'll need to see someone else this time."

Ally gestured to the drawing in Lucy's hand. "What did you draw, kiddo? You wanted to show us something?"

Lucy nodded and held up the picture in her hand. "This."

It wasn't like the ones before. There were no demons or flames. It was a simple pencil drawing, but Nora recognized the dark lines and patterns immediately. The image resembled the one from her dream. It showed a hole in the ground surrounded by walls of stone, which could only be the quarry. Smoke rose from the opening.

Ally looked into Lucy's eyes. "What does it mean?"

Lucy shrugged. "I just remember it."

"Have you seen it somewhere before?"

"A dream." Lucy waited for a moment and then turned away.

Ally turned to Nora. "Who should we call?"

"There's only one person—Father Tony. I'll call him and see if he can talk with us today." Ally turned away and spoke softer. It was better that Lucy didn't hear everything that she had to say. "At the very least, maybe he can steer us in the right direction. He should be able to tell us whether or not this is connected to what happened."

Nora's eyes confirmed she understood what Ally was alluding to. Maybe this was connected to what had happened at the quarry a few months earlier when Tess had almost killed Lucy. Some degree of trauma had certainly affected the girl, either PTSD or something darker.

"Impossible." Nora shook her head. "I'm sure that's in the past. She's done so well since then..."

A loud siren filled the air and grew louder. Fire trucks were on their way somewhere, but the noises crescendoed and stopped just a short distance down the street. More flashing lights and approaching sirens added to the chaos.

Lucy rushed to the front window and peered outside. Ally and Nora came up behind her. The traffic and pedestrians had come to a stop. Everyone was staring at something just out of view up the street. Rushing out the door, they joined a small crowd of curious pedestrians who had gathered along the sidewalk.

A swarm of police officers, EMTs, and firefighters were rushing toward a woman whose car had slammed into a telephone pole and caught fire. As far as Ally could tell, no other car was involved. Some of the rescuers were struggling to save the woman's life, but the flames were holding them back. One of them was reaching out to her through a broken window when a woman's scream filled the air. The engine exploded. Flames consumed the car a moment later.

The screams stopped.

Ally couldn't see the woman's face, but the car looked familiar.

Orange.

Tammy's car.

You're going to die soon.

❈   8   ❈

Nora was filled with relief when Father Tony arrived. She ushered him inside and closed the door behind them even before he had a chance to speak.

Nora greeted him with a hug. "It's so good to see you, Father."

"It's been a while." He smiled warmly and glanced at each of them. "I hope your family is doing well."

Daniel shook his hand. "Could be better."

Blanco emerged from the shadows a moment later and rushed toward the priest. Instead of stepping back, Father Tony crouched down and lifted Blanco into his arms, holding him like a baby. He whispered into Blanco's face, "Hello, my old friend. Are they treating you well?"

The cat purred and settled into his arms.

Father Tony stroked Blanco's fur a few times before placing him on the floor again and then turned back to Nora. "You said it was urgent?"

"I'm so sorry to call you on such short notice," she said.

He held up one hand while brushing away a few stray cat hairs from his black clerical shirt. "It's no problem at all. How may I serve you?"

"Lucy," Nora said. "She needs your help."

He glanced curiously toward the living room.

Daniel gestured toward the stairs. "She's up in her room. We tried to get her to come down, but she's... nervous, I guess."

"That's perfectly all right," Father Tony said. "After everything she's been through recently, I don't blame her. You said she wasn't feeling well?"

Nora swallowed. The father had brought a black bag with him, and she glanced down at it. "It's hard to explain."

He tilted his head. "How so?"

"She hasn't been herself lately," Daniel said.

His smile faded. "I'm sorry to hear that."

"It's hard to explain," Nora said. "Like I mentioned on the phone, her behavior..."

He nodded once and stepped forward. "I'll have a talk with her."

Nora led Father Tony upstairs. They found Lucy in her room, sitting at her desk. She was drawing circles with colored pencils and didn't look up when they came in.

"Lucy, honey," Nora said. "Father Tony's here."

She didn't respond.

Father Tony stepped forward but stopped short of getting close to her. "Hi Lucy, I haven't seen you in a while. Do you remember me?"

Instead of answering him, she pressed her pencil harder against the paper, making wide, exaggerated strokes.

"I had a chat with Blanco downstairs a moment ago," Father Tony said. "He's worried about you."

She stopped drawing but didn't look up.

He inched forward. "Blanco said you haven't felt like yourself lately. Is that true?"

After Lucy still didn't respond, Nora spoke in a soft voice, "We're all worried about you, honey. Can you please answer Father Tony?"

Lucy finally glanced over at him but didn't smile. "I remember you."

"Your mother said you had a little trouble at school," he said. "Is that correct?"

Lucy shrugged.

"Whatever you did," Father Tony continued, "or didn't do, I'm not here to judge you. I'm just here to listen and support you. Your mother said you bit one of your classmates. The boy sitting in front of you. Is that correct?"

Lucy shrugged again and continued drawing without a pause. "I don't remember."

"What *do* you remember?" He narrowed his gaze.

"I remember waiting for my turn," she said finally. "Mrs. Anderson was making us stand up and talk about ourselves."

"And then someone upset you?" he asked.

Lucy shook her head.

"Okay," Father Tony continued, "when it was your turn, did you stand up and speak?"

Lucy seemed to think about it for a moment and then shrugged. "I don't remember."

"So that's when you lost track of time?"

Lucy nodded.

"Okay, I see," he said. "I'm sure you were a little nervous waiting for your turn."

Lucy nodded again.

"Was anyone teasing you?" he asked. "Anything like that?"

"No," Lucy said softly.

"Maybe the boy in front of you had said something earlier that morning? Something mean?"

Lucy shook her head.

"Okay," Father Tony gestured to Lucy's arm. "I see you have some bandages on your arm. Did he injure you?"

Lucy shook her head again. "I cut myself."

"By accident?"

"I don't remember."

"Maybe that's a good thing," Father Tony said. "Some things are better left forgotten. What did you use to cut yourself with?"

"My pencil."

Father Tony winced and then nodded. "How do you know you cut yourself if you don't remember?"

"They told me."

"Who told you?"

"The nurse."

Father Tony leaned back and looked at Nora curiously. "She's been through a lot lately. The memory of what happened this summer will take a long time to heal."

"Do you feel this is something psychological?" Daniel asked. "Maybe PTSD?"

"From all I've seen," he answered, "that's my best guess."

Lucy stared up at them. "Am I going to hell?"

Her chilling words hung in the air between them for a long moment before anyone answered.

"No, dear." Father Tony inched forward. "I promise you're not going to hell. I've already blessed and sanctified you. Nothing can harm you now."

Lucy nodded and then started a new drawing. "Good."

Nora moved in next to her. "Honey, I'd like to show him your arm... under the bandages."

She extended her bandaged arm toward him. "Here it is, but don't hurt me."

"We won't, honey."

Nora gently peeled back the bandages to show Father Tony. The marks were still clear, although they'd scarred over a bit. They were still fresh, but at least the blood was gone and they'd started to heal. She peeled them back far enough so Father Tony could get a look at them, and then she stepped aside.

He examined the wounds for a few seconds in silence before his eyes widened, and his mouth dropped open.

"What's wrong?" Nora leaned forward.

"I... It's nothing," he said. "You say she cut this into her skin with a pencil?"

"That's what her teacher told me." Nora followed his gaze, staring at the wound more closely until a familiar pattern took shape within the inflamed lines. A spiral. It was the same symbol she'd seen in the dream with her mother. It was clear as day now. "Do you see it?"

"See what?"

Nora traced her fingers over the lines, careful not to touch Lucy's tender skin. "I saw this same design in a dream last night."

"Yes, I've seen it before," he said, "many years ago at the quarry. But I'm not saying it has any connection to anything. I'm just pointing it out."

Nora swallowed, and her heart beat faster. "What about the quarry?"

He held up his hand. "It's an old symbol. She could have seen it in any number of places while growing up surrounded by mediums."

Nora turned to Lucy. "Honey, I know you said you don't remember doing this, but... have you ever seen a pattern or a symbol like this in a book, or somewhere else?"

Lucy glanced at the wound and then shook her head. "No, Mommy."

"She must have seen it while Tess held her at the quarry," Father Tony said. "It must have been part of the woman's ritual. The image stuck in her mind."

"What does it mean?" Nora asked. "My mother showed me something like this in my dream. I remember it now."

"Your mother?" He pivoted to face her, and the color drained from his face. His eyes held a rising panic.

"Yes, she was leading me through the quarry toward the pit. I followed her all the way to the edge, and I could tell she wanted me to go down there into the darkness, but something... stopped me. And that's when I woke up."

His face tensed while pushing his lips together, and he stared down at Lucy's arm again. "It's nothing."

"Are you sure?" Nora asked. "If it's connected—"

"It's not." He shook his head. "It's not relevant to anyone anymore." He met her gaze for a long moment. He must have seen the helplessness in her eyes, because his expression softened, and his shoulders drooped as if surrendering. "Many years ago, Tess brought a group of teens with her to the quarry one evening. I heard about it when one of my parishioners confessed their plans, thank God. They went there with the intention of contacting things that are better left untouched."

"What sort of things?"

"It's all in the past now," he said. "There's so much superstition surrounding the quarry. Its history is notorious. They were... tempted to play with the occult, like many teenagers are, but I stopped them just in time. Before it got worse. I sealed it up. It's over."

"What did they do?" Nora leaned closer.

"I'd rather not go into the details, because it's not important anymore. It was a terrible mistake on their part, but I corrected it. They never went back—until recently... with Tess and Lucy."

"Then why would she cut something like this on her arm?"

He shook his head. "I don't know, but I can assure you that I stopped it in time. Everything is sealed away forever. I made sure of that."

Nora covered Lucy's wound again, pressing the bandages against her skin.

Lucy winced. "It hurts, Mommy."

"I'll put on a fresh bandage soon, honey, after the father is gone."

Father Tony was still staring at Lucy's bandages. "I'm afraid this is an unfortunate consequence of her traumatic experience in the quarry with Tess."

"What can we do about it?" Nora asked.

"Be patient," he said. "This too will pass."

Daniel shifted in place and frowned but stayed silent.

A sinking feeling spread through Nora's chest. His words were cold comfort. "But don't you think there's something more to this? I saw it in my dream, and she's not behaving the way she used to."

He swallowed. "I understand your concern. I can offer another blessing if you'd like?"

"Yes." She took a deep breath. "We appreciate anything you can offer, but... she's not *herself*."

He shook his head, and then stepped over to Lucy's bed with his black bag and opened it. "What happened with Tess in the quarry was certainly traumatic. She may need professional counseling."

"Will that... be enough?" she asked.

Father Tony dug out his cross and began to perform the blessing. "To be pragmatic, I suggest starting there. The healing process takes time."

Daniel shook his head. "I'm not sure more time is needed here. Please, look deeper. Don't you see it? There's something... off."

"Of course." Father Tony scrutinized Lucy a little closer but continued with the blessing. "I'll do all I can."

With the father's cross raised in the air, Nora caught sight of Lucy. The girl wasn't paying any attention or showing any reaction to what he was doing. She seemed quite comfortable in his presence. Maybe Father Tony was right. Maybe this was all just part of the healing process and nothing like she feared. Lucy was just struggling to make sense of the world again after such a traumatic experience. It would take anyone time to move past what had happened to her with Tess.

Father Tony's process took only a few minutes. When he was finished, he put everything away and offered a silent prayer with his eyes closed. When he opened them again, he turned to face Lucy.

"You're a brave girl, Lucy, and I feel your recent experiences will only strengthen you." He watched her for a moment and then turned back to Nora. "Please call me anytime, day or night, but I'm confident that all of this will soon be a distant memory."

"I hope so," Nora said. "Thank you, Father."

He nodded with a smile, closed his bag, and glanced around the room. His gaze stopped at Lucy's drawing. "Lucy, may I ask what you're drawing?"

She scribbled the circles faster now. "It's a hurricane."

"Yes." He smiled nervously. "I can see it now. That's the eye at the center."

When he turned away from her, Daniel gestured toward the door with a solemn expression. "I'll walk you outside."

"Thank you." He glanced back at Lucy one last time before leaving. "God bless you, Lucy. I will pray for you."

Lucy didn't respond. Instead, she tightened her grip on the pencil, pressing it even harder against the paper with her eyes blinking rapidly.

They left her like that, with her scribbling circles again and again with a growing intensity.

Nora followed Father Tony and Daniel out into the hallway, but she stopped before going down the stairs. Lucy was making noises now. Playful giggles or a tuneless hum coming from the back of her throat.

Glancing back, Lucy was still sitting at her desk. When she saw Nora was watching her, she turned toward her and proudly held up the drawing she'd made, gripping the top corners with her little fingers. A wide grin stretched across her face. Even from that distance, the image was clear now. Father Tony was wrong. The dark patch at the center of her drawing wasn't the eye of a hurricane. It was a deep hole. The same one she'd dreamed about.

The pit.

❧   9   ☙

When Nora stepped into the parlor the next morning, the bell over the door rang, and it startled her for a moment. The sound was different. Daniel had upgraded it to a newer bell, something a little louder, but she hadn't gotten used to it yet. It didn't have the same familiar charm that she'd come to expect when stepping inside their family business. She missed the old one. Something about it had always comforted her, in a way, a reminder that she was home.

Lugging Blanco's carrier inside first, Nora held the door open for Lucy, who trailed behind her. Instead of rushing ahead to greet Ally at the front desk, like she always did, Lucy kept her head down and said nothing as she hurried toward the break room in the back. She didn't even wait for Nora to let Blanco out of the carrier. That room had become her refuge over the summer, a place where she'd spent hours reading and playing with Blanco to hide from the chaos of the renovation. But now, Lucy seemed to use it as an escape from everyone—including them.

Ally had too, judging by the look of disappointment on her face. She'd also noticed Lucy's antisocial behavior. "At least she knows what she wants."

"She hasn't been feeling well all night," Nora added. "After Father Tony left, she barely spoke a word."

Ally glanced back toward where Lucy had disappeared. "Aw, she's probably just scared we're judging her for what happened at the school. I'm sure she feels awful. She didn't say anything else about it after I left?"

"No." Nora put Blanco's carrier on the floor and let him out. The cat immediately rushed toward the back room to join Lucy.

"Well, *something* must have triggered her to act like that," Ally said. "I'm betting that boy must have bullied her."

"I hope that's the case." Nora stepped toward Ally and lowered her voice. "I'm just afraid the quarry affected her more deeply than we realize."

Ally met her gaze but stayed silent.

Quarry.

The word hung in the air between them. It was the code word now for all the trauma Lucy had gone through at the hands of Tess. The girl had come back from the brink of death at only nine years old. She'd survived a nightmare no child should ever have to face, but she had seemed to recover since then. And until the incident at the school, they'd held out hope that she'd gotten through the worst of it, but how could anyone be expected to ever recover after such a horrible trauma?

"It'll take time," Ally said.

Nora scoffed. "Father Tony recommended the same thing during his visit last night, but that won't cut it. We can't play wait and see. After he left, Daniel and I had a long talk—a *real* talk. We both agreed that he wasn't telling us everything. Then I told Daniel everything about the dream with my mother, and he didn't try to brush it off. I could see in his eyes that he was listening with an open mind, that he truly believed me."

Ally smiled warmly. "He's gone through a lot too. It's impossible to ignore."

"He's certainly changed a lot recently, along with everyone else." Nora placed Blanco's empty carrier behind the front desk, out of sight from the clients. "Maybe it's better that she's here with us for a few days."

Ally nodded and glanced over at the clock on the wall. "The first client will be here soon. I wanted to talk to you about something."

"About what?"

Ally gestured toward the hallway leading to the apartment in the back. She had the same look on her face when she wanted to say something important—good or bad.

"What?" Nora glanced toward the front door. "The client is scheduled to be here in ten minutes. Shouldn't we be—"

"Never mind that," Ally said. "They can wait."

Ally led Nora past the break room, where Lucy and Blanco were playing on the floor just inside the door. Blanco glanced up at them as they passed. Lucy didn't.

Entering Ally's apartment, they crossed over to the kitchen table where Ally had laid out several old newspaper clippings. Without sitting down, she pushed one of them toward Nora. "Look at this. I found it mixed in with some of Dad's old things last night. I was planning to wait until this evening, but after what you said about Lucy... Trust me, you need to see this."

Nora slid the article closer. The headline immediately caught her attention.

UNHOLY DISCOVERY AT HOLLOW BEND QUARRY.

A chill swept down Nora's spine.

"This is from the '80s," Ally said. "A bunch of kids broke into the quarry, just like what Father Tony mentioned, and everything checks out. It says the police thought some vandals broke in, or maybe it was part of some local cult. Whoever it was, they left some graffiti and weird symbols on the walls, but... well, I'll let you read it."

Nora did. She scanned the faded black-and-white text of the newspaper article, although it didn't give much more information than what Ally had said. Still, just from the brief description, her stomach churned. She knew in her heart the identity of one of the vandals, even though the article didn't list the names. "This was Tess, wasn't it?"

Ally nodded. "I'm certain of it. But there's more." She grabbed a printed black-and-white photo and placed it between them. "I grabbed this off the internet. It's from an old high school yearbook."

The caption read:

Hollow Bend: The Art of Memory and Rebirth—Student Exhibition, 1983.

The photo was grainy and not very clear, but the woman standing near the edge of the photo stood out immediately.

It was their mother.

She was unmistakable, standing with a wide smile beside Tess and a few other students. They were in what looked like an auditorium, proudly displaying their table exhibit, along with a crowd of other students. Limestone sculptures sat on pedestals, tagged and organized. Nothing was clear from that distance, but some of them were abstract, and others more lifelike.

"Where did you find this?" Nora asked.

"Digitized archives online. From Mom's high school. They used limestone from the Hollow Bend Quarry for their exhibit. I cross-checked the dates. The exhibit happened two months after the break-in."

Ally grabbed another printed photo from the edge of the table and placed it above the first one. It showed a close-up of one of the stones. Someone had cut it open to reveal the veins. "Look at this. Do you see the pattern here?"

Nora focused on it a little more. It showed the same odd marks that she'd seen in her mother's dream. The same marks Lucy had cut into her skin.

"They called it 'The Stone That Screams,'" Ally said. "Do you see it?"

Nora nodded and tapped the photo. "This is exactly what I saw in my dream. But Mom and Tess? It's impossible to think they would have hung out together. That woman was—"

"Insane," Ally finished. "I know. It's hard to believe."

Nora shook her head. "No. Mom couldn't have been part of what happened at the quarry. We would've heard about it... at some point."

"I'm sure she wouldn't have wanted us to know. It wasn't something to brag about."

"Maybe she didn't actually go there," Nora said. "Father Tony didn't mention her yesterday when he talked about the quarry."

Ally shrugged and pulled out another printed photo. "Look at this one."

It showed another stone carved into the shape of a gargoyle or demon.

"This looks something like the statue we had," Ally said. "It's clear that she took this from the quarry."

"So this is part of some satanic ritual?" Nora asked. "I can't believe Mom would have taken anything that far—or been associated with it—despite her family owning the parlor."

"It is hard to believe," Ally said.

Nora glanced around the room as if she might find the answers hidden within the shadows around them. "Do you think Mom was trying to tell me something in the dream?"

Ally met her gaze. "I guess that's for you to answer."

The door creaked open, and Lucy's little head peeked around the edge. "A man is looking for you."

Ally's eyes went wide. "Oh shit, my client!"

Nora rushed over to Lucy and nudged her back into the parlor. "Thank you, honey. We'll be out in a moment. Please go back into the break room for now."

Lucy looked up. Her eyes were tired and... afraid.

"Is everything okay?" Nora asked.

Lucy looked at the floor, nodded, then hurried away without answering.

While Ally rushed out of her apartment, Nora forced her to stop for a moment. "I need to see it... for myself."

"See what?" Ally asked.

"The quarry. The carvings. The stones. Whatever's left. Mom was there. She was trying to show me something in the dream. She wanted me to find something."

"Nora," Ally said, "if there's still something *alive* down there —some dark energy, a demonic force—you know what happened last time."

The image of Lucy's wound flashed through Nora's mind. The idea that their mother had been involved in what had happened with the rituals at the quarry decades ago seemed impossible. But the dream had seemed almost real. It wasn't just Nora's imagination. Her mother had called to her—connected with her—on a deeper level, and it tugged at Nora's heart.

She had to go there to find whatever her mother wanted her to see, even if she had to go alone.

"After work," Nora said finally. "We have to go back to Hollow Bend Quarry."

❧ 10 ❧

Moments after the last client had left the parlor, Daniel stepped in. Nora glanced up from the front desk and met his tired face. His shirt was stained with dirt and grease—his usual appearance after working a long day at the school.

"Hey, babe," he said. "Everything alright?"

Daniel normally went straight home after work, but she had asked him to stop by the parlor today instead. She watched his face, trying to gauge his mood, and then smiled and nodded. "Everything's fine."

He looked at her curiously, then with a bit of suspicion, holding her gaze a little longer than normal. His expression changed when Lucy charged into the room. A broad smile swept over his face, and he crouched to her level as Lucy ran into his open arms. "Hey, I missed you, kiddo."

She laughed. "I did too."

Blanco strolled in but stayed near the hallway, watching all of them with his tail gently brushing the floor.

"How was your day at the school?" Nora asked Daniel.

"The usual," he replied, gesturing toward Lucy. "How's *she* been today?"

"A perfect little angel."

Ally stepped out of the hallway where she'd cleaned up after her last client for the day. Despite the day's busy schedule, her smile radiated warmth and vitality. She glanced at each of them and then joined Nora behind the front desk. "It's all ready to go in there for tomorrow."

"Were you really a perfect little angel today?" Daniel lifted Lucy in his arms. She squealed with delight.

"She's fine, Daniel," Nora said. "Just a little... quieter than usual."

Lucy laughed. "I wasn't quiet. I was busy."

"Busy doing what?" he asked.

"Playing with Blanco."

"Is that all you do? Play with the cat?"

She nodded and grinned. "But I miss my friends at school."

He pressed his lips together. "I'm sure you do, but it's just a few more days. You'll be back in class before you know it."

Lucy went quiet again, and all the joy of the moment seemed to drain from her face.

"Are you afraid to go back?" Nora asked her.

Lucy nodded.

"Just apologize again," Nora said, "and be super nice to everyone."

"I will," Lucy said.

"Everyone has bad days." Daniel kissed Lucy's hair, then gestured to Ally. "Help Aunt Ally close up the parlor so we can go home."

He stepped toward Nora with that same curious stare. "You look like you didn't get a good night's sleep."

"You do too." She smiled and glanced at Ally before turning back to Daniel. "There's something I want you to see."

"Uh-oh," he said.

"What do you mean, 'uh-oh'?"

"You've got that look on your face. Like you're about to drop something heavy in my lap."

"Well, let me just show you and get your opinion on whether or not it's heavy."

"All right, sure."

Nora lifted a folder off the counter and opened it in front of him. She'd prepared it just for this moment. It contained everything that Ally had shown her, everything they had found about her mother's involvement with Tess at the quarry.

She showed him the "Unholy Discovery at Hollow Bend Quarry" old newspaper article first and waited patiently until he finished reading it.

"What's this?" he asked.

She didn't answer. Instead, she flipped the page to the first photo. "And this. Look at the background."

Daniel leaned closer. "Some old news clippings. So what?"

"Just look closer." She pointed to one woman and then another. "That's Tess. And that's my mom, right there."

He leaned back and furrowed his brow. "Are you sure?"

"We're sure." Ally inched closer.

"I didn't know your mom—so she knew the woman that..." Daniel glanced over at Lucy, then forced a smile. "Lucy, why don't you take Blanco into the back apartment for a few more minutes. We need to talk about some business things."

"About Grandma?" Lucy stared at them.

"Yes, honey," Nora said. "We found some old photos, and we need to... sort them out. Can you please go play in the apartment for a little while longer? Can you do that for me?"

"I suppose," Lucy said. "Can I have your phone?"

Normally, Nora would shake her head. She didn't like Lucy using her phone—ever—but under the circumstances... and Lucy knew the answer before Nora said anything. Digging out her phone, Nora handed it to Lucy with a smile. "Yes, honey. Just for a little while."

Lucy accepted it and hurried away. Nora waited until the door leading to Ally's apartment clicked shut before continuing their conversation with Daniel.

"So your mom knew the woman who tried to kill Lucy?" Daniel asked.

"It looks like it," Nora said.

He thought for a moment, then dropped the paper. "Well, that's pretty messed up, don't you think? But thank God it's over. Tess—that psycho woman—is dead, and she'll never hurt Lucy ever again."

"You're right," Nora said. "She won't. But it's ironic that you said it looked like I hadn't gotten enough sleep because... I haven't. Remember that dream I told you about last night? The one about seeing my mother at the quarry? I can't get it out of my mind." Nora gestured to the folder of papers. "I said I thought she wanted me to see something there. Something important."

Daniel slowly started shaking his head. "I hope this isn't going where I think it's going, because the answer is no."

Nora sighed. "It was so *real*, Daniel. I need to understand what my mother was trying to tell me in my dream. I need to go back there."

"You nearly died there, Nora. Lucy nearly—" Daniel cringed. "Why go back to that place? You probably dreamed about the quarry because of what happened with that Tess woman. A traumatic experience like that takes a long time to process."

"That's why I need to go back there. I need to face the trauma again. One last time."

He kept shaking his head. "I'm sure it's locked up now, fenced off, especially after what happened there. Maybe they even installed cameras and alarms—"

"I have to see for myself."

"Is it *that* important to you?" Daniel asked.

"My dream was so vivid, like my mom was standing right in front of me," Nora said. "It's hard to explain."

He took a deep breath. "I don't think it's a good idea."

"I'll go with her," Ally cut in.

Daniel grimaced. "You've got your mind made up already, haven't you?"

"I do," Nora said. "And I'd like to go now, before it gets dark."

"Maybe we can talk about it over dinner?"

Nora shook her head. "Now."

"In that case, I'll take you." He faced Ally with a somber tone. "Would you mind watching Lucy and Blanco for an hour or so?"

Ally smiled warmly. "I'll be happy to."

"But we're only going to look around for a few minutes," Daniel added. "No digging or breaking into anything. If we can't get inside easily, or if there are cameras, then it's not happening."

"Got it." Nora nodded once. "But... it might take longer than a few minutes."

"You just want to look around though, right? That's the plan?"

"That's the plan."

Daniel glanced back at the parlor's front window. "We'll go now. There'll be some traffic, but we can take the back roads. I'm guessing we won't get past the front gate."

"I still have to try." Nora glanced back toward Ally's apartment. "I'll go tell Lucy. I'm sure she won't mind staying here a while longer."

Without saying another word, Nora walked back to the apartment alone. Stepping through the door, there was no sign of Lucy at first. A few lights were on in the back, but everything was still. Then came the sound of running water from the bathroom.

"Lucy?" Nora called out.

No answer.

She walked toward the open door. "Lucy, I have some good news."

Stepping into the bathroom, she found Lucy leaning forward in front of the sink. The girl's face was smeared with black makeup paint, and she was staring at her reflection in the mirror.

She was humming softly while pressing paint-smeared fingers into her cheeks and lips.

Nora's phone was lying on the floor. Had it fallen off the counter? A little water had splashed across its screen, but at least nothing was broken. Nora picked it up, wiped it off, and then slipped it into her pocket.

Lucy had also filled the sink to the top so that it nearly overflowed. If it weren't for the overflow drain near the rim, it would have flooded the room.

Nora's heart skipped a beat as she lurched forward and turned it off. "Lucy? What are you doing?"

The girl barely reacted. Instead, she continued to stare into the water as it slowly settled, the excess still flowing down the drain near the edge. "Mommy, it's deeper than it looks."

"Lucy..." Nora touched her daughter's shoulder.

The girl shuddered at the touch. She turned sharply as if awakened from a dream and faced Nora with wide eyes. "Mommy?"

"Yes... honey," Nora said. "What are you doing?"

Lucy glanced around, her face full of confusion, then looked down at Blanco. He was sitting at her feet, staring up at both of them.

"I..." Lucy stepped back from the sink.

Nora hit the drain stopper, and the water slowly started to drain, creating a vortex in the water. "You can flood the bathroom by playing with water like that. Where did you find that makeup?"

"In Aunt Ally's closet."

Nora recognized the old plastic grease makeup case—the same brand her mother had used for séances years ago. It was open, and the palette of colors was smeared together. Nobody had bothered to throw it out, but now it had fallen into the wrong hands. Tiny, mischievous hands.

"Sorry, Mommy." Lucy bowed her head.

"Just... don't do it again. I need you to stay here with Ally for maybe another hour or two. Is that okay?" Nora gestured to Lucy's face and hands. "You'll need to clean all of that off, understand? Your dad and I need to go somewhere for a bit. She can take care of you until we get back."

"Yes, Mommy."

"We won't be gone long, but Aunt Ally will need to give you a bath or something. Don't... do that again." She glanced back at the sink. The water had only drained halfway. It spiraled on its way down and let out a loud gurgle, like someone gasping for air.

Father Tony removed his collar and dropped it on the kitchen table. The day had gone smoothly at church—no more hectic than any other day—but he couldn't stop thinking about his visit with Nora's family. It gnawed at the back of his mind as he poured himself a whiskey with ice, took a sip, and tried to relax. His hands trembled. He'd been like that all day. And he knew why. He just didn't want to think about it.

Carrying his drink with him, he headed down the hallway to his home office near the back of the house. Stepping through the open doorway, he scanned an older section of his cluttered shelves. Near the bottom, there was a file box he hadn't touched in decades. Its label was faded, but he knew exactly what it contained.

Why had he saved it all these years?

For just such an occasion.

A shadow of a doubt had always lingered in the back of his mind. Now, it was front and center, and he had to deal with it. At least, if what he feared was true.

He set down his drink on the desk and pulled out the file box, blowing away some of the dust that had gathered across the top over the years. After carrying it to his desk, he opened the lid and stood in front of it. It was all just as he remembered, stuffed with file folders, loose papers, and notebooks. The smell brought back some of the memories. It was the smell of old ways and fear.

Lucy's words echoed in his mind.

Am I going to hell?

A chill went up his spine. Lucy's voice had held so much fear.

And Nora was hungry for answers. Her dream about her mother at the quarry had shaken him. She had seen something *real*, not just a dream—a vision.

"Our Father, who art in heaven," he whispered, making the sign of the cross over his chest. "Give me the strength to prevail."

Lifting out the first of the file folders, he went through them in order. Many were papers he never expected to see again—old church reports on the Hollow Bend Quarry incident, hand-written notes about the ritual and the symbols found at the site, and photos of the limestone figures showing the faint, unique markings on each of them that were characteristic of the unique vein someone had discovered in the quarry.

And then there were dozens of photographs of Tess and the other young adults involved, pictures of them at the church during better times. They were smiling, unaware of the dangers ahead and what they had unleashed that night.

The sights, the sounds, the smells—it all came back to him in waves. But he pushed the feelings away for now, choosing to focus on the documents in front of him. He had to make sure of something.

A doubt had gnawed at the back of his mind all day. It was a twisted kind of relief to finally have the time to go through everything, despite the painful memories. Somewhere down in those papers were the Latin phrases he'd written down and used during his rite. The words to stop them from completing their demonic ceremony. Despite his pleas, Tess and Nora's mother, Claire, had refused to stop. He had warned them over and over, but they had continued as if the whole thing were nothing more than a game.

Let's see how far we can push the priest before he snaps.

Digging out the contents, he went through each folder and notebook one by one.

Finally, he found it. Yes. These were the words he had written. All the information was prepared before their confrontation. He'd scrutinized it to make sure he hadn't missed anything...

But now, all the years of experience reciting Latin phrases, all his studies, revealed something that sent his heart racing. There was something incomplete in his rite.

He'd said all the words properly, but he hadn't said enough. He hadn't finished the rite properly. Panic swept through him.

The rite he'd performed at the quarry wasn't effective in banishing any demon, not like he thought. He had just sealed it away beneath the earth. He hadn't said any of the phrases to remove it, only to contain it in that place.

"God help me," he whispered. His hands trembled.

He hadn't ended it. Whatever Tess and Claire had brought to the surface, he had trapped it within that place. And now, everything that Nora had said about dreaming of her mother made sense.

The woman had come back to warn them of his mistake.

But why now?

Tess. Everything she had done at the quarry with the incinerator months earlier—all of it—flashed through his mind. The things Nora and Ally had told him about what had happened with the statue. It all made sense now. Its dark energy had weakened the binding. Weakened the seal.

How long before it finally broke through—like Tess and her friends had intended decades earlier?

Father Tony dropped into his chair and leaned back. He whispered a prayer, but his voice trailed off after a few seconds. He had to go back and finish what he had started.

The weight of the discovery pressed down on him, and he closed his eyes. The memories of that night flashed through his mind like an old home movie. He remembered stepping out of the trees, shouting their names. They had scattered in every direction. All but two of them had run away by the time he'd arrived at the pit.

Tess had remained, with her eyes wild and her hands gripping an old book. She kept glancing around in every direction as if something else were there with them. Had she seen something he hadn't?

Claire had also remained, but she'd backed away, folding her arms over her chest.

"Dear God, what are you doing here? Tess? Claire?" he had asked. "Is this how you were raised? You have no idea what you're doing."

"We know enough," Tess snapped. "What are *you* doing here?"

He didn't answer, but the moment he'd learned what they were planning, he knew he had to act. One of his parishioners had come to him that very morning, shaken and afraid, and had confessed their plans—one of the same young men who had fled as Father Tony arrived at the quarry. He had pleaded with the fearful young man, even then, never to take evil lightly. But he'd said Tess was determined to go through with it, and there was no reason to doubt him. Father Tony knew the young woman's stubbornness all too well.

He raised his crucifix into the air and thrust it toward them, as if that alone might scare them off. "You cannot stay! Go home now! GO HOME!" he yelled.

Tess only laughed. "We have every right to be here."

Something churned inside the pit. The water sloshed and splashed against the sides.

"What did you do?" Father Tony demanded.

Tess smirked. "Raise a little hell."

Claire pulled at Tess's arm. "Let's go."

A gust of wind blew through the area. It seemed to tug at Father Tony's jacket, nudging him back a few inches until he caught himself.

"Someone snitched on us." Tess turned to Claire. "Did you do it?"

Claire leaned back. "I didn't tell him anything."

Tess walked over to the edge of the pit and stared down into the water as it bubbled higher. "He's here anyway. You're too late, Father. He's already here."

"You don't know what you've unleashed," Father Tony said.

"I know enough. I hope he comes to get you," Tess replied with a laugh.

He closed his eyes and started to pray. The Latin came back to him—everything he had studied that day in preparation for this moment. Without that confession that morning, he would have never known. He shuddered to think what might have happened if he'd arrived even a minute later.

The commanding words flowed from his mouth, both in English and then in Latin.

"In the name of the Father, and of the Son, and of the Holy Spirit. In nomine Patris, et Filii, et Spiritus Sancti. Step back, unclean spirit. Vade retro, spiritus immunde."

Opening his eyes, he took another step toward the edge of the water and extended the crucifix. A searing heat rose from the pit and spat scalding steam in every direction. A burst of the hot water touched his skin, and in a blind panic, the crucifix slipped from his hand. It splashed down and disappeared in an instant. The water boiled higher, as if swallowing it up.

Father Tony gasped and stepped back. He would have to finish it another way. He closed his eyes again and recited the same Latin phrases over and over.

"You have no power here. Non habes potestatem hic. This ground is consecrated. Hoc solum sanctificatum est."

This was everything he could do to push back the demonic

forces, to neutralize the horrible mistake Tess had made by coming down there.

Children playing with the fire of hell.

Digging out a smaller crucifix from his jacket pocket, he held it out over the water in the same way, but squeezed it tightly. The boiling water splashed up again, burning his face and arms, but he held firm this time, without backing away.

He spoke the lines louder and louder.

"What sin opened, faith now closes. Quod peccatum aperuit, fides claudit."

Slowly, he opened his eyes.

Yes—that was it.

The water began to cool now. It seemed to settle a little more after every word. He continued reciting the words with renewed strength, until a silence filled the air and the water was a perfect sheet of glass that reflected the moonlight.

When he stopped, he turned to face Tess and Claire. But they were gone.

At least he had succeeded.

The memory of that night faded, and Father Tony opened his eyes with a gasp. The realization that he was in his office again—and that he'd been wrong all these years—pierced his heart.

There was still time to complete the correct rite, but after what Nora and Ally had described about Lucy, his mind reeled. How would he face the evil again after all these years?

"Lord," he whispered, "I failed you once. Let me not fail again."

❧ 12 ❧

When the front gate to the quarry came into view, Nora's heart sank. Getting inside wouldn't be as easy as she'd hoped. Not only had they put up a fresh barricade over the entrance, but they had also erected a new fence around the perimeter of the abandoned property. A large "Trespassers Will Be Prosecuted" sign hung prominently on the gate, along with a few smaller signs placed at regular intervals on the fence in both directions. The message was clear: Stay out.

Still, the wire mesh was bent in a few areas along the top—someone had already attempted to climb over it. It wouldn't be possible for them to do the same, except they had only brought along flashlights, and Nora doubted Daniel would dare to push things that far.

Daniel stopped the car in front of the gate, with the headlights beaming straight at the sign, and glanced over at her. "We can come back another time."

Nora shook her head. "We have to find a way in tonight."

He leaned forward in the driver's seat, craning his neck upward to see out the windshield. They had installed a new light at the top of the pole, which was now working and illuminated the area. "They might have installed a camera up there."

Nora peered out her side window. The trees and thick growth also posed a natural barrier against intruders. "There's another way in. The last time we were here, Tess had parked her car down near the river. There's got to be a back road somewhere."

"Either way, they've probably got that blocked too."

Nora opened her car door. "Then we'll have to find a way in."

Daniel switched off the engine and climbed out of the car too. After switching on their flashlights, he came around and met her on the other side. "Are you sure this can't wait until this weekend? Maybe it'd be better to stop by during daylight hours?"

"It can't wait." Nora hurried to the fence and peered through the chain links into the trees beyond it. She caught a glimpse of the quarry, the moonlight reflecting off the stones, and the memories came flooding back. Lucy, Ally, Tess, and Eve—their faces appeared clearly in her mind. Lucy had almost died that night. A chill swept up her spine.

Did she really want to go back down there and face it all again?

No, not really.

How would she handle the flood of emotional pain after arriving in that spot again?

The dream of her mother came back and washed away the fear. She *had* to go there. She had no choice.

She followed the fence into the trees, pushing through the brush and branches. The city had taken drastic steps to seal off the area this time. It seemed to extend forever into the darkness.

Daniel followed her, shining his flashlight ahead of them as the ground sloped a bit toward the quarry. As it descended, they searched for flaws or openings, while brushing away the mosquitoes that buzzed around their ears.

Daniel didn't complain, but he grumbled a few times. "We *could* ask the city for permission, you know. After what happened with Tess, I'm sure they'd grant us access to the place if we suggested it was to heal emotional wounds."

Nora nodded in the darkness but continued forward. "They might, but we wouldn't get full access to the place. At least, not where I plan to look."

"Where do you plan to look?"

"Under every stone, if I have to."

A short time later, Nora found what she was looking for. The ground dipped sharply between the fence poles in one spot, providing an opening just large enough for someone to crawl through.

Daniel turned his light to where she had already focused hers. "Looks like you want me to crawl now, don't you?"

"I'll be right behind you."

Daniel dropped to the ground and crawled under first, scraping his elbows and chest against the weeds and dirt until he came out on the other side. He lit up the area while Nora crawled under after him. In moments, they were both standing on the opposite side. She'd scraped the back of her jacket against the wire mesh, but it hadn't ripped, as far as she could tell. It didn't matter anyway. They were in.

Pushing through another wall of trees, they finally stepped out into the open. They'd arrived close to the river, and the sound of the water flowing filled the air.

"If we'd gone any further," Daniel said, "we would have had to swim."

Nora smirked at him in the darkness but kept quiet. The quarry was straight ahead now as they followed a bumpy terrain toward the old utility shed she'd seen on her last visit. Graffiti covered its boarded-up windows, and the city had posted even more "No Trespassing" signs for those who had made it past the first barriers.

Walking a little further, she finally caught sight of the pit she had seen in her dream. It was there several yards behind the utility shed. A fence circled the opening, but the same weathered cement barrier still covered it.

Glancing toward the incinerator, her gaze stopped at its

wide, open mouth at the base. The stone tower loomed over them as they moved toward it. Daniel's flashlight caught the opening. The infinite darkness inside it seemed to swallow up his light.

The stone table was there too. The sacrificial table where Tess had attempted to kill Lucy. A layer of dirt and bird droppings caked the top and sides. There were more stains along one side. Dark splattered stains. Blood.

Nora reached out and wiped her fingers across the cold stone. The dried bloodstains had survived the summer weather, but the harsh Minnesota winter would clear it all away. Still, the memories of what had happened that night would stick in her mind forever.

Daniel aimed his flashlight toward the incinerator, stepping toward it and leaning his head into the opening, peering up into the tower from the bottom. "This thing's... creepy. Why do you think she did it?"

"Get away from there," Nora said.

Daniel didn't argue. He backed away and stepped toward her again with a grin. "Alright, so let's find what you're looking for and get the hell out of here."

Nora stepped toward the pit, shining her flashlight around the perimeter. "Down there."

"What's down there?" he asked.

"I don't know... yet."

He followed her gaze. "You're not thinking of climbing down there, are you?"

Nora couldn't stop staring at the sealed opening. The dream of her mother flashed through her mind again. "Whatever my mother wanted me to find... it's down there."

"Not going to happen," he scoffed.

Nora spotted an opening on the other side, a section of the cement that had cracked apart. She hurried to it, dropped to her knees, and dug her fingertips into the crack. Pulling with all her strength, she shifted it until it gave way. The broken piece of stone cracked and dropped into the depths of the hole. A second later, the sound of it crashing against the bottom of the pit filled the air.

It didn't splash. It had hit something solid. Aiming her light toward the bottom, she could see there was no water inside, just a pile of rubble along the bottom.

"Would they have drained it?" she asked.

He stepped over and stood beside her, also shining his light into the hole. "It probably drained naturally. The stones are fractured, and the cave system in this area goes down a lot further than this."

The opening Nora had created provided enough space for someone to slip through, but the darkness below was daunting.

Daniel aimed his light down inside and then backed away. "There's nothing down there."

"She showed me," Nora said. "In the dream, my mother wanted me to find something. It's there."

He let out an exasperated sigh. "Do you have *any* idea what it is? Lost treasure?"

"I didn't see what it was... in my dream."

"Well, we didn't bring any rope." He swatted a mosquito on his arm. "And we planned to make this short, remember?"

Nora scanned the area, turning her attention to the utility shed. The door was locked with a large padlock, but the weeds were strewn with abandoned items. Boards, a sheet of rusted metal, and matted against the ground, almost obscured completely within the dirt, was an old, crusty rope. It looked more like a massive snake at first until she started ripping it away from the earth.

Uncoiling it, she gestured to it. "Do you think it's long enough?"

Daniel stepped over and lifted a section of the rope. It was crusty, stiff, and weathered with age. "This must have sat here for decades."

"Will it work?" Nora asked.

He worked with it, tugging at it and stretching it over the ground, until it caught on something in the darkness. One end was already tied to a rusted iron ring jutting from a limestone wall near the utility shed, secured with a tight knot. Daniel pulled at it with all his strength, but it held.

"It might work," he said. "*If* it reaches all the way to the bottom."

Nora took the rope from him. "I'm going down there."

He pulled it away. "No, you're not. There's no way I'm going to let you go down there. I've done some rock climbing. You haven't, but it doesn't give me a lot of confidence knowing that you don't even know what I'm supposed to look for."

"You'll know it when you see it," she said.

"That doesn't help," he said.

Dropping the rope through the opening, they watched the end hit the bottom. There was plenty of length.

"I feel we aren't the first ones to try this," he said.

"Do you think you can make it?" Nora asked.

"As long as I don't fall."

"Then don't fall."

He smiled and squeezed his legs through the opening Nora had created. "Here goes."

"Do you have your phone?" she asked.

He nodded and tapped his pocket. "Here." Holding the flashlight in his teeth, he descended into the hole, wrapping the rope around his waist and letting it unwind as he rappelled into the darkness slowly.

Each breath and movement he made echoed against the walls as he descended. Finally, his boots tapped against the rubble at the bottom.

"Ew." He took his flashlight from his mouth and scanned his surroundings. "This place stinks... Lots of dead animals down here."

The tale of the eight miners who had died in a collapse a

hundred years earlier popped into her mind. "Do you see anything else?"

"Like treasure or something?" he said. "Nope. There's nothing valuable. If your mother wanted you to find something here, she should have told you what to look for."

"Keep looking," she said.

"Beer bottles... cigarettes... an old shirt. Someone lost a base-ball cap—Minnesota Twins." He shook off the dirt and pretended to slip it on his head. "Fits me."

"Don't touch that awful thing."

He laughed and then tossed it aside. Turning his flashlight suddenly toward the lower section of one wall, he stopped. "Here's something. I think I found where all the water went, out through this hole." He stepped over the rubble and crouched near the opening.

Nora's heart beat faster. It was exactly the same as she remembered from her dream. "Look in there."

Daniel froze. "Holy shit."

"What?"

He reached for something near the opening and tugged at it. He pulled harder and then rubbed his fingers over it. The object glistened in his light.

"There's a crucifix down here. It's like... melted into the stone. How is that possible?"

"Can you get it?"

"No, not without tools. It's almost swallowed up by the rocks." He took out his phone and snapped a few photos. The flashes exploded through the darkness.

"Anything else?" Nora asked.

Daniel inched forward, his boots scraping through the rubble. He turned the flashlight into the hole again. "This thing goes down a lot further, but I can't see the bottom."

"Don't go in there," she said. "But do you see anything near the opening?"

He shone his flashlight in every direction. "No, but—"

He went silent, then he leaned forward and pulled something up out of the debris. It dangled from his hand.

"What's that?" Nora asked.

Daniel lifted it in front of his face and turned it over. "Oh, wow... I'll bring it up."

"What is it?" she asked.

"Just a minute." He slipped it into his pocket, along with his phone, and glanced around the area again. "I hope that was it. I'm definitely not coming down here again anytime soon. This place is really creepy."

He turned his flashlight toward the opening again.

After a few seconds of silence between them, Nora asked, "What do you see?"

He shook his head but kept staring. "Nothing."

"Tell me if you see anything else."

"It's nothing," he repeated. "This place is not right."

"I agree."

"Alright, I'm coming back up." He put the flashlight in his teeth again and pulled himself up a step at a time, using his feet for leverage. Dropping his flashlight along the way, he didn't stop to retrieve it. Instead, he climbed faster until he reached the top.

Nora grabbed his arm and helped to lift him to his feet. "Are you okay?"

"I—" He struggled to stand, then dug into his pocket and pulled out the item he'd found. "At least I didn't come back empty-handed."

He dropped the item into her hand. It was a pendant, still caked with dirt and grime. Brushing away a bit of the soil, she'd need more time to reveal the details.

"Something..." He shivered and glanced back down into the hole as he discarded the rope. His abandoned flashlight lit up the rubble along the bottom of the pit, pointed straight toward the opening he'd stood in front of minutes earlier. Digging out his phone again, he snapped a few photos of the opening and then put it away.

"Something wrong?" Nora asked.

"No," he said. "Nevermind."

"What's wrong?" Nora slipped the pendant into her pocket.

"That's... strange."

"What's strange?"

"It felt like something... pulling me down on the way up."

❧ 13 ☙

Shortly after Nora and Daniel left, Ally nudged Lucy toward the bathroom. "Alright, kiddo, let's get you cleaned up."

The girl didn't complain, and Ally led her to the bathroom, switching on the water in the bathtub. Blanco came in a moment later, right behind Lucy, but he stayed near the doorway as the tub started to fill.

"Are you mad at me?" Lucy asked nervously.

Ally laughed. "No, but it looks like you went a little crazy with Mom's old makeup, huh? Of course, I'm not mad. I was a kid too, remember? You were just goofing around. That's what kids do."

Lucy stepped beside Ally and stared into the tub as it slowly filled. Ally dipped her hand under the faucet to test the temperature—it wasn't too hot. She inspected the makeup on Lucy's wrists and fingers.

"I'm not sure it's all going to come off with just a bath, but we'll try. You might need to scrub at it for a while." Ally gestured to the edge of the tub where a few different bottles of soap sat. "Would you like some bubbles in your bath?"

Lucy smiled and nodded.

"We've got to make it fun, right?" Ally reached over and

poured some soap into the water. It immediately started foaming as the water hit the liquid. Instead of getting undressed for the bath, Lucy stood there, staring at the water as it flowed. Ally glanced back and stared into Lucy's eyes. The water seemed to entrance the girl as it poured from the faucet and exploded into a growing layer of bubbles.

Her little lips were moving. She was whispering something under her breath.

"Something wrong?" Ally asked her.

Lucy made no sign she'd heard.

Ally repeated herself. "Lucy?"

This time, Lucy flinched slightly and met Ally's gaze, though she remained silent.

"Is something wrong?" Ally asked again.

"No," Lucy said, with all the innocence of a precocious little girl.

"It's been a long day, huh?"

Lucy nodded. "Can I bring Blanco in with me?"

Ally shook her head. "That's not a good idea. You can save that mess for your mother at home." She laughed lightly. "I think we should just focus on getting you cleaned up tonight so your mom and dad can relax when they get back."

"Okay," Lucy said.

Blanco shifted near the doorway, pushing against the edge of the door. Ally glanced back at him, although he was staring at Lucy the entire time.

Turning her attention back to the tub, the water was almost high enough now, and the bubbles had spread across the top. Shutting off the water, Ally stepped back and averted her gaze to give her some privacy. "You should get undressed now and hop in."

Lucy didn't argue and began to undress.

Ally waited until the girl was completely in the tub and covered by bubbles before she turned back. As soon as Lucy sat in the water, the bubbles started rising around her. She immediately started splashing, raising her hands and letting the foam run through her fingers and down her arms toward her shoulders.

After only a few seconds, some of the makeup came off. Ally shut off the water and handed Lucy a sponge from nearby. The girl used it for a few moments, then started splashing again. Some bubbles and water landed on the floor near Blanco, and Lucy let out a little squeal of delight.

"I'm not sure he likes that," Ally said.

"It's okay," Lucy replied. "He plays in the tub with me all the time at home."

"Does he?"

Lucy nodded emphatically. "As long as I keep his head above water, he doesn't mind."

"Tomorrow we'll go to the store and buy you a paint set," Ally said, "so you have something fun to do while you're out of school."

"I'd like that." Lucy smiled.

She started washing off the ink from the girl's hands, even scrubbing. Ally tried to help, grabbing her hand in hers and scrubbing over the top and between her fingers.

"It's coming off," Ally said.

Then Lucy grabbed Ally's wrist. At first, the little girl's fingers tickled. Ally broke into a laugh and even played along, allowing the girl to tug at her arm for a few strained moments. But then she pulled with surprising strength.

Meeting Lucy's gaze, the girl's face had changed back to that same blank stare she'd had when she'd watched the water pour from the faucet. Darkness filled her eyes.

Before Ally could move back, Lucy yanked her forward. It might not have mattered, except the floor was slippery from the soapy water. Ally lost her balance and fell, nearly hitting her head on the far side of the tub. Instead, she curled forward and dropped inside the tub with Lucy.

Ally found herself flailing a moment later, facing up toward the ceiling, her back against the bottom of the tub. Her face hovered just a hair above the water. She gasped for breath within the soapy blur of the water. Her hands reached for anything solid to grasp. Lucy laughed as Ally tried to sit upright, splashing along with her as if the whole thing were a game.

"It's deeper than it looks," Lucy said playfully.

Ally's head throbbed from hitting the side of the tub. She struggled to stay above the water, but Lucy wasn't helping. Instead, the girl seemed to hold her down, almost climbing on top of her. Lucy's wild giggles filled the air, even as she struggled to push her away.

Rising for a moment, she gasped another breath before slipping beneath the water again. Panic flared. Her pulse thumped in her ears. Lucy's arms pressed down on her head. One foot still hung over the edge of the tub, but she couldn't catch her balance or get leverage to sit up. Water flooded up her nose.

Lurching forward with all her strength, Ally rose above the water and gasped another breath. "Lucy!"

Her muscles burned. Dropping back, the water covered her face again. Through the murky haze, Lucy was staring down at her. The girl's face was almost angelic and glowing while blocking the harsh bathroom light.

Ally struggled to turn on her side. If she could push up with her elbows, she could lift her face above the water. But Lucy pressed down on her shoulders and leaned into her.

It was almost like...

She was doing this on purpose.

Rising again, Ally took in another lungful of air and then went under again.

Her ears were plugged with water. Every desperate cry was muffled, but through it all came the sound of splashing and Lucy's laughter growing louder.

Ally couldn't breathe anymore. She couldn't scream or cry for help.

And Lucy wouldn't relent.

The dull thuds of Ally's arms hitting the sides of the tub echoed through the water. Again and again, she pushed at Lucy.

It shouldn't have been this difficult. Lucy was only nine, after all, and no more than sixty pounds. But there was something intentional about the way she lay across her chest...

Ally kicked her legs against the sides of the tub, but there was nothing to hold on to, nothing to help her right herself.

A scream filled the air. Not from Ally or Lucy. Someone else had stepped into the bathroom.

Nora.

14

"Oh my God, Ally!" Nora reached into the water, grabbed Ally's arms and pulled. She didn't pause until her sister's head was above water, but then continued dragging her out of the tub as water splashed around them.

Lucy laughed hysterically throughout the ordeal, continuing to play in the water, even as Ally crumpled against the bathroom floor. Ally was alive, gasping for breath and clutching at Nora's arms, but it was clear she'd come dangerously close to passing out. Her eyelids fluttered, and her eyes rolled in their sockets.

"Are you okay?" Nora asked.

Ally nodded weakly.

Spitting out some of the water, Ally gasped and coughed with each breath. Her head rolled lazily on her shoulders. The soap slowly drained from her face and dripped to the floor.

Nora dragged her sister across the floor and laid her out flat while keeping her head propped up and to the side. Water drained from Ally's mouth. She was still struggling for air, but at least she was breathing.

Nora stroked her sister's head and spotted blood beneath her hair. "You're bleeding."

Ally didn't answer. She coughed again, then finally took her first deep, uninterrupted breath since Nora had pulled her out. Ally inhaled slowly and let it out. She wiped her eyes with the back of her wrist, squinting while glancing around the bathroom.

Nora grabbed a towel from the floor, wiped her sister's face, and sat her upright. "Is that better?"

Ally nodded again.

Daniel came in a moment later. "What happened?"

"I think she fell," Nora answered.

He studied her for a moment, his face full of concern, then grabbed a towel from the rack and opened it in front of Lucy. "Time's up."

Lucy stood and wrapped the towel around herself. Instead of getting out, she stood in the water and stared down at Ally lying on the floor. "Are you okay, Aunt Ally?"

Ally didn't answer.

"I didn't mean to," Lucy said in a small voice.

"What do you mean, you didn't mean to?" Daniel narrowed his gaze on her.

"I thought she wanted to play."

Ally shook her head. "No, that's not right."

"What's not right?" he asked.

But Ally didn't answer. Instead, she struggled to sit up all the way, still trying to catch her breath. When she shifted her weight to the other side, it revealed a patch of dark skin under her arms —bruises.

"Do you need an ambulance?" Daniel asked.

Ally shook her head. "I'm just... I just need a minute."

Daniel turned to Lucy and helped her out of the tub. "Let's get you out of here." He walked her across the wet floor toward the door, stepping carefully around Ally.

When Lucy approached Blanco, he recoiled and hissed.

"Blanco," Lucy said to him. "It's okay."

Instead of moving toward her, he darted out into the hallway.

Lucy frowned. "I think he doesn't like water."

"Maybe." Nora turned her attention back to Ally, still propping her up.

Despite Daniel leading Lucy away, she stopped in the doorway and stared back at Ally. "It was just an accident."

"No," Ally coughed. "She pulled me in."

"What do you mean, she pulled you in?" Daniel paused beside Lucy.

"It sounds crazy, but—"

"You slipped and fell in," Lucy said with a sympathetic smile.

Ally shook her head. "No. She pulled me in. Forcefully."

"What do you mean, forcefully?" Daniel gave a confused expression. "She's only nine."

"I'm aware of that." Ally smirked and scrutinized Lucy. "But something's different with her. Can't you feel it?"

Nora couldn't lie—she *could* feel it. As soon as she'd stepped into the bathroom, there was something about the way Lucy looked at each of them. Even now, as she stood there in her towel, the water dripping down her shoulders, there was a deviousness in her eyes, like she was hiding something.

"Is that true?" Nora asked Lucy. "You pulled her in?"

Lucy's eyes widened. "I didn't, Mommy!"

Nora met Ally's gaze, and it was clear in her sister's eyes— Ally was telling the truth. A wave of unease spread through Nora's chest. Still, she nudged her sister forward a bit. "Let's get you off the floor."

Working together, Nora and Daniel helped Ally to her feet. The water had soaked the bathroom floor from all the splashing. The bath mat was drenched, and water had pooled all the way to the door. They carried Ally out into the hallway and over to her bedroom.

Ally sat on her bed, clutching the towel that Daniel had wrapped around her.

"Is that true?" Daniel asked.

Ally opened her mouth to speak, then paused. Her gaze jumped to the doorway. "We can talk about it later."

When Nora glanced back, Lucy was standing in the doorway, her hair still dripping wet. "Are you okay, Aunt Ally?"

Ally paused and then answered. "Yes."

Silence filled the air. Lucy looked so small standing there. So fragile and innocent. But something had changed. Her eyes held a darkness. Had she failed to remove some of the grease makeup? Instead of stepping into the room, she turned to face Blanco, who was curled up in the corner. He growled at her this time.

"Something's wrong with him, Mommy," Lucy said.

"He's just scared," Nora said, "from all the commotion."

Lucy turned back to them. "What did you find at the quarry, Mommy? Did you find something you like?"

A chill swept down Nora's spine. It was just the way she said those words. Not something Lucy would normally ask—and definitely not in that tone.

"Yes, honey," Nora said. "We found something."

"Was it nice?"

There was a flicker of a grin on Lucy's face. It was so small, it almost went unnoticed.

"A pendant," Nora answered.

"Can I see it?"

Nora glanced at Daniel, who shrugged. She retrieved the pendant from her pocket and held it up in her palm, but didn't offer it to Lucy. Instead, Nora examined it under the overhead light in Ally's room. She hadn't had time to examine it until then, so she took a moment to wipe away the dirt. "There's not much to see."

Still, there was an unmistakable quality about the pendant's style, something familiar... but she couldn't quite place it.

"Let me see that—do you mind?" Ally asked, holding out her hand.

Nora handed it to her.

Ally turned it over in her hand. "I think this belonged to Mom."

"How do you know?" Nora asked.

"She had some other jewelry just like it," Ally said. "Don't you remember?"

Nora shook her head.

Ally wiped more dirt from the front of the pendant. Beneath the small design, her sister pointed to some nearly imperceptible markings. Somehow, Ally could read them. "The initials—Mom's initials. CV. This belonged to her. I know it."

Daniel stepped toward Lucy. "Honey, why don't you get dressed? We'll take you home soon. I know you have spare clothes here. We can talk about all of this later."

"Can I stay with Ally tonight?" Lucy pleaded.

Another silence passed between them.

"No," Nora said definitively. "Not tonight."

"What else did you find down there?" Lucy asked. This time, she wasn't speaking to Nora. She was looking at her father.

"Nothing," he replied.

"Nothing?" she repeated.

His face turned white, then red, before he nudged her away. "It's time to get dressed."

"I bet you found something really nice down there. Didn't you, Daddy?"

"No," he snapped. "Get dressed."

Lucy walked away, but the tension still hung in the air.

Ally handed the pendant back to Nora and gestured in a slow circle around them. "All of this... This isn't normal."

"I couldn't agree more," Nora said. "We have to call Father Tony first thing tomorrow."

Ally nodded. Her face was still pale, and she was trembling a bit.

"Are you going to be alright... alone?" Nora asked.

Ally nodded again but glanced at the floor. "Keep an eye on her. It's probably too late to see him tonight but call him anyway.

Maybe he has time tomorrow morning. This can't go on like this."

Nora glanced toward the open doorway. She heard Lucy laughing. A soft, distant laugh came from the kitchen. Blanco wasn't with her. He was still there in Ally's bedroom, huddled in the corner.

❧ 15 ❧

Nora couldn't sleep. The sight and sound of her sister struggling to catch a breath in the tub while Lucy held her down still haunted her. If she hadn't walked in at that very moment...

A chill swept through her, and she sat up in bed. Daniel was snoring beside her, but there was no sense in waking him up. Let him sleep. They'd both had a long day, and at least one of them should get a good night's rest.

The room was perfectly quiet for a moment... until a noise came from somewhere down the hall. Had Lucy come out of her room? Or was Blanco pushing himself against the bathroom door?

They'd come straight home after leaving the parlor. They'd gone about their evening routine without a word about what had happened, either at the parlor or at the quarry. Still, it never left her mind. Lucy had stayed quiet and avoided eye contact with both of them. It was clear she regretted her actions, although it wasn't clear she understood what she'd done. She hadn't played with Blanco all night. That wasn't normal. He'd become her incessant companion recently. But now he'd avoided her most of the night too, instead choosing to hide beneath the furniture and only come out to eat, drink, and use the litter box. Something was off.

Nora had tried so many times to fall asleep, but now it seemed pointless. The events of the day flashed through her mind like endless fireworks. And then she couldn't stop thinking about the pendant she'd discovered at the quarry. In the dream, her mother had led her there to find it. But... why? It seemed like a miracle that Daniel had even stumbled across it at the bottom of the pit. Nora had placed it on her dresser when she got home. She would examine it closer in the morning with a clear head. It was better that way. Let everything go until then. She was exhausted, so why couldn't she let it go?

A sound came from down the hallway—a toilet flushing. The noise startled her, although Lucy had probably just gotten up in the middle of the night to use the bathroom. Nothing to worry about.

Nora took a breath and tried to clear her mind. The silence swelled as she listened for the sound of Lucy coming out of the bathroom. It never came. Instead, a soft voice caught her attention. Lucy was whispering something.

Then, the toilet flushed again.

Did she need help?

Nora climbed out of bed and walked to the bedroom door. Before opening it, she glanced back at Daniel. He'd stirred when she'd gotten up, but his breathing slowed again into a gentle rhythm.

Opening the door slowly, she glanced down the hallway. Despite the sound of someone in the bathroom, the door was open, and the light was off. Lucy's bedroom door was also open.

Nora waited in her doorway for her daughter to emerge.

Instead, another flush.

Three times?

Was Lucy sick?

A guttural groan came from the bathroom. It wasn't coming from Lucy, but from something smaller. An animal. A cat.

An uneasy feeling swept through Nora's chest. It came in waves that nudged her forward, but for some strange reason, she resisted. Something was wrong in there. Very wrong. Her maternal instincts kicked in, but for a moment she couldn't make herself move forward. Dread held her back. She wished—prayed—that Lucy would just step out, wipe the sleep from her eyes, and go back to bed. But somehow, she knew that wouldn't happen.

Heading toward the bathroom, she stopped in the doorway and flipped on the light.

Lucy was there, on her knees in front of the toilet. She wasn't sick. Instead, she was holding Blanco with both hands. He was meowing and hissing while struggling to escape her grasp. She was dunking him again and again in the water. Each time she pushed him down, she flushed the toilet.

"Lucy!" Nora cried. "What are you doing?"

Lucy didn't seem to notice. Instead, she continued uninterrupted, even as Blanco clawed at her hands and arms.

Nora dropped beside her daughter and pulled at the girl's arms. Lucy fought back. She didn't let go of Blanco, even then, holding him with one hand while struggling against Nora with the other. Blanco finally broke free and charged out of the bathroom with a loud hiss. He left behind a long scratch down Lucy's arm.

"Lucy!" Nora cried again. "My God, what's going on with you?"

Lucy didn't flinch or turn toward her. Instead, she faced forward, fixated on the toilet bowl as the water swirled down the drain.

Daniel came in a moment later. His face was full of confusion and concern. He grimaced as he stared down at the toilet. "Is she sick?"

"No." Nora pulled Lucy in against her chest. "Not in that way."

"In what way, then?"

She tried to answer, but she couldn't bring herself to say it.

Something's got her. Something evil.

Daniel didn't press her. Instead, he swallowed and touched Nora's shoulder. "We'll talk about it in the morning."

Embracing her daughter, Nora's hands trembled. The warmth in Lucy's body was gone, and she was still staring into the toilet bowl.

"What do you see in there, honey?" Nora whispered into her daughter's hair.

"Where does the water go, Mommy?" she asked in a somber tone.

"To the sewer," Daniel answered.

"And then where?" Lucy asked.

"I don't know," he said. "To a lake, I guess. Or somewhere underground."

"Deep underground." She turned her face up to meet Nora's gaze. "You can't stop it, Mommy."

"Stop what, honey?"

"The darkness. It's deeper than it looks."

❧ 16 ❧

Somehow, they'd gotten Lucy to fall asleep. Nora had sat with the girl for another hour before she'd finally closed her eyes and her breath had dropped into a slow, steady rhythm.

Afterward, Nora had gone through the house, shutting off most of the lights. She left a few on to illuminate the stairs in case of an emergency.

What kind of emergency was she imagining? She tried not to think about it.

It was clear something was very wrong with Lucy. Nora planned to call Father Tony first thing in the morning. If they could only just get through the night... Nora even left her bedroom door open so she had a clear view of the hallway. If Lucy even opened her door, Nora would hear it.

But after putting Lucy to bed, everything had gone silent, except for the sound of the furnace whirring to life. Her mind still echoed with the events of the night before. She tried to rationalize it. Ally had slipped and fallen in. Yes, that sort of thing happened all the time. Except it just wasn't true. Not this time. Lucy had somehow managed to pull her in and bury Ally's face below the water. Her sweet angel of a daughter had done that.

Still, Nora tried to make sense of what she'd seen, replaying the events over and over, trying to process how something so horrendous could have happened. It was a tragedy narrowly averted. But... why? Something still gnawed at her, something like dread, knowing that it could happen again without notice.

~

NORA AWOKE THE NEXT MORNING TO THE SOUND OF SOMEONE whispering in the hallway. It didn't sound human. More like a guttural cry from someone in distress. Had Blanco gotten in trouble, or had he spotted something in the darkness?

She couldn't remember when she'd fallen asleep. Had Daniel gone out to check on Lucy? No, he was still in bed beside her. She pushed her eyes open wider and climbed out of bed. Under the circumstances, it was better to act on that nagging feeling at the back of her mind that something wasn't quite right.

The silence broke. The sound was there again, coming from downstairs, echoing up the stairway.

"Lucy?" Nora called out into the hallway.

No answer.

It was almost morning, judging by the soft light streaming in through the blinds. She glanced back at her phone on the dresser. Her alarm would go off in only a few minutes anyway. She switched it off, circled the bed, and nudged Daniel's feet.

"Daniel," she said.

He groaned and then sat up with a start. "What time is it?"

"It's okay," she said. "You're not late, but I heard something downstairs."

He looked toward the open door. "Downstairs?"

"Maybe it's just Lucy, but..."

"I'll check." He stood and headed toward the hallway. She followed him, and then she hurried past him and turned into Lucy's room. The door was closed—just how she'd left it—but when she opened it, Lucy's bed was empty. Her blankets were pushed aside, and there was no sign of Blanco either. Nora's stomach sank.

"Oh God," Daniel said. "Not again."

Nora rushed across the hallway and then checked the bathroom next. The towels from the previous night were still in a heap by the tub. The smell of soap and Lucy's shampoo still lingered in the air.

She turned back to Daniel. "I'm sure she must have gone downstairs."

"Let's hope so."

On their way down the stairs, Daniel called out, "Lucy!"

No answer.

Arriving in the kitchen, they circled around the area, but there was no sign of Lucy.

"Maybe she's with Blanco?" Daniel suggested.

Nora frowned, staring across the living room. Blanco was there in the corner and staring back at them with wide eyes. His tail twitched a few times until his gaze jumped to the basement door. It was open.

Nora swallowed.

That indistinct sound came again. It was like a low growl now, echoing up through the air ducts.

"Do you hear that?" Nora asked.

"Yes." Daniel reached the basement door first and opened it.

"Lucy?" he called down.

The sound stopped.

Nora came up beside him and flicked on the lights.

"Lucy?" Nora called out. "Lucy, honey, are you down there?"

Still nothing.

Without a word, Daniel charged down the basement stairs, with Nora following closely behind.

The three exposed lights that lit the basement failed to reach every corner. The shadows were harsh, revealing a long-neglected area of the house that had become nothing more than storage space. It was small, dank, and they rarely went down there unless it was absolutely necessary. Lucy had called it the "scary place" when they'd moved in a few years earlier, and Nora couldn't argue with that. The place had bad vibes.

But that's where they found Lucy, sitting against the back wall behind a pile of boxes. She was beside a floor drain, with her knees pulled up into her chest, her face turned down. She didn't look up, even when they approached.

"Sweetheart?" Nora asked softly. "What are you doing down here?"

Lucy didn't answer, although her head tilted slightly.

Nora stepped cautiously forward. "Honey, are you alright? We're worried about you."

Lucy still didn't answer.

Daniel moved ahead of her, reaching Lucy first. He sat down beside her and wrapped an arm around her shoulders while checking her forehead.

"She doesn't have a fever," he said.

Nora moved in next, crouching in front of Lucy while delicately touching her daughter's arm. "Why are you down here, sweetie?"

She didn't answer again.

Nora stroked the side of Lucy's hair. "Let's get you back upstairs. You can spend the day in bed, okay? Please tell me how you're feeling."

Lucy shook her head. A wave of relief swept through Nora. At least the girl was responding.

"Is something wrong?" Daniel nudged her a little closer.

Nora moved around to the other side of Lucy and sat beside her, trying to get her to look up. Nora wanted to see Lucy's eyes —to see her face again.

Lucy nodded slowly several times.

"Can you tell me what it is?" Nora asked.

And then Lucy made the same low, groaning noise Nora had heard all the way upstairs in her bedroom. A sickening sound that rattled Nora's stomach and reverberated through the basement. It was unnatural—nothing like any sound Lucy had ever made before.

Nora swallowed. "Whatever you're feeling, honey, we can talk about it upstairs."

"Blanco misses you." Daniel leaned closer. "And we do too."

Nora glanced around for Blanco. She thought he might follow them down into the basement but he hadn't. Instead, he was sitting near the top of the stairs, peering at them from a distance.

"Did you come down here to be alone?" Daniel asked.

Lucy nodded.

"Weren't you a little... scared?"

"I like the dark," Lucy said in a gravelly voice. "It reminds me of home."

Nora met Daniel's gaze. His face was paler than usual.

"Let's help her upstairs." Nora tugged on her hand.

Daniel nodded, and together they each grabbed one of Lucy's arms and lifted her just a bit.

At the same time, Lucy threw out her arms, knocking her fists against both of them with a force they'd never imagined possible. It wasn't the strength of a nine-year-old, but like a grown man on steroids. Her fist crashed into Nora's chest, knocking the air from her lungs. The force threw her back against the cement wall. Daniel did the same, although he recovered quicker, grabbing Lucy's wrist and not letting go.

Lucy struggled for a bit, then turned to face Nora. "I will do as I please."

And for a second, Lucy's eyes were gone. Not just the pupil or the iris, but the entire eye. They were hollow sockets, blackened and oozing with blood. Despite the empty sockets, she was staring at Nora with an intensity that peered into her very soul.

Nora gasped, and her heart raced. Could Daniel see what she was seeing? It seemed not.

Daniel grabbed her other wrist, and then Lucy's eyes were normal again. She was back, staring at each of them in terror.

"Call Ally," Nora cried out to Daniel. "I need to call Father Tony. He needs to get over here right away."

17

Nora greeted Father Tony at the front door. He was dressed in his priest uniform, carrying a black leather bag, and wearing a large crucifix around his neck. The same crucifix she'd seen on his office desk at the church months earlier.

"Hello, Father." She put on a brave face. "I know you've got a busy schedule, but... this is important."

"By the sound of your voice on the phone," he said, "I believe you." His usual confidence was gone, replaced by a solemn intensity as he stepped inside and glanced around nervously.

"She's in the basement." Nora gestured toward the basement door near the kitchen. "Ally's down there with her."

"The basement?" His eyes widened. "Is she all right?"

"She's... struggling, but we're concerned she might hurt herself. She doesn't talk much, and when she does...."

He nodded, as if understanding exactly what she meant. After stepping inside, Nora shut the door behind him and led him across the dining room toward the basement door but stopped short of going down the stairs.

"We're hoping you can solve this," Daniel said. "She tried to drown Ally last night."

"Drown?" Father Tony stiffened as shock flashed across his face.

"In Ally's bathtub," Nora said softly. "It's a nightmare. Lucy's not acting normally, not in any way."

"I don't blame you," he said. "Have you—"

"If this doesn't work," Daniel interrupted, "we'll need to consider other options. Things are spiraling out of control. She's sick."

"I'll do my best." Father Tony met his gaze. "I promise. But I was going to ask, have you talked with anyone else about this?"

Nora shook her head. "Who else can we turn to about something like this?"

Father Tony nodded sympathetically. "That's understandable."

"Tell me," Daniel demanded. "Is she possessed?"

Father Tony tensed, and his gaze dropped to the floor. "It's impossible to know until I see her."

"Before we go down there," Nora said, "the dream I had, about my mother..."

"Yes?" He looked at her curiously.

"Daniel and I went back to the quarry."

Father Tony's expression changed. A bit of anger flashed across his face. "Why did you go back there?"

"I felt I had to."

He shook his head. "It's a dangerous place for anyone, especially someone with your background."

"That's exactly what I want to know," Nora said. "There's something you're not telling me, isn't there? Something about my background?"

"Please try to understand my position. Many people have confided their darkest secrets to me over the years. It's a sacred obligation to keep them well hidden, but it's also for the common good. Some secrets are better left kept between me and God."

Nora scoffed. "You can't hide the truth forever. We found

something while we were there." She pulled the pendant from her pocket and held it up, turning it over in her hand to reveal the initials carved into the base. "Daniel climbed down into the pit and found this. It belonged to my mother."

"Yes," Father Tony mumbled. "Your mother…"

"She was there at the quarry with Tess, wasn't she?"

"Yes." He sighed. "Unfortunately, she was there, and she must have dropped the pendant."

Nora held it out. "Why would she want me to find this?"

He gestured to it. "You saw this in your dream?"

"Not exactly, but I know she wanted me to find *something* in the pit. In my dream, she led me straight to it. I needed answers, and this is what we found."

"We found something else," Daniel said. "A crucifix."

Father Tony's eyes widened.

Daniel pulled out his phone and brought up the photo of the crucifix on his screen. It showed the silver relic embedded in the limestone near the bottom of the quarry. He zoomed in on it.

Father Tony scrutinized the photo, his face turning pale. He seemed to waver in place, his mouth slowly opening.

"Is it yours?" Nora asked.

He nodded. "It's mine."

"What happened that night?"

He stared at the photo for a few more seconds and then met Nora's gaze. "When I arrived, your mother and Tess were about to commit a horrendous act—one that would have had deep implications for all those involved if I hadn't stopped them."

"What were they doing?"

Father Tony swallowed. "One of them had dived to the bottom of the pit to retrieve something for their ritual. They nearly succeeded in summoning a demon."

"A demon." Daniel's gaze jumped to the basement door.

"It's not like you think." Father Tony made the sign of the cross over his chest. "I sealed the gateway before Tess and your mother could complete the ritual. I sealed it within that pit forever."

"But... why?" Nora asked. "Why would my mother ever do something like that?"

He stared into Nora's eyes. "You. I heard from another parishioner that your mother was having trouble with her pregnancy. She almost lost you a few times... until this happened. She was desperate, I heard, and went there to beg for Moloch's help when all else had failed. The demon Moloch is known to grant favors to those in need... for a price. Tess led the ritual, and the others went along for the thrills. Most of them scattered when I arrived, except for Tess and your mother. They were determined to go through with it at all costs."

"So, the pendant is causing this?" Nora asked. "Causing Lucy to act like this?"

He shook his head. "I don't think it has anything to do with the pendant, but before I say anything else, I need to talk with your daughter to see if she's exhibiting the symptoms you explained to me on the phone. Then we can know how far things have progressed."

"Of course." Nora clutched the pendant and placed it back in her pocket. She led him down the wooden stairs into the cool, musty basement. The exposed overhead bulbs created harsh shadows around them.

Lucy was sitting against the far wall with Ally beside her. They were hunkered near an old utility sink, with the drain in the floor at their feet.

"How's she doing?" Nora asked on the way over.

Ally stroked Lucy's hair. "She's quiet. I think she even fell asleep for a while."

Nora leaned down in front of her daughter and spoke in a gentle tone. "Honey, do you want to come upstairs now?"

Lucy shifted slightly but didn't answer.

"How long has she been like this?" Father Tony asked, kneeling down in front of her but giving the girl plenty of space.

He removed the crucifix hanging from his neck and held it up in front of Lucy. She didn't react.

Thank God, she didn't react.

"We found her down here like this a few hours ago after looking everywhere. Daniel almost called the police, but then we saw the basement door was open. Blanco was sitting in front of it, but he wouldn't go down. That's when we knew something was wrong. He's been acting strangely toward her lately."

Father Tony nodded, still clutching the crucifix, and turned his gaze to Lucy. "How are you feeling?"

Again, she didn't answer. Instead, she turned her face away and picked at a crack in the cement wall, pulling out small pieces of stone and dropping them into the floor drain.

"I'd like to talk with you for a moment, if you don't mind," Father Tony said. "I'd like to help you."

"You can't help me," she said in a sweet, soft voice.

He cracked a smile. "I'm sure I can."

She shook her head. "It's going to kill me."

"No," Father Tony said gently. "Who told you such a horrible thing?"

She pointed to her own mouth. "He did."

"Who? Someone talking through you?"

She nodded. "It wants me to let go."

"Let go?" Father Tony asked. "You mean surrender to it?"

She nodded again. "He wants me to go home with him."

"Where is home?"

"The quarry." She pointed to the floor. "Underground."

"Who wants you to do that?"

Lucy's expression changed. She frowned and spoke in a deep voice, not her own. "You know damn well who I am."

Ally leaned back to give the girl some space.

Nora's stomach churned at the harsh words coming from her daughter.

"No, I don't know who you are." Father Tony inched closer. "Please tell me your name."

"I like to play games," Lucy said in the same dark voice. "I like to play 'Drag Lucy to Hell.'"

"Let's not play that game." Father Tony stared into Lucy's eyes. "Am I talking with the demon Moloch?"

Her face exploded with outrage. "Ezeran! Moloch will have her when I deliver her to him. She's mine for now."

"Moloch can't have her, and neither can you."

Lucy grinned and narrowed her eyes at Father Tony. "You're too late. I already have her."

"No," Father Tony said. "Tess already provided a sacrifice at the quarry. It's over."

"It's not over. Moloch is not satisfied with what Tess offered. I've come here to deliver this one instead. She is bound to him, and the deal cannot be broken."

"You're wrong." Father Tony raised his voice.

Lucy struggled within Ally's grasp, but the girl's expression had softened.

Ally held on. "She's fighting me."

Nora gestured for her to let go. "No, it's okay."

When Ally released her, Lucy stumbled forward with her arms outstretched. "Mommy, Mommy, I'm scared."

Nora broke into tears and rushed forward, but Father Tony held out his arm to stop her. "Please, no. Not yet. Give us a moment."

Nora stopped and spoke through her tears. "Don't be scared, honey. Listen to the father. He'll help us get through this."

Daniel also moved closer. "Lucy, we'll get through this. I promise."

"Am I going to die?" Lucy's face flushed with terror.

"No, honey." Nora shook her head. "I won't let you die. Never."

"I won't either," Father Tony added. He pulled a bottle of holy water from his pocket and opened it.

Before he could splash any of it on Lucy, Nora held out her hand to stop him. "Is this going to...?"

"It won't harm her." Father Tony touched her arm. He was trembling too.

"But remember what happened at the church? With the statue?"

"This isn't the same," he said. "I promise. If anything, this will keep the demon at bay."

"She... *is* possessed?" Daniel asked incredulously.

"Not fully, but... it's happening. It hasn't taken complete control of her yet. There's still time."

"How do we stop it?" Nora asked.

"Keep her here, if possible," Father Tony said. "Don't let her leave the house, but no matter what you do, don't let her get back to the quarry."

"That'll never happen," Daniel said. "We watch her all the time."

Father Tony glanced up at him. "Don't underestimate the stealth of the demonic force controlling her. She's not acting alone."

"Are you saying we should... restrain her?" Nora asked.

He gave a stoic stare. "If necessary. If only to keep her from hurting herself."

"Maybe she'd be better off with someone else," Daniel said with a bit of desperation in his voice. "At a hospital... with professionals."

Father Tony shook his head. "I understand your concern and skepticism, but I'm the best defense against such things. Getting a priest with more experience than me... I'm afraid there's no time."

Nora's voice wavered. "How did this happen?"

Lucy laughed long and hard. Her shrieking laugh filled the air for several seconds. "How did this happen?" She mocked in Nora's voice. "The priest is a failure. Little Lucy is going to die because... he's a phony. Did you know that? Tell them the truth, Father. Tell them!"

"Stop." Father Tony held out the cross, aiming it toward Lucy's face.

"He lied. To the church. He lied to everyone. He's not a real priest, are you, Father Tony?"

"I'm as real as you are." He splashed the holy water across Lucy's face.

She recoiled with a small scream and turned away. When she turned back, the water had left scattered red patches on her skin that resembled a sunburn.

Panic spread across Ally's face. She lurched toward Lucy but stopped short of touching her.

"Stop!" Nora reached out. "You're hurting her."

"It's for her own good." Father Tony paused for a moment, as if reflecting on what he'd done, but then prepared to splash more. "It will save her."

Nora jumped forward and embraced Lucy, squeezing her with as much motherly love as she could manage. "She's only nine."

"Yes," Father Tony agreed, "and if you want her to see ten, then you'll move away. The girl needs more cleansing before its hold on her grows worse."

"Cleanse how?" Nora cried. "I won't let you burn her alive."

"This isn't like the statue," he repeated. "It will keep the demon at bay."

Daniel stepped forward. "Nora's right. There's got to be a better way."

Father Tony shook his head. "This isn't something to be solved through traditional channels. This isn't a mental illness, or a phobia, or a bad dream. An evil energy—a demon, a *true* demon—is attacking your daughter."

"Why?" Nora cried. "Why *Lucy*?"

"I don't know."

"He's lying," Lucy mocked the father in a dark voice. "He knows *exactly* what he did. You know, Father! Tell them! Tell them! Tell them!"

Nora turned to face him. "Tell us what?"

"Don't listen to her," Father Tony ordered. "She's not herself."

"Tell us how to stop this," Nora demanded.

"Mommy..." Lucy gasped, grasping Nora's arms, speaking in her normal voice, "he's going to kill me..."

"I won't let anyone touch you," Nora cried.

Father Tony raised the cross again and started chanting a prayer. "Our Father, who art in Heaven..."

Lucy responded by cowering closer to her mother.

He sprinkled a bit of holy water again. This time, Lucy shrieked. Her voice filled the basement.

Still grasping Nora's arms, Lucy convulsed violently. Her eyes rolled back into her head, and foamy saliva dripped from her mouth. "Mommy!"

"Lucy!" Nora cried.

Only a moment later, Lucy convulsed and collapsed into Nora's arms.

18

Nora pulled Lucy's limp body closer and squeezed her hand with a panicked shake. "Oh God, no. Lucy, honey, wake up."

The girl's eyes were fluttering. At least she was alive.

Nora turned to face Father Tony with her heart racing. "Father, whatever you're doing, it's not working."

"Give it time." He made a downward motion with his hand and continued splashing holy water across Lucy, but his hands were shaking. "... hallowed be thy name..."

"We should bring her upstairs." Ally nudged Nora's arm. "Out in the open."

"It won't make any difference." Father Tony shook his head. "It's better that she stay down here, away from the doors and windows. It will keep the demon confined."

Nora crowded in beside Lucy, sweeping her arm around her daughter's back.

Daniel's face tensed, and he dug out his phone. "We should call 911."

"No," Father Tony said. "Not yet. I just need more time."

"She's out of time," Nora cried.

"Please move away from her." Father Tony gestured for Nora to step aside. "I need to finish this."

"Finish what?" Nora pleaded. "She's unconscious, for God's sake!"

Father Tony shook his head. "The demon is here, in this place. He still has a hold on her. Don't let her lack of movement fool you."

Nora squeezed Lucy tighter. "Then do something else. Tell it to leave!"

"Yes." He moved in closer and made the sign of the cross. He sprinkled more holy water over Lucy's clothes again. The same reaction happened—Lucy's skin showing faint splotches of red when the water touched it. "In the name of the Father, and of the Son, and of the Holy Spirit."

Lucy's eyes rolled back into her head, and her eyelids fluttered. The air moved in and out of her mouth in raspy breaths.

Father Tony inched closer to Lucy and spoke in a commanding voice. "Ezeran, look at me."

She made no motion at first. Instead, she started to hum, and a low gurgling sound erupted deep in her throat. It wasn't a childish melody, but something drawn out, long and fierce, like a low growl. Like something wanted to speak through her but couldn't quite form the words.

The father dangled the cross in front of her face. "I command you, demon, to leave this child!"

More holy water rained down over Lucy. The girl cowered against Nora's chest, wincing and shrieking in pain. Again, the droplets hissed when they touched her skin. The splotches turned red on contact, and tendrils of smoke floated off the surface like snakes escaping from a pit.

"You're hurting her!" Nora cried.

"It's necessary," he said. "It won't be long now. Please keep her steady."

Despite Lucy's desperate pleas, Nora held her arm. "Stop! She's hurting!"

Lucy gasped, then gave another chilling growl. The sound welled up in her throat, full of anger and hate. The demon's voice roared through her small throat. "Tell them about the deal, priest. The girl is bound to Moloch. You know there is no escape. Why do you waste my time? Tell them before I do the same to you!"

Father Tony froze. He didn't answer. Instead, his hands dropped to his sides.

Nora stared at him, waiting for a response. "What deal? What is she talking about?"

Instead of answering right away, he shook his head and stared at the basement floor for a few seconds. "I must confess—I'm afraid she's right. This is my fault."

"What do you mean this is *your* fault?"

"I told you before that I was at the Hollow Bend quarry the night your mother, Tess, and their friends went there. I thought I had stopped them in time. I was wrong." Father Tony looked up again and met Nora's gaze. "Tess and your mother did something—opened something—moments before I arrived. I heard your mother cry out to the demon, pleading for it to save her unborn baby's life. I found out later she'd been told her baby would likely die in the womb. You, Nora. She was pleading with the demon to spare *your* life."

The words hung in the air between them. Nora couldn't speak, but she gasped. Had her mother damned another so she could live? It seemed impossible.

"What are you talking about?" Daniel asked from somewhere behind them. "What does that have to do with Lucy?"

"Everything. I'm afraid the demon is correct." Father Tony slumped forward. "I failed."

"You can't fail." Nora glanced back at Lucy. Her daughter's face was turning pale, but she was still breathing. Lucy's mouth twitched wider until a small grin broke out.

The father continued speaking in a softer voice. "Tess made the same bargain, but for a different reason. Her daughter would be born many years later. Tess wanted a daughter—healthy, intelligent, exceptional—but she tried to outrun her obligation. Instead, the demon took payment on its own terms." His jaw tightened. "Eve's tragic crash... I'm certain the demon caused it to pressure Tess into keeping her word. After that, Tess grew more desperate to save her daughter—to find a sacrifice worthy enough to make the demon return what it had taken from Eve."

Father Tony hesitated and then stepped back.

"So that's it?" Ally frowned. "You're going to give up now?"

He turned to face her. "Your mother made the deal, and the demon fulfilled its end of the bargain. Nora survived. Your mother must have known there was a price to pay. Or maybe... she didn't care at the time. Caught up in her emotions, maybe the price seemed so far away. Maybe she thought someone else would pay the debt in her bloodline. *Your* bloodline."

"My mother wouldn't have done that." Nora shook her head. "She wouldn't have... made a horrible deal like that."

"How far would you go to save the life of your child, Nora? A mother's love for her child holds no boundaries. She made the deal... and I tried to stop her, I swear. I pleaded with her to stop before she finished the ritual. But she continued, even as I began my rite to bind the demon to that place. I thought if I could just keep it there, none of this would ever come to pass. So I did the only thing I knew. I bargained with it too."

Nora's stomach churned. "What... did you bargain?"

"I couldn't force it from that place with my limited knowledge of demonology. I was never an exceptional student, even in seminary school. That's what the demon was referring to. I was never ordained... properly. I struggled to finish my training, so... I falsified some documents. A bishop—a friend—signed off on it anyway. Every mass I've celebrated, every confession, my authority over demons... All of it means... nothing. I'm not a real priest in the technical sense, but that secret—that disgrace— only propelled me to work harder. I fumbled through the rites at the quarry as best I could. I bound the demon to that place—to the pit—hoping the darkness would hold it inside like a cage. It worked... or at least, I thought it did."

Daniel's mouth dropped open. "So... it's loose?"

Father Tony nodded once. "God help us."

Lucy stirred in Nora's arms. Her eyes fluttered open again—but they seemed darker now, blackened along the edges. She mouthed something, but Nora couldn't understand the words.

Nora's eyes watered as she pulled her daughter closer, trying to listen. "You need to save her. Whatever you did, undo it. That thing can't have my Lucy."

Father Tony stared down with tired, sympathetic eyes. "The demon has come to collect her soul. Moloch remembers every debt. Ezeran will possess her until the debt is paid. There's no stopping him—not with what I know. I'm sorry."

"Sorry?" Ally shouted. "That's it? Sorry? *Do* something!"

He stared down at the holy water vessel in his hands. "The water—it won't work, nor the crucifix. She is bound to him."

"Well, *unbind* her," Daniel yelled.

Lucy opened her eyes wide, now staring at Nora with a sparkle in her eyes for just a moment before turning her gaze to Father Tony. A grin erupted on her face. "Look at you! You finally spoke the truth and crushed her heart at the same time. I couldn't have done it better myself. You were so bold when we first met, railing against the might of Moloch. We will have the child... and take the rest with us down the road."

Nora squeezed Lucy against her chest. The panic was swelling again. She wanted to run with her daughter out of the house—run anywhere as far as she could go—until the sweet light in her daughter's eyes returned. But she knew, no matter how far she ran, that thing would always be there. This was their best chance—maybe their only chance—to free Lucy from whatever bargain their mother had made with the demon.

"No," Nora said in a casual tone, as if a simple refusal was enough to end it all. "It can't have her."

Ally moved in closer and faced Father Tony. "Keep praying, keep trying... You can't give up on her!"

Father Tony stared back, then nodded once. "I won't give up." He continued with the prayers, holy water, and crucifix, reciting the words louder this time, with more force. His posture straightened. "... deliver us from evil. For thine is the kingdom..."

Lucy struggled within Nora's embrace, and then broke free and pointed at Father Tony. "Do you think a simple crucifix will stand between you and Moloch? You're weaker than this child."

"... the power and the glory—" Father Tony's eyes shot wide open. They bulged in their sockets, and his mouth gaped. Stumbling backwards, he clutched at his chest. The crucifix slipped from his hand, hitting the cement floor with a clang that echoed through the basement. The vessel of holy water fell next, landing at his feet. The water splashed over his shoes and pooled near the basement drain as he stumbled forward.

"Father?" Nora reached her hand toward him. "What's wrong?"

Ally rushed to his side at the same time.

He collapsed. His knees buckled as he fell sideways. Just before he hit the floor, Ally caught his arm. It stopped his head from hitting the ground, but his shoulder bore the full impact instead. On the ground, writhing and crying out between gasps for air, his eyes stretched even wider, and his stare fixated on some distant point beyond them. Terror filled his eyes—the same horrific stare she'd seen just before her own father had died.

Daniel lifted his phone. "I'm calling for help."

Lucy laughed wildly. If she had laughed like that at any other time, Nora would have joined in.

Air wheezed into the old man's lungs. His face went pale, and his lips trembled.

Ally and Nora each held him by one shoulder, trying to get a grasp of the situation.

Then Father Tony went silent and pale. His eyelids fluttered closed, and then he went still.

"Tell them to hurry!" Nora screamed to Daniel.

He stepped forward, the phone pressed up against his ear. "They're on their way."

"They won't make it in time." Ally leaned forward and lowered her cheek near his mouth. "He's not breathing."

Nora kneeled beside him, preparing to do CPR. She checked his pulse first, pressing two fingers against the side of his neck. Nothing.

Ally kneeled on the opposite side. "Oh, my God."

"It's not over yet." Nora started chest compressions on him, her own pulse thumping in her ears. She glanced at Father Tony's face every few seconds, praying silently that he would come back.

Lucy crawled away a few feet before Daniel grabbed her arm with his free hand.

Instead of resisting, her little grin widened as she stared down at Father Tony's lifeless body. "Is he gone? Is the old fart finally dead?"

Nora couldn't answer.

The doorbell rang a moment later.

"They're here." Daniel released Lucy for just a moment. She broke away from him with a shrieking laugh, skipping toward the stairs as if they were all just playing a game.

Daniel raced to catch her again. "Lucy! Stop! Where are you going?"

"Upstairs." Lucy charged up the stairs, stomping her feet on every step. "To celebrate."

❧ 19 ☙

Only moments after the police left, Nora stood behind the closed door with one hand resting on it. She leaned against it, pressing her forehead against the wood. The ambulance was long gone, with Father Tony's lifeless body inside. It seemed unimaginable that he was gone.

Daniel came up beside her and put his arm around her waist. "You should get some rest."

Nora shook her head. She didn't feel like resting. There was still the weight of Lucy's voice drifting down from the top of the stairs. Her piercing giggles had never ceased—not even during the police investigation or when they had carried out Father Tony's lifeless body on a stretcher.

Maybe they hadn't heard it.

But she couldn't not hear it.

On top of everything, her head ached. The sudden tragedy had jolted her in a way that felt disturbingly familiar. Déjà vu? Hadn't her own father died the same way months earlier in the parlor? It was too similar.

How could she be expected to rest now?

When they'd first seen Father Tony lying on the floor, the police hadn't questioned them thoroughly. They'd only asked how and why he'd ended up in their house in the middle of the night—and in the basement.

Daniel had done all the talking. "He came to check on Nora. She'd been... under a lot of stress since her father passed away."

And she *had* been under a lot of stress lately. That part was true, and she'd gone downstairs to find solitude. He'd gone down to sit with her, to pray and to listen.

They'd believed him.

After they'd carried Father Tony's body upstairs, the officers had quietly wrapped up the investigation, questioning each of them briefly without the slightest hint of suspicion. After all, he was an old man. He had a heart attack. It was just his time.

Ally had scooped up the melted crucifix before anyone arrived. She'd placed it behind a box as the paramedics rushed down into the basement. When she turned back, Ally whispered to Nora, "They shouldn't see it. They might take it or ask questions we can't answer."

Nora had agreed.

And after they'd left, Ally had gone down to retrieve it. When she returned, she handed it to Nora with a solemn nod. "It survived, and so will we."

Nora accepted it. The metal chilled her skin. She imagined Father Tony holding it only moments earlier, gripping it frantically as death consumed him. She'd seen the fear in his eyes before he died—the terror. He had seen something in the darkness.

Something she didn't want to imagine.

Nora met Ally's gaze. "I'm sure you're exhausted."

Ally shook her head. "I can stay all night."

"You don't have to," Nora replied.

"I need to," Ally insisted. "We're all in this together."

Daniel didn't argue. He walked over and rubbed the back of Nora's neck. "Somehow, we all should get some sleep now."

Nora glanced toward the top of the stairs. "What about

Lucy? We've all been up for what, forty hours now? None of this is helping."

"I'll sleep outside her door," Daniel said. "If she tries to step out—"

"What about the window?" Nora cut in. "She'll get out somehow. She'll get outside and go back to the quarry before we can stop her."

Daniel shook his head. "I'll make sure that doesn't happen. I'll sleep on the floor next to her bed if I need to."

"What if she tries to hurt you?" Nora asked.

"I'll take that chance," he said.

"She's not asleep yet," Ally added. "I can... stay up with her. There's some... sodas in the fridge... or I can make some coffee while you two sleep. I'll go home after you wake up. We'll tag team. I can do it."

Nora looked at Daniel.

His eyelids drooped over his eyes, and he nodded in agreement. "Okay, we'll take this one step at a time. We'll *try* to get some sleep."

Nora's eyes watered. Pressure welled up in her chest, her throat, behind her eyes. The tears started to flow. "What are we going to do?"

She dropped into Daniel's arms, and he pulled her closer against his chest. "It's late," he said. "We can't answer those questions now. We'll deal with it in the morning."

She closed her eyes for a moment, but the commotion still echoed through her mind. The chatter, the police, the detectives, the strobing lights—it all flashed repeatedly against the back of her eyelids. How was she supposed to sleep after all of that?

Daniel glanced back toward the top of the stairs. "We should check on Lucy."

Nora nodded and met his gaze.

He touched her cheek. "We're going to be okay."

Nora fell against his chest again. She wanted to believe him, but she stood on the verge of collapse. How would she even get up the stairs? Still gripping the crucifix in her hand, she stepped back and stared at it. The twisted metal was a reminder of what could happen if things went wrong. Father Tony's death had revealed that the stakes were too high now. They had to protect Lucy from whatever had—

Possessed her.

It was hard to imagine her daughter being possessed by a demon. It seemed unimaginable.

He extended his arm. "I'll help you upstairs."

She took it, slipping her arm under his. He didn't try to take away the crucifix or ask her to set it down. Instead, he gently helped her navigate the stairs.

Her tears blurred her vision. By the time she reached the top, she'd wiped them away.

Ally rushed ahead of them and peeked into Lucy's room. Pushing the door open wider, Lucy was sitting upright on the side of her bed. She was staring forward, expressionless, mumbling to herself over and over.

"Lucy?" Nora asked.

The girl went silent.

Ally cautiously approached her. "How are you feeling? Tired?"

Nora wanted to believe that Father Tony had ended whatever had possessed her, that maybe the warped crucifix or the prayers had somehow broken the demon's hold. But just by seeing her sitting there, she knew it wasn't true. Lucy was someone else now. Someone she didn't recognize.

Strangely, she'd behaved perfectly during the police visit. Just her normal little angel, answering every question with innocent eyes, smiling at everyone, and then retreating to the corner of the room as the officers conducted their investigation. Lucy had grinned as they carried Father Tony away on a stretcher. The girl had even giggled a few times near the end.

They hadn't said anything about it. They must have thought

the girl was just exhausted or stressed and dealing with it the best she could. But she hadn't stopped giggling, even after they'd left.

And now, she laughed again in long, hysterical bursts. Not a single laugh, but two voices mixed together. Two tones.

One not her own.

A cold, unnatural sound flowed from somewhere deeper—somewhere darker. It was layered beneath her sweet, small voice, and it chilled Nora to the bone.

"Lucy?" Nora took a step toward her daughter.

Lucy stopped laughing and turned to face Nora almost mechanically. "Yes, Mother?"

Nora swallowed. "It's time for bed. For all of us."

"Yes, Mother." Lucy lay back on her bed and stared at the ceiling. She folded her hands across her chest. "Nighty-night. Sleep tight."

❧ 20 ❧

Lucy had laughed all night.

After a few hours of the little girl's relentless giggling, Nora had searched their bedroom for some earplugs. She found a pair in the top dresser drawer. Daniel had used them recently at the gun range. They'd been the only thing keeping her sane throughout the night.

She'd slept soundly for the most part, but every so often, Lucy's small voice had come through. In those moments, she cracked her eyes open to stare into the darkness until the sounds stopped, then adjusted the earplugs again. The darkness always, mercifully, drew her back each time.

She woke in a daze the next morning. For a moment, she actually believed the whole thing was just a dream, until she saw Daniel was gone, and she snapped back to reality. Climbing out of bed, she immediately hurried to Lucy's bedroom. Peeking inside, she found her daughter's bed empty, and her heart skipped a beat.

"Daniel? Ally?" she cried out. "Lucy's gone!"

This was everything she had feared. She dropped to the floor, searched under the bed, and checked the closet. Nothing.

She charged out of the room and called down the stairs in a panic. "Lucy's gone!"

"She's okay," Ally answered from somewhere in the living room.

"Where is she? Is she with you?"

Ally stepped into view and appeared at the bottom of the stairs, holding up her hands. "Yes, she's with me. I'm keeping an eye on her. She's down in the basement again, in the same place as before."

"The basement?" Nora hurried down the stairs and stopped in front of her sister. Ally's eyes were bloodshot, her clothes were wrinkled, and her hair was a tangled mess.

"It's okay." Ally smiled sympathetically. "I've been down there with her all night. I came up only to use the bathroom, and I'm heading back down now."

Nora stared deeper into her sister's eyes. "You've been up all night?"

Ally nodded once. "Of course."

"What's..." Nora glanced back toward the basement door and lowered her voice. "What's she doing down there? We shouldn't leave her alone."

Before Ally could answer, Lucy's shrill laughter floated up through the floorboards. It was louder than before.

"She's alright," Ally said in a calm, reassuring tone.

Nora glanced back toward the kitchen. Daniel was there, making breakfast in his pajamas. "You stayed home from work?"

He nodded but didn't turn to face her. "I called in sick."

Judging by the way he was slumped over the food, she doubted he'd gotten enough sleep. Pausing for a moment, he glanced back and gestured to the pancakes, eggs, and bacon on the stove. "I'll take some food down to her soon."

Lucy's laughter came again.

Nora cringed and rubbed her forehead. "How is she still laughing? She's been going at it all night."

"I think she slept," Ally said, "for a few hours... I think. It was hard to tell because she sometimes talked in her sleep."

"What did she say?"

Ally shook her head. "I didn't understand. Not a single word."

Nora pressed her eyes shut for a moment. The darkness helped to clear her mind. She opened them again and looked at Daniel. "Does she have water?"

He nodded. "She has two water bottles down there. Don't worry. She'll wear herself out... eventually. At least she's safe."

"Everything's going to be okay." Ally stepped closer and touched Nora's hand. "We'll find someone else to help us. Father Tony said to keep her in the house, and that's what we'll do for now."

Nora stared at the floor. Powerlessness swelled through her body. Lucy was down there in the darkness—cold, alone, scared —suffering against unimaginable evil, and they had no idea how to help her. She spoke in a weak voice. "Who can we call now?"

At the same time, something thumped against the floor just below them. Nora looked up and met Ally's gaze. Lucy's voice rose through the floorboards. Not laughter this time. Now she was crying. Pleading. Calling out in a desperate voice.

"Mommy! Mommy! Help me! Help me!"

Nora instinctively lurched toward the basement door, but Ally grabbed her wrist and held her back.

"No, don't go down there," Ally said. "She's been doing that all night, too—toying with my emotions, just to... let her out."

Nora tilted her head. "Let her out?"

"It's better that you not go down there." Daniel turned away from the food and wiped his forehead with the back of his hand. "We just put a few weighted blankets on her. She's wrapped in them—swaddled like when she was a baby. It seems to calm her down."

"She slept on a mattress we found," Ally said. "She's okay."

"That old mattress?" Nora let out an exasperated sigh.

"It's fine for now."

"I suppose, but how long can we keep this up? We need to talk to somebody—today."

Another thump against the basement ceiling sent Nora's heart racing.

"How...?" Nora's eyes widened. "What is she doing? Climbing on the ceiling?"

Without waiting for an answer, Nora broke away from Ally and charged down the basement stairs. Lucy was sitting upright in the same spot on the mattress as the night before, next to the furnace, and she was covered in layers of blankets, just like Daniel had said. Only her little head poked out. The girl's skin was pale, and beads of sweat dripped down her forehead.

Seeing Lucy like that pierced Nora's heart. "Oh, my God."

Lucy stared into Nora's eyes. Sad, longing eyes. "Mommy, what's wrong?"

"I'm worried about you, honey."

Ally rushed down the stairs a moment later and came up behind Nora. "She's been... like that all night. Don't worry. She's got plenty of water and snacks, and I've even walked her to the bathroom a few times. But she keeps coming back to this spot."

"I like the darkness," Lucy said. "It reminds me of home."

"This *is* your home, honey," Nora said. "Upstairs with us."

There were cups and paper plates beside the mattress, scraps of food along with snacks, wrappers, and the bottles of water that Daniel had mentioned.

"I've been trying to keep her comfortable," Ally said. "I *think* she'll eventually fall asleep."

"I don't want to sleep," Lucy said with a little giggle. She held a dull stare, like someone who hadn't slept for days.

Nora crossed her arms over her chest. The cool basement air brushed against the back of her neck. "We're going to get someone to help you, honey. I promise."

Lucy stared back. "I don't need help. I don't need anything."

Nora swallowed. Those weren't Lucy's words—she was sure of

it. The tone of her voice—its *texture*. It just sounded all wrong. Her eyes held a dull stare, as if she were focusing on a distant object.

"Whoever is controlling you, honey," Nora said, "fight it with everything you've got."

Lucy laughed again. "What a stupid thing to say, Mommy. I belong to Moloch now."

"You can't have her!" Nora shouted.

A harsh voice erupted. "I already do." Then Lucy giggled, lowered her face, and spoke in a small, mischievous voice. "You can't watch me all the time. I'll get out when you let your guard down. Then, who knows what I'll do."

Nora took another step forward. "Don't say that."

"Don't say what?"

"I know it's not you saying that, Lucy, but whatever is in there with you, please fight back. Do you hear me, honey? Whatever is inside you, we're going to stop it."

"You can try." Lucy laughed even louder.

Daniel came down the steps as her laughter tapered off. The smell of eggs, bacon, and pancakes filled the air. Stepping over to Lucy with a tray of food, he approached her from the side and cautiously squatted next to her. "See? I made you breakfast."

"Yum!" She squirmed in the blankets until Ally and Daniel worked together to unwrap her, just enough so she could get her arms out.

The cup of milk wobbled as he lowered the tray onto her lap. "You don't need to eat it all, but—"

Lucy threw up her hands. The tray flew into the air and crashed against his chest. Everything went flying—across the blankets, the floor, his chest, his face.

Daniel's expression flashed with anger. "What—?"

Lucy laughed again, but then she snarled at him in a low, guttural tone. "You can't expect me to eat that garbage."

Daniel stepped back and wiped the mess off the front of his shirt, letting the food drop to the floor, but the milk saturated his clothes. He met Nora's gaze. His expression was a mix of shock and desperation. "Nora... can you call someone? They're going to take her away. When they see—"

"They won't take her away," Nora insisted. "I won't let that happen."

"Please," he said. "No more priests. No more rituals. That's what got Father Tony—"

Lucy broke into laughter, and all three of them froze. "The father. The old priest... He went down like an old tree. Didn't you see that? I'll do the same to all of you."

"Lucy, stop!" Nora cried.

Lucy laughed even louder. The sound was deafening in that small space.

"Stop!" Daniel reached forward and grabbed Lucy's arm while leaning into her face. He wasn't gripping her with force, but he was losing his patience. "Stop!"

She didn't seem to hear him. Her pale face turned red as the screams roared from her throat. The veins bulged in her neck until she gasped in a long breath and then started laughing hysterically as if the whole thing was just a joke. One big practical joke.

Instead of resisting her father, she allowed Daniel to lift her into a standing position on the mattress, and the blankets fell away. She looked almost emaciated in her pajamas, standing hunched forward with her face down. She shivered in the chilly air. Her teeth chattered, and she wavered like a rag doll, until her laughter finally died down.

When Daniel finally released her arm, he stared at her with wide eyes. "Lucy, honey. Something awful has gotten into you. Your mother's right. You need to fight this. We'll get you some help. I promise."

"Yes, Daddy," she said with a sheepish grin.

He ran a hand through his hair. "I just don't know... what to do anymore."

"You can die," Lucy said in a small, soft voice. "That would help."

At the same time, a loud thump came from upstairs. Something heavy had fallen. Then the sound of shattering glass. The floor above them shook, and dust drifted down from the ceiling. All three of them glanced up.

Lucy charged forward. She slipped past Daniel and Ally, but Nora grabbed her before she reached the stairs.

"Leave me alone!" Lucy screamed, thrashing within Nora's grasp.

"No!" Nora cried. "I won't!"

Daniel grabbed her a moment later and pulled her away, dragging her with his arms wrapped around her chest from behind, back to the mattress. She kicked him a few times in the chest. He winced but struggled to keep her under control. "You can't leave, honey. I'm sorry. Not yet. We're going to solve this."

"Ally," Nora said. "You should go home and get some sleep. We'll watch her for now. Come back as soon as you can."

Ally stared at Lucy for a long moment and then nodded. "Yes. You're right. I won't be gone long. I'll come back in a few hours, and then we can decide what to do."

Nora smiled sympathetically. "Thank you."

Ally rushed up the basement stairs but stopped in the doorway and turned back. "When you come up, watch your step. There's glass everywhere."

21

Ally stepped into her apartment and locked the door behind her. She was more than exhausted after staying up the whole night with Lucy in Nora's basement.

The girl had stirred all night, sometimes even breaking into shrieking fits of laughter. Ally had sat up the whole time with her back against the cement wall, keeping an eye on her niece. Sometimes in the darkness, Lucy had stared back at her, as if she were waiting for Ally to fall asleep and...

And what?

What did she think Lucy would do? Ally swallowed. Lucy's behavior was deteriorating, growing more violent, but how much worse could it get?

Ally was running on fumes. She needed food, water, and sleep, but something kept nagging at her mind. She needed answers before she could drop into bed.

Crossing the apartment to the spare bedroom, she opened the door and glanced around inside. The room was stacked with clutter, everything that her father had hoarded over the years. This was where her parents had put everything they no longer needed but couldn't quite get rid of.

She'd intended to go through it all someday, but the process would take weeks, if not months. She had already thrown out a lot of what her father had accumulated over the years. Most of it was worthless junk, but there was plenty more. Boxes, totes, old furniture—and a few things her mother had owned.

Her father had thrown out or sold most of her mother's possessions, but what he had saved were the most valuable pieces—the ones with sentimental value. Unfortunately, he'd tucked those things far into the corner, as if he'd tried to bury them away, hide them from sight and mind.

Slogging forward through the clutter, she pushed aside stacks of boxes to get to the farthest corner, where she'd seen some of her mother's things. When she finally reached them, most of the boxes were unlabeled, but a few bore faint titles in fading marker:

Frames and Photos. College Stuff. Old Friends.

She started with the last one, pulling out the box and brushing dust from the lid before peering inside. It was stuffed with loose papers—notebooks, receipts, envelopes. Lots of business-related things. And then beneath it all, there was more.

She dug deeper, past a few old photo albums, and found a small stack of old notebooks. The covers were neon pink, electric blue, and neon green. All the colors that echoed her mother's eccentric personality.

One of them was labeled: *1990s.*

Pulling it out of the box, she flipped through the pages. Judging by the neat, cursive handwriting, it was one of her mother's old journals. She sat down on the floor, taking the notebook with her.

At least it was something.

There was page after page of thoughts, notes, memories. Ally remembered her mother writing in notebooks over the years, keeping journals, though she never quite saw the point.

Once, she had asked why.

"Oh, just to remember," her mother had replied. That was it. That was all she'd ever said about it.

Ally flipped through the pages. Many of the entries were mundane comments about whom she'd met, about what they'd done as a family that day, about the weather. Some comments mentioned their family business:

Had three customers today. One of them wanted to speak with their pet dog, of all things. Said we couldn't do it. They got upset and walked out.

But as she reached the end of the notebook, there was something stuck between the pages. Old newspaper clippings—some folded and loose, some taped to the pages. Several articles with yellowed edges, stories of missing children. Then, there were more pieces about the Hollow Bend quarry.

Ally's throat tightened.

This... *this* was what she'd been searching for.

Her father had saved all this. He could have easily tossed it out like everything else. But he hadn't.

Why?

The articles about the quarry were mostly historical:

Built in 1907...

A list of basic facts, but nothing especially useful.

Placing the journal back into the box, she dug even deeper. There were more items, and a wooden box, eerily familiar. It was similar to the one from Gabriel's house, the one Father Tony had once asked her to dispose of, but it wasn't etched with demonic designs. This one was more... ordinary.

Opening it, she found a rosary coiled at the bottom, its blackened beads no longer reflecting any light. They weren't dirty—they were scorched. Burned? She lifted it out gently. Ash smudged her fingertips.

More objects lay beneath it—occult items connected to rituals. Chalk. A folded scrap of paper with hand-drawn symbols in ballpoint pen. Burned herbs.

A small glass vial of dirt.

From the pit itself?

One by one, she turned them over in her hands. Why would her mother have these? But there was nothing that explained why her parents had kept something like this. No notes. No reasons.

Was this what Father Tony had been referring to when he mentioned seeing her mother and Tess at the quarry performing rituals? Were these the same items they'd once used?

Digging further into the box, she found another notebook. This one was clearly labeled: *Hollow Bend.*

Every page inside was written in her mother's unmistakable cursive handwriting. This wasn't like the other diaries. It was structured. Detailed. A record of what they had done at the quarry—the ritual with her mother, Tess, and others.

The pit is awake again. It's deeper than it looks.

Those last words.

Ally froze. A chill raced up her spine.

Lucy had said those exact same words.

There was also a crude map drawn inside the journal. Her mother had marked the location of the pit—near where the incinerator now sat, and the stone slab in front of it—the altar where Tess had tried to sacrifice Lucy.

The map sketched out a path down to the quarry—the hidden back road Tess had used to slip in undetected.

The pit was circled several times in thick black ink, and then marked with a black X.

Stepping back, Ally's heart raced. This was everything she'd hoped to find. She pulled out one of the photo albums she'd seen earlier and opened it slowly. Inside were several old Polaroids of her mother from her college years, smiling beside three young women and two young men.

Tess was one of them, standing beside her mother with her arm around her waist, as if they would stay best friends forever.

Ally's heart sank. Instead of a lifetime of loyal friendship, the woman had nearly cost Lucy her life.

Were the others in the photo the ones Father Tony had referred to? The ones who hadn't taken the binding seriously?

Flipping over one of the photos, she found their names scrawled on the back.

Tess, me, Marcy, Jonah, Derek

Marcy, Jonah, and Derek's names were crossed out with a year written below them. The year they died? Only Tess and her mother had no dates. Not yet.

And then newspaper clippings of the obituaries for those whose names were crossed out. The reason for death was absent in all of them, but her mother had filled in the missing details, listing the fates for each one:

Marcy - burned inside car fire, 1993

Jonah - burned in a house fire, 1997

Derek - lightning strike, charred internally, 1998

All of them had died by fire.

The images that Lucy had drawn—the ones showing the incinerator and flames—flashed through Ally's mind. Tess had died in the same way at the quarry, but her mother had somehow avoided a similar fate, instead succumbing to leukemia. So, was that what the demon had in mind for Lucy? Sacrifice in hellish flames?

There were only two photos of the group. One taken in front of the incinerator. One near the edge of the pit.

In one, her mother held an item—the very same object Ally had just found in the box. The burnt rosary.

Yes, these were the same ritual tools her mother had used back then.

Ally flipped through more photos at college—one of her mother, visibly pregnant—Nora. Another of her father, smiling —a rare expression for him—his hand resting gently on her swollen belly.

And there were even more pictures of her mother dressed in

her old séance outfit outside their parlor. She looked *so* much like Nora back then. They could have been twin sisters.

Setting the photos aside, Ally unearthed the last bundle of papers. They were better organized this time. Some of them were stapled, and some were clipped inside a folder.

References to binding rites. Blood seals. Moloch's offspring. Even the name Ezeran appeared.

Her mother had underlined one phrase in her distinctive handwriting:

Vessel prepared in innocence.

Vessel? Ally's stomach churned. This was what she'd wanted to find, but now that it was in front of her, it sickened her. Her mother hadn't stumbled into this. She had known precisely what she was doing.

But then her mother had written more. She'd written lines of text deeper into the paper, as if under stress.

I will not willingly give up anything in exchange for my child. You can take my blood, my breath, my name. But when I die, my daughter will remain unburdened by this debt. There will be no sacrifice, not to any god or demon.

I refuse...

And their father... He must have known about it too.

It was clear now: Tess had lied to Ally about Ezeran. The demon had never been a protector. It was only there to deliver Lucy to Moloch, coming to prepare the sacrifice for its master.

That explained why her father had discarded so many of her mother's things, especially the books tied to her college years. He must have known about what her mother had done, and the deal her mother had made with the demon.

But he'd kept this box with the items tied to the ritual. Maybe he feared they would need it again someday.

Stepping back, Ally carried the box out of the spare room and set it on the kitchen table. She'd go through it more thoroughly later. Right now, the weight of sleeplessness pressed down on her whole body. It was overwhelming. She needed to lie down, even just to take a nap.

But it was crystal clear what needed to happen next. As soon as she woke up, she had to find out what Father Tony had done. What rite had he performed to put the demon to sleep, to seal it at the pit? If his work had failed, Ally needed to understand why. But she also needed to understand how to fix it. And more than that, she needed to ensure she would never repeat his mistakes.

$\maltese$ 22 $\maltese$

Nora and Daniel returned to the top of the basement stairs after Lucy had crawled under a blanket and fallen asleep. At least, it seemed that way. Silence filled the house for the first time in hours. They'd crept up the stairs, but Nora had peeked over her shoulder several times to make sure Lucy was still breathing.

After the door closed behind Nora, a fragile sense of relief rushed over her. Maybe things would get better now. Maybe the worst was over. The morning light filtered in through the closed blinds she hadn't had time to open yet, but the light seemed to brighten her heart.

Her brief optimism faded a moment later when she spotted the broken glass on the floor that Ally had mentioned. A bookcase had toppled over, along with a framed photo of her family. The shards had scattered everywhere. Nothing that couldn't be replaced, but the incessant accidents had taken a toll on them both.

"I'll get a broom." Daniel stepped around the debris on his way to the garage and emerged a minute later with it.

The picture frame had survived the crash, but the glass had torn the photo beyond repair. Still, their beaming faces showed through the pieces. It was a perfect analogy of their shattered lives.

"We have to keep her down there," Daniel said without expression while sweeping up the glass. "We have to lock the door."

Nora didn't argue. "I know. But then what? How far are we going to take this? We can't keep her locked down there forever. She's not a monster."

He paused and stared into her eyes. "Do you know what's wrong with her?"

For the first time, she could see him truly searching for answers, truly willing to do anything—supernatural or not—to face whatever had taken over Lucy.

"Is she really possessed?" he asked.

Nora nodded. "I think so."

"So what can we do about it?"

She hesitated to answer him. Without Father Tony, she had no answers. Not anymore. "Let me think about it."

"Think fast. Maybe Father Tony had friends we can call. Someone else at the church must know who we can call to help us, to finish what he started."

"I don't know any of his friends, Daniel. But... we'll get someone. I'll make some calls. I'll go to the church and talk with everyone there, if I have to."

Daniel nodded without looking up. "Can you go right away? I can handle her alone."

The thought of leaving Lucy alone in the basement while she headed into town sent a jolt of panic through her. What if something happened while she was gone? But Daniel was right. He could handle anything that came up, and the longer she waited, the worse things would get. "I'll leave now."

He glanced around. "Where's... Blanco?"

Nora searched the kitchen and then walked toward the living room. She found the cat hiding beneath one of the end tables next to the couch. He was crouched in a corner, staring up at her with wide eyes. There was no fear in them. He was just watching them from a distance, as if he knew what was happening.

"Blanco." Nora stepped forward and crouched in front of him. "Maybe you're safer in the laundry room today."

She picked him up and cradled him in her arms while walking him into the laundry room. He seemed content to let her carry him. After shutting the door, he meowed from the other side. Still, it was better that he stayed out of sight, just in case Lucy made her way upstairs.

A disturbing thought struck Nora. Lucy had attempted to harm Blanco before. Would she try again to finish him off?

It was impossible to rule it out. Lucy wasn't herself anymore. It was hard to believe they'd come to that, but it was better to stay cautious... under the circumstances. There was no telling what Lucy might do, the way she was acting.

When she returned to Daniel, he was sweeping up the last bits of glass. He smiled at her, but she could see the exhaustion on his face. "I won't be gone long."

Pausing for a moment, he leaned on the broom and met her gaze. "Do you think anyone will listen?"

"I won't stop until they do."

His smile stretched wider. "That's why I married you—you never give up. After you get back from the church, we'll take turns watching the door. If she comes up to eat or use the bathroom, one of us will be there to meet her." He rubbed the back of his neck. "I hope you come back with some answers."

Nora nodded slowly and headed toward the front door. "I won't come back until I do."

❦   23   ❦

Nora walked into St. Michael's Catholic Church. It just wasn't the same without Father Tony there, although she could still sense his presence on some level. Staring straight ahead, she avoided the staff near the entrance and headed toward Father Tony's office—his *old* office.

It was strange to think that she would never see him again, and yet she was there to get his help. Keeping her chin up, she passed the sanctuary and turned down the hallway toward his office. The door was partly closed, although the light was on.

When she stepped inside, his secretary glanced up and met her gaze. It was the same old woman she'd met months earlier during her last visit.

The woman's eyes widened, and she smiled, although it didn't reach her eyes. "Oh... may I help you?"

"I need to talk to someone about Father Tony. He was helping us."

"Oh, yes." Recognition swept over her face. "I remember you, Miss Vale."

"That's right," Nora said. "He was helping us—my family. I'm hoping you can show me any notes he might have kept about my family a couple of decades ago—especially my mother. I know he kept a journal. He mentioned it once."

The old woman glanced toward the hallway door, and then leaned forward and lowered her voice. "I'm afraid Father Tony's records are private, but I'm not sure I'm allowed to..."

A loud thump came from inside the closed door to Father Tony's office. Voices came through the walls, and then another thump.

The old woman flinched. "They're retrieving his personal belongings and some furniture. It may seem insensitive to move so quickly, but I'm afraid it's the only way to make a smooth transition. Father Tony took on a lot of responsibility—even more in his later years—and we need to ensure that his hard work is not lost. Another priest will pick up where he left off. He'll be arriving soon."

Scraping sounds filled the air, like furniture being dragged across the tile floor.

Nora gestured toward the door. "Can I go inside just for a moment?"

The old woman held out her hand. "No, it's better—"

But Nora had already turned away and opened the door.

Behind her, the old woman called out, "Miss Vale, wait!"

Two custodians were busy working inside Father Tony's office, boxing things up and cleaning off the shelves. His office looked much smaller without him in it. The curtains were half-drawn, letting in only a fraction of the light that usually poured through the stained glass windows behind his desk. They'd stripped the walls of everything he'd placed there, as if someone were erasing his identity. Even the crucifix above his desk was gone.

One of the men turned and looked at her. "Ma'am, you can't be in here."

Nora stepped inside. "I'm just looking for something."

He shook his head. "You're not going to find it in here, I'm afraid."

"Where is all of this... going?"

The old woman hurried in behind Nora and touched her arm gently. "Please, they're just doing their job. If you have questions—"

"I have lots of questions," Nora said.

She glanced around at the piles of paper, folders, and boxes. They had already packed away much of it. Somewhere in that mess were the answers she was looking for. If she just had time to glance through it before everything was shoved into a dark closet forever...

"He was helping my daughter before he died," Nora said.

"I'm aware of the circumstances—"

"He would have kept notes on her—on what happened—and he might also have pulled up notes on my mother recently."

"I'm sorry." The old woman tugged on Nora's sleeve. "Please, dear, let them finish."

Nora's gaze snapped toward something half-concealed under a stack of hymnals on a shelf beside the door. Something she hadn't seen in a long time: a small, portable cassette player. Next to it were rows of old cassette tapes, each labeled with hand-written masking tape.

One of the labels jumped out at her.

Claire, 1997.

Her mother?

Father Tony had never mentioned recording anything with her mother. But maybe it wasn't her. There were probably other women named Claire in their community. Still—

Her hand jumped toward it before she could think. Grabbing the cassette off the shelf, she turned it over in her hand.

The men didn't seem to notice, but the old woman did. Nora met her gaze for a long moment.

Nora pleaded silently.

Don't take this from me. Don't take the last thing he left behind.

The old woman's throat bobbed as if she might speak, but then she glanced away.

"I'll go now." Nora slipped the cassette into her pocket.

"Yes," the old woman said, leading her out of the room. "It's better that way."

The pressure of the cassette tape in Nora's pocket satisfied her. If it was her mother's recording, it might help answer some of the nagging questions that hovered at the back of her mind.

What had her mother done out at that quarry with Tess? What had they unleashed, and what could Nora do to stop it?

Moving out into the hallway, the old woman followed her.

"Nora," the woman whispered urgently. "Whatever you think that is—"

Nora turned back to her. "It has my mother's name on it."

The old woman pressed her eyes closed. "You don't want to hear it."

"Why?"

The woman opened her eyes again, a little wider. "Because... he wouldn't want you to. I'm sure he died trying to help your family—he would have risked his life to save anyone—but this was something he battled before you were born. He wouldn't want you to get involved."

"Get involved? My daughter is—" Nora's heart raced faster, but she lowered her voice. "—*possessed* by something he was involved with. My daughter might die. How much more involved could I get?"

The old woman swallowed hard and glanced back inside the office. "Please wait here." She hurried back into Father Tony's office and returned a minute later holding the cassette player, a crucifix, and a folder thick with papers. She handed Nora the cassette player first. "You might need this. They're not so common these days."

Nora accepted it.

The woman continued, "He didn't tell me everything, but I've sat behind that desk long enough to know when to bend the rules." She handed the folder to Nora. "These are his notes regarding your mother. I believe he kept most of them at his house. This is all that's left here."

Nora accepted the folder and nodded. "Thank you."

The old woman handed her the crucifix last. She smiled, and it seemed genuine for the first time. "He spoke highly of you. May God bless you and keep you safe."

Nora turned away, pressing the folder, the crucifix, and cassette player against her chest. She hurried down the hallway, out of the church, and headed back to her car. As soon as she climbed into the driver's seat, she slipped the cassette into the old player and started the tape. The voices were instantly recognizable—her mother and Father Tony.

The conversation started after some soft clicks, a hiss, and some shuffling. Father Tony cleared his throat.

Father Tony: *Claire, I asked you to come in here to talk with me about what happened that night on June 7, 1997.*

Claire: *What do you want to know?*

Father Tony: *I'd like to know what really happened at the quarry between you, Tess, and the others. What were you doing there before I arrived?*

There was a long silence until her mother sighed.

Claire: *I think you already know.*

Father Tony: *I do, but I'd like to hear it from you. What did you expect to accomplish?*

Claire: *Well... we all went there for different reasons. I went because I was pregnant, and what the doctors told me about my baby... that it would die.*

Father Tony: *They said it would die?*

Claire: *Yeah.*

A brief silence passed.

Claire (continued): *Tess went there for something similar. She was having some trouble getting pregnant. She fell in love with a guy and wanted to have a baby with him.*

Father Tony: *What about the others?*

Claire: *Jonah, Marcy, Derek... They were just along for the thrill of it, I think. I doubt any of them believed anything would happen. But Tess did. Tess always believed in it—yes, wholeheartedly.*

Father Tony: *And you believed.*

Claire: *Yes. I believed in Tess. She knew all about that stuff, and of course I wanted to see if it was real. I mean, selling the psychic stuff at the parlor is one thing, but I... I wasn't raised to really believe in it. It's just for show, you know. Tess told me she'd found a way to make it happen— for real. I could save my baby, and she could get pregnant too. You know the history of the quarry, right? The rocks there?*

Father Tony: *They're special in some way.*

Claire: *Some of the stones—the ones way down there—have a connection to something... evil. They've got weird lines in them. The veins —they look like little screaming faces. I'm sure you've heard all the stories. They say the place is cursed. I don't doubt it, but Tess said she could give us all what we wanted—anything—if we paid the price.*

Father Tony: *So she took you all down there?*

Claire: *Yes. She had Jonah dive to the bottom of the pit. He retrieved some of them, including a stone with screaming veins in it. He brought it up to the surface, and Tess started the ritual.*

Father Tony: *The one I interrupted.*

Claire: *Yes. But we'd already finished most of it. Before you got there, Tess had us cut our palms and bleed onto it. Then she started reading out loud from the book she brought along—a bunch of old ritual stuff.*

Her voice faltered.

Claire (continued): *Everyone made a request. Well... when she demanded that we all cut our palms on it and bleed onto it, the others backed out. So it was just me and Tess from that point on. And then, when you showed up... they ran away.*

Father Tony: *They ran away before they completed the ritual?*

Claire: *Yes. I guess they got scared and tried to back out at the last minute. There's something special about it... that the stone at the bottom is demonic or something.*

Father Tony: *During the ritual, you demanded that it save your baby?*

Claire: *Of course.*

Father Tony: *Even though you knew it would require a sacrifice.*

Claire: *We're still in college. Who takes anything seriously at our age? I would have given anything to save my baby. So... we didn't really think about it. Not seriously.*

Father Tony: *Did Tess explain to you what this sacrifice might entail?*

Claire: *She said it didn't matter—that we didn't need to worry about it.*

Father Tony: *Did she ever tell you that the demon would require something living? Something innocent?*

Claire: *She mentioned that.*

Father Tony: *And that didn't bother you?*

Claire: *I don't think you get it. My baby was going to die. And I didn't think it meant something human. Tess told me we could deal with it later... kill an animal or something.*

Father Tony: *Did you ever attempt a sacrifice?*

Claire: *No, never. I couldn't hurt a fly, much less a wild animal. I thought if I just ignored it, maybe it would forget about me.*

Father Tony sighed, and some papers rustled.

Father Tony: *About the demon... Closing your eyes doesn't erase the pact. The debt stays open until it's paid.*

Claire: *But you bound it anyway. You told me you sealed the pit.*

Father Tony: *I did, as best I could. The rite holds... as long as nobody disturbs the seal that I placed there. The thing is not banished, but instead it is like a sleeping giant. However, the debt is always there, and if you die before the debt is paid... your child inherits it.*

Claire: *Nora? No... no. That can't be right.*

Father Tony: *I'm afraid that's the way it works. But I will watch it —keep an eye on things. If you see anything happen over the years, please contact me immediately. Do you understand the seriousness of what you've invoked?*

Several seconds of silence passed.

Claire: *Tess said... everything would be alright.*

Father Tony: *You opened the door—all of you. You must understand that. You don't simply walk away from something like that untouched. Thank God I arrived in time to stop it.*

Claire: *So everything is okay then?*

Father Tony: *It appears so. Is your baby healthy? Was it... worth it?*

Claire: *Nora is doing wonderfully. The doctors were amazed. There's nothing wrong with her—a perfect, beautiful girl. It was worth it.*

Father Tony: *For now, but eventually, the price must be paid.*

Claire: *Then I'll just worry about it then, won't I?*

Father Tony: *Maybe you won't need to worry about it, but maybe your children will.*

Claire: *Tess will know what to do if anything happens.*

Father Tony: *I pray Tess never sets foot in that quarry ever again.*

Claire: *What happens if she does?*

Father Tony: *God help us.*

24

Daniel hated leaving his daughter alone in the basement, even for a few minutes, but he needed a break. Lucy was finally asleep, and there was no telling when Nora or Ally might return.

Pausing in the bathroom on his way to the kitchen, he checked the cuts and bruises Lucy had inflicted on him during their struggle. Nothing serious, but the bruises were already forming where she had kicked him in the chest.

In the kitchen, he found some leftover pizza and sat at the table eating it. The relative calm helped to soothe his nerves, but he never let the basement door out of his sight for long. Every creak made his pulse jump.

Ten minutes later, he found himself standing in the basement doorway again. It was silent down there. No signs that Lucy had awakened.

Perfect.

His paternal instincts kicked in. He wanted to call out to her, to ask if she was okay, but instead pushed his lips together. It was better to leave well-enough alone.

Despite the relative calm, she wasn't okay. Not in any sense of the word. Something had taken control of her.

Possession?

Was this the real thing? It was hard to believe any of this was happening. He'd heard plenty of stories over the years and had seen most of the movies of priests exorcising demons from writhing innocents. It never ended well, but those were just movies. He never imagined he'd actually come face to face with it someday. His heart ached knowing that Lucy was down there shivering, alone, and confused, and there was nothing he could do about it. This wasn't anything he could have prepared for. Nothing he could have foreseen. His little girl's life was on the line, and he didn't know how it would end.

Forcing himself to go back down the stairs, he took his time and gently lowered himself onto each step to avoid making noise. It was better to let her sleep, but it was quiet. Too quiet. He needed to check on her again.

The light was on, but everything seemed darker than usual. The clutter they'd accumulated over the years sat stuffed against every wall of the small space. It seemed to close in on him.

Reaching the bottom, he crossed the basement and reached Lucy's corner a moment later.

At first, he couldn't believe it. His stomach churned. The mattress was empty.

He scanned the twisted pile of blankets for her little frame, but he couldn't deny it. She was gone.

"Lucy?"

His heart raced faster. There wasn't much space for her to hide, but he searched the area with growing intensity. Where the hell did she go?

Finally, he spotted her near one of the basement windows. She'd climbed onto a pile of stacked totes and was pushing against the glass with her shoulder. She had already slid the lock open. The window frame bowed outward. One more shove and she would have been outside.

Daniel rushed over, grabbed her around the waist, and pulled her back.

Shrieking and limbs flailing, she struggled wildly within his grasp. One foot caught him in his ribs, and another against the back of his head. The pain was sharp, but he recovered quickly. Was this really his daughter? She had the strength of someone twenty years older, and it caught him off guard.

But once he pulled her away from the window, she went limp —instantly boneless, like a rag doll dropped after playtime.

"Lucy... stop! Why are you acting like this? You know I can't let you leave the house. You'll hurt yourself. I'm sorry."

He carried her back to the mattress, cradling her in his arms like he had when she was an infant. It would have felt the same, except for his aching muscles and bruises. Her breathing fell into a steady rhythm, and her eyelids fluttered gently along the way.

Somehow... her surrender was worse.

He squeezed her wrists and wedged her legs under his arm in case she awoke again. He *had* to keep her restrained, but she wasn't fighting anymore. He was the bad guy, and it tore at his heart.

After placing her on the mattress, he sat beside her in a defensive position for several minutes just to make sure she wouldn't try anything again.

Eventually, she retreated to a spot beside the furnace a few feet away. Slumped forward and wavering, she turned onto her side and curled up in a ball. He couldn't see her face from that angle. Her hair draped across it like a curtain.

Daniel watched her like that for a long time. What the hell was going on inside her head? The answer came back—*Do you really want to know?* Not really, but there seemed to be no way he could help besides holding her there until Nora or Ally returned. What else could he do? He desperately wanted to rescue Lucy from her nightmare, but he was powerless. He considered bringing her upstairs, back to the comfort of her bedroom, but decided it was safer for everyone to keep her down here. Less of a chance she would try to escape again.

Escape.

The word churned his stomach, but Lucy *was* a captive now in her own home.

He stood after a few minutes of watching her lie completely still. He wasn't about to leave her down there alone again, but he wanted to check on her. Her chest had stopped rising and falling, but he couldn't see her all that well back in the corner like that. The shadows gave the appearance that she hadn't moved at all for a long time.

Leaning down, he pressed his hand against her forehead. Her skin was cold.

"Lucy?" he said softly. "Honey?"

Still nothing. One of her hands rested slack against the mattress. Her little fingers looked pale in the dim basement light, but she didn't even twitch.

"Sweetheart, can you look at me?"

After a few seconds, she finally moved. Her arm shifted a bit. It was enough to know that she wasn't—

Dead?

Shaking off the thought, he let out a sigh of relief. Of course, she was alive. Her face was turned away from him, but he could tell by the way she'd raised her head that she was awake now.

Instead of turning over to answer him, a harsh, low voice erupted from her throat. "It's not me you should lock away."

A cold wind swept across Daniel's face. The window wasn't open. Lucy hadn't gotten it open. But the chilly air filled his lungs. Her words hit him like a slap in the face. His heart raced. He imagined himself scooping her up in his arms and rushing her to the hospital. Maybe someone there could wake her from this nightmare. Instead, he froze, and his mouth dropped open.

"I love you," he said.

Lucy didn't speak at first. Not until a low grumble again filled her throat. "Before the night is over... you will burn me alive."

At the same time, Blanco let out a deep, pained cry from the top of the basement stairs. He hadn't come down, but something had clearly upset him.

Daniel leaned toward Lucy. A scream welled up in his throat. Instead, he spoke in a soft, steady tone. "Lucy, you're scaring me. Don't say things like that. Look at me. Please."

She turned toward him slowly. Her body twisted first, then her face. With a blank stare, she met his gaze, and a twisted grin spread across her face. "Yes, Daddy?"

He swallowed. "I just... want to see if you're okay."

The corners of her mouth tightened. "Do I look okay?"

He hesitated to answer. "No."

"Correct!" She turned a little more to face him directly. "And whatever happens to me, remember, it's *your* fault."

"Nothing's going to happen to you, I promise."

"Promises made, promises broken."

Something thumped against the floor straight above him. Footsteps. Nora? Ally? But they were heavy... and slow. Nothing like their footsteps.

He followed the sounds with his ears. More footsteps, heading across the floor toward the kitchen. Something thumped again upstairs. Loud and sharp.

Had Blanco left his post by the door and gotten into trouble? Somehow, he doubted it.

"Nora?" Daniel called out, hoping—praying—that it was her or Ally up there.

No answer.

He turned back to Lucy. She hadn't moved.

"Are you going to leave me down here alone, Daddy?" she asked in a sweet, frightened voice.

"I'll never leave you."

"You're a liar." She growled and turned her face away from him. "You left me down here all alone earlier. All alone, with the bugs and the mice and the monsters..."

Daniel shook his head. "I'm right here, honey."

"Too bad. I liked it when you were upstairs. It gave me time to *think*."

More footsteps thumped against the floor above him.

Heavier this time—like an overweight man charging from room to room. Every footstep shook the house.

It couldn't be Nora or Ally.

An intruder? He hoped so this time.

He turned to face the stairs.

"You're leaving now, aren't you?" she asked.

"I need to... check on something."

"On the man upstairs?"

He swallowed. "How do you know it's a man?"

"What do *you* think it is?" She glanced over her shoulder and grinned at him.

He reached for the phone in his pocket but stopped. He couldn't call the police. It didn't matter whether this was an intruder or not. They wouldn't understand the... *situation*. They would arrive to find a father holding his daughter hostage in the basement. And what if Lucy said something damaging during their visit? She wasn't herself at the moment—not in any sense of the word. What might she say to them?

Officers, my father locked me in the basement. Don't you see the mattress and the scraps of food? Take him away, boys!

If they found her like this, they'd not only take her away, they'd drag him and Nora off to prison.

No, they had to deal with this nightmare alone, at least without the help of the police.

Please, Nora. I hope you found something. God, I hope there's a solution to this madness.

"And while you're up there," Lucy added, "can you turn up the heat? I'm freezing."

Her request caught him off guard. He backed away and stood staring at her form hunched over in the shadows. "I'll... see what I can do."

Then, the lights went out.

Not just the basement lights but the furnace. All of it—gone. The house's power had gone out.

Daniel pulled out his phone and switched it to flashlight

mode instead of calling anyone. He would have to deal with this alone.

Making his way back toward the stairs, the darkness weighed on him more than before. The shadows shifted on all sides.

The circuit breaker box was out in the garage. He'd need to go upstairs to reset the tripped circuit, but he agonized over leaving Lucy alone.

Did he have a choice? It needed to be done.

Something grabbed him from behind. A dark and powerful force. It yanked him backwards, and he tumbled sideways. He hit the wooden railing first, then the stairs, and finally landed on the cement floor. His head crashed into a pile of boxes, breaking his fall from the worst of it, but his right arm and shoulder bore the full weight of his body. Something cracked in his arm, and pain flooded his mind.

He screamed.

Lucy laughed. "I told you there were monsters down here."

Writhing in pain on the ground, he struggled to sit upright. His phone had slipped out of his hand and landed nearby, face up, with the light still illuminating the area. Instead of lighting the way, it blinded him for a few seconds. Whatever had struck him was still out there.

Its shadow moved in the darkness, but he couldn't focus on it.

Reaching for his phone with his good arm, he stopped after another wave of pain shot up his spine. He imagined bruises were already forming on his back. "Lucy..."

"I'm right here, Daddy."

The sound of shuffling clothes moved closer. It was the sound of Lucy's pajamas, but he couldn't see her from where he sat. She was coming toward him, and when she stepped into the light, he gasped.

Lucy's body jerked sideways, her head and hair tossed back violently. Something invisible yanked her toward the ground, forcing her onto her hands and knees. She crawled toward him then, like a wounded animal with broken limbs. Her knees and palms scraped across the cement as she advanced, leaving a streak of blood behind.

"Stop!" he cried. "Lucy, you're hurting yourself!"

She continued toward him like an animal stalking its prey. Her gaze fixed on his.

Then she lunged.

Slamming into his chest, a fresh wave of pain exploded through his ribs. He crumpled while struggling to take in a breath.

Lucy's small fingers clutched his throat and squeezed. Her nails cut into his skin.

"Lucy, don't—" He pulled at one of her wrists. He couldn't move his other arm.

Her pupils expanded, swallowing the color of her eyes. "It's too late. You can't stop me."

The front door slammed shut upstairs.

A moment later, Nora's voice sliced through the air. "Daniel?"

He struggled to call out, but he was out of breath.

Lucy turned sharply toward the stairs. Her face was repulsive in that light, almost feral, with her little teeth bared in a wide grin.

"Daniel?" Nora shouted again.

Lucy released him and sprinted toward the stairs.

Daniel took a labored breath and screamed, "Nora! Look out!"

25

Nora stepped inside the house carrying the cassette recorder, crucifix, and the folder of notes she'd received from Father Tony's secretary. She had briefly flipped through the notes in the car, but she couldn't focus. The echo of her mother's voice on the cassette still rang through her mind. Would the discoveries finally provide the answers she so desperately needed?

The house was dark and silent when she entered.

Flipping the light switches, she found that none of them worked. "Daniel?" she called out. "Daniel?"

Closing the door behind her, a flurry of noises came from somewhere under her feet. A struggle? The basement door was open. Blanco was sitting in the doorway, hissing into the darkness.

Hurrying over to the basement stairs, she called out down, "Daniel?"

Instead of his voice, thunderous footsteps filled the air. A moment later, Lucy appeared out of the shadows, charging up toward her.

"Nora!" Daniel's voice came from the basement. "Look out!"

Something was off about Lucy. Her face was pale and wild,

and her hair flew in every direction. Her pajamas were twisted, with one of the top buttons missing. She was breathing sharply and heavily, like she hadn't exhaled in minutes.

"Lucy?" Nora stepped back. The girl's eyes were wide and distant. "What's wrong?"

But Nora already knew the answer to that.

Gripping the crucifix a little tighter, the metal suddenly felt warm in her hand as she took another step back.

Lucy seemed to notice. She stared at the crucifix and stopped in her tracks when she reached the top of the stairs.

Nora lifted it slightly higher. "Okay, honey... try to calm down. Where's—?"

Lucy lunged.

Nora wasn't ready. The girl's forehead collided with her chest. Lucy's nails scraped across Nora's shoulder, and both of them stumbled backwards. Squeezing the crucifix, Nora thrust it up between them. Terror spread across Lucy's face, and her reaction sent a chill up Nora's spine. Her daughter recoiled and... *snarled.* The sounds came up her throat in guttural gasps—something demented and animalistic. Something evil. Baring her teeth, the girl stopped and trembled.

Nora caught her breath. "Lucy, where's your father?"

Lucy didn't answer. Instead, she glanced toward the front door and then took a step in that direction.

Nora cut her off. "Where is he, honey?"

A moment later, footsteps echoed up the basement stairs.

"Keep away from her," Daniel's voice came through the darkness. "She's gone."

Nora extended the crucifix again. Lucy backed away further, turning her face and covering it with one arm.

Daniel's footsteps echoed up the basement stairs, and he appeared in the doorway a moment later. He was clutching his phone with one hand. He'd switched it to flashlight mode, and the beam bounced off the walls. His other arm hung at a strange angle, stiff and swollen. The collar of his shirt was torn, and long red scratches ran down the side of his neck.

"Oh my God, Daniel!" Nora moved toward him.

His gaze stopped first on Lucy, and then shifted to the crucifix in Nora's hand. "We'll need more than that."

Nora reached toward his injured arm. "What happened?"

He held up his hand. "Stay there! Don't let her outside."

Nora stopped. Lucy shifted her stance as if preparing to bolt out the door. "Did she—?"

He nodded. "She's out of control. She's gone."

Nora tried to look into Lucy's eyes, but the girl avoided her gaze. "She's not gone."

He stepped toward them, nursing his injured arm. "Trust me. She's gone. I think... she broke it."

Nora's heart raced. "We'll call an ambulance."

He shook his head. "Not... just yet. Get her back downstairs first."

Nora caught a glimpse of Lucy's eyes when she glanced up. They were wide, bloodshot, and full of malice. Daniel was right. She wasn't herself anymore. Maybe she wasn't *gone*, but whatever controlled Lucy now had pushed the girl's beaming spirit into a dark corner.

Lucy lunged for the door.

Nora blocked her and extended the crucifix again.

Daniel lunged forward at the same time. Despite his injury, he looped his good arm under Lucy's shoulder and pulled her back. Together, they dragged her away from the door. She writhed in their grasp, kicking and screaming.

"Hold her!" Daniel gritted his teeth.

"I am!" Nora shouted.

Lucy fought them for several seconds, until something snapped, and her body went limp. She let out a few exhausted gasps and then sagged in their arms. Her eyes snapped shut, as if she'd fallen asleep.

"She did this before," Daniel said between sharp breaths.

"She falls asleep for a few minutes, like she's recharging, but then she comes back even worse. We need to take her downstairs. That's the only place she's safe."

"But what about your arm?"

He glanced at it briefly, winced, and then met Nora's gaze. "It'll have to wait. Can you hold her for a minute? Alone? I need to reset the breaker. You got her?"

Nora squeezed Lucy a little tighter. "Yes."

He took a step back, winced again while drawing a breath through clenched teeth, and then hurried out into the garage.

The power came on a minute later. Despite the sudden glare of the overhead lights, Lucy didn't stir. Her breaths came slowly, although her eyelids fluttered a bit.

"Hang on, Lucy," Nora whispered. "I know you're still with us."

Daniel rushed back inside, still holding his limp arm. After putting away his phone, he grabbed Lucy's arm again and together they half-guided, half-carried Lucy down the stairs into the basement.

When they reached the bottom of the stairs, Lucy seemed to wake a little. Her toes touched the floor, and she drifted toward the mattress like a sleepwalker. The moment she stepped onto the mattress, she settled back into the same place as before, curling into a ball again even without their help.

When she stopped moving, they both cautiously stepped away.

Nora waited until Daniel looked at her before gesturing to his arm and whispering, "What happened?"

"She tried to get out of the window. I stopped her, but... it didn't go well." He gestured to his broken arm and winced, sucking in a breath. "We'll need to block the windows from the outside, or she'll try again."

Nora nodded, despite the disturbing thought of trapping Lucy down there alone like an animal. "Yes, of course."

Daniel gestured to the crucifix in Nora's hand. "How did it go? I hope you have some good news."

"Not exactly good."

Lucy shifted on the mattress, turning her face up. For a brief second, she looked almost normal again—her sweet, usual self. Vulnerable and small.

Nora stared at Daniel's wounds as he leaned against a stack of boxes. How had their little girl done something so horrendous? And what else was she capable of? The harsh light illuminated the scratches across his neck and the bruises forming around them.

"You need a doctor," Nora said.

He nodded. "But we can't leave."

"I'll call an ambulance."

"I don't want them coming in here." Daniel glanced around nervously. "Nobody should come in here. Not now."

"We'll meet them outside when they arrive... on the front porch."

He didn't respond for a few seconds, but then he nodded. "I'll say I fell down the stairs."

"What *really* happened?" Nora asked.

He turned his gaze to Lucy. "Something caught me off guard. I didn't see it—I felt it. It knocked me down from behind. And then she attacked me."

Lucy started giggling—low and quiet to herself—and then stopped.

❧ 26 ❧

Nora stood by the door and stared out of the window. The ambulance had left moments earlier. It was racing away now, down the road, with Daniel inside. She couldn't go with him this time. It was impossible. Lucy was still in the basement.

Turning away from the window, Daniel's words echoed in her mind.

Don't turn your back on her. Block the windows.

Nora stepped over to the basement door, closed it, and then locked it. Her actions felt like a betrayal. Did she really need to take such drastic steps? Yes, it was necessary. After everything she'd experienced recently, this wasn't just a precaution. This was protection. For her. For her daughter.

While pausing to eat a sandwich at the kitchen counter, she caught a glimpse of the folder containing Father Tony's notes on the table. She wanted to go over there immediately, sit down and flip through every page. There had to be something in there that would help them, either to guide them or just offer clues on how to deal with Lucy's behavior. Anything would help. Even just something to point them in the right direction.

But all of that would have to wait. She had something more important to take care of.

Nora grabbed her coat, slipped it on, and headed out into the garage. Stepping through the doorway, she walked over to the stack of cinder blocks along the side. Daniel had purchased them to build a small playhouse for Lucy in the backyard. It was a summer project he'd talked about for years. He'd intended to start working on it that very summer, but now it seemed he might never finish it—not with a broken arm.

Dragging out a small red wagon, she smiled softly. This was the one they'd used to pull Lucy around the neighborhood when she was younger. It still even had some of the stickers Lucy had placed along the sides. Some had worn away. They'd talked about giving the wagon away at a garage sale. Now, Nora was glad they hadn't.

Lifting the first cinder block with both hands, she placed it in the wagon and reminded herself of why she was going through so much trouble.

This is all to save Lucy.

Grabbing three more blocks, she fit four into the wagon before the small wheels started to buckle under the weight. It was enough. At least enough to cover all four of the basement windows if she put one block behind each. She could always come back if she needed more.

Pulling the wagon across the grass around to the side of the house, she stopped in front of the first window. The small pane was barely large enough for someone to slip through. It seemed impossible to think that Lucy might ever attempt to escape through it. Their house was old. It had come with small hopper windows, common features when they'd built the house decades earlier. Nothing fancy about them, but in this case, that was a good thing. Smaller windows meant there was less of a chance Lucy would find her way out.

Lifting the first cinder block from the wagon, she placed it in front of the glass.

This is for my daughter.

But it somehow felt *wrong*. She was building a wall between herself and the child she'd so many times cradled in her arms and vowed to love until the end of time. Her stomach churned.

I'll be glad when this is over.

Working her way around the house, she stopped in front of the last window and placed the final cinder block in front of it. She brushed the dust from her hands, stood straight, and then took a deep breath.

Maybe now she could—

A sharp thud rattled the window she'd just reinforced, followed by a second, more frantic pounding.

Nora froze.

Behind the foggy glass, someone's small pale face appeared. They were desperately clawing at the pane.

"Lucy," Nora whispered.

The scraping intensified. Lucy's small fingernails scratched and pulled at the wooden frame. The girl let out a tight, strangled cry, and it pierced Nora's ears and heart. Had she really locked her daughter in the basement like an animal in a cage? It seemed so.

Nora leaned down and pressed her palm against the cinder block. It was vibrating from Lucy's efforts. "You can't get out this way, sweetheart... stop. Please stop."

Another violent blow.

The glass almost shattered.

Then—silence.

A chill swept down Nora's spine. Slowly backing away, she expected the frenzied pounding to start again at any moment. Her heart raced faster with anticipation.

Okay... Don't panic. That's not her down there. I haven't locked my little Lucy in that basement. I've locked that thing *inside of her down there. She's not my girl. Not right now.*

Nora hurried back toward the front door, leaving the wagon behind. She dropped its handle somewhere along the way and didn't look back.

But stepping onto the porch, her gaze fixed on the front door. It was wide open.

Nora's stomach dropped. "No."

She rushed inside.

"Lucy?"

The living room was empty. The kitchen too.

The basement door was still closed, but it was unlatched. Unlocked. Somehow, she'd gotten out.

"Lucy!?" Nora shouted.

No answer.

Until someone shouted outside. A familiar voice.

Nora turned and ran back out the front door. Ally was there, her arms wrapped around Lucy's thrashing body. The girl was resisting with everything she had. If anyone else had seen her like that—kicking, clawing, baring her teeth, and screaming wildly toward the sky—they'd have thought Ally was abducting the girl.

"Nora! Help!" Ally shouted.

Nora rushed toward them. Lucy's face was ghost white. Her eyes were wild.

Nora grabbed Lucy's wrists. "Calm down, Lucy! For God's sake, calm down!"

Glancing around the yard, there was no sign that any of the neighbors had noticed the commotion. But the thought still haunted her. If anyone had seen them, they might have already called the police. The police might already be on their way. They would take Lucy away.

And who could blame them?

Together, she and Ally wrestled Lucy back into the house. Lucy's strength came in waves—wild, powerful bursts that pushed both women to their limits. But as soon as they crossed the threshold, her body went limp again. Her head rolled gently against Nora's shoulder.

A wave of relief washed over Nora. Now they could get her

back down to the basement. They would have a bit of time to exchange ideas and plan out a strategy.

Carrying Lucy inside, the smell of smoke filled the air.

Ally sniffed. "Do you smell that? I think something's burning."

"Shit," Nora whispered.

The smoke alarms erupted a moment later. The relentless, shrill sound pierced her ears.

A gray haze drifted through the air near the kitchen.

Before Nora could object, Ally scooped Lucy into her arms. "I'll take her."

Nora broke away from them and ran to find the source. In the kitchen, she spotted it right away. The oven door was cracked open. A thin line of fire burned inside.

Nora grabbed a dish towel, yanked the door open, and staggered back. A burst of smoke poured out in front of her. A black, charred mess lay on the oven rack. It was all clumped together. Ash, paper, and melted plastic. Father Tony's folder. The cassette. The recorder. All of it had burned, and it was still smoldering.

The plastic device had melted into a lump of sizzling goo, dripping onto the bottom of the oven. A burst of thick gray smoke erupted with every drop.

Nora switched off the oven and backed away. There was nothing she could do now except wait. Even the fire extinguisher in the pantry wouldn't help. It was too late. The fire sputtered and died on its own a short time later, but the damage was done.

After opening the nearest windows, the smoke began to clear. A soft breeze filtered in, clearing enough of the haze that the alarms finally fell silent.

Stepping out of the kitchen and into the living room, Nora paused.

Through the smoke, she spotted Ally on the couch, cradling Lucy in her arms. Lucy was like an infant again. Her precious little head leaning against Ally's shoulder. Under any other circumstances, she would have hurried to get a photo of the moment. But then she lifted her head and met Nora's gaze.

"Mommy," Lucy said calmly. "What's burning?"

Nora stared into her daughter's eyes for a long time before speaking. Was there a glimmer of devious humor in the girl's eyes? Yes, it was there. "I think you know."

Lucy grinned.

❧ 27 ❧

They returned Lucy to the basement without a struggle. After only a few minutes, the girl seemed to calm down. Nora finally forced herself to turn away and head back upstairs. Ally followed right behind her.

They were almost to the top when Lucy called out to her in a desperate voice, "Mommy, don't leave me down here with the monsters! I'm scared, Mommy! Please don't go!"

She didn't say it this time in the low, coarse tone of the demon, but in Lucy's fragile voice. Despite the emotion behind her words, it was clear the thing was mimicking her. The tone wasn't right, but for a moment it tugged at Nora's heartstrings.

Nora didn't answer, but the maternal pain slowed her enough that she needed to stop and take a breath.

Ally nudged her forward. "Don't listen to it."

"Please come back, Mommy," Lucy continued. "It's freezing, and I'm starving."

Pausing again at the top of the stairs, Nora *almost* turned back, until it ended their conversation with, "See you in hell, Mommy. I'm already there."

It was easy then to close the door behind them, and Nora locked it.

After taking a few steps toward the kitchen, Ally turned to face her with a stoic stare. "Try not to think about it."

"How can I *not* think about it?"

"We'll get through this." But despite her bravado, it was clear the events had rattled her too. She kept glancing back to the basement door, as if Lucy might come charging through it at any moment.

"Thank God you showed up when you did."

Ally glanced around. "Where's Daniel?"

Nora looked down. "Yeah, you missed a little drama. He broke his arm."

Her eyes widened. "Broke his arm!"

"Something pushed him down the stairs."

Ally narrowed her eyes. "... Lucy?"

Nora shook her head. "Daniel said there was something else down there with her, but she *did* attack him. He's at the hospital."

At the same time, her phone vibrated. She pulled it from her pocket and glanced at the screen. Daniel. He'd sent a text:

I'm fine. Stay with Lucy. Don't let her leave the house. Please.

A second message appeared a moment later:

If she wakes up... don't be alone with her. Wait for Ally.

Nora showed the message to Ally, who nodded.

"He's scared," Nora said.

"I don't blame him," Ally replied.

"So am I."

"But we'll get through this anyway." Ally took Nora's hand. A moment later, she sniffed at the air and looked toward the kitchen. "So, what *did* burn?"

The toxic smell of burnt plastic still hung in the air, despite the fresh air still coming in through the open window.

Nora led her to the kitchen, opened the oven, and gestured to the charred remnants inside. "It *was* Father Tony's interview with Mom."

Ally gave a curious stare. "How did it... get in the oven?"

"I'm guessing Lucy put it in there while I was outside."

"Why would she...?"

Nora shrugged. "Maybe she—*it*—didn't want us to have it. But..." Nora lowered her voice. "I already listened to it, fortunately."

Ally glanced back toward the basement door again. "An interview?"

"Well, it was more like an interrogation. Father Tony recorded it, probably to preserve the details of what Mom did at the quarry."

Ally's eyes narrowed. "What did she say?"

"Not a lot. She admitted going there with Tess to contact demonic forces. She intended to make a covenant with them. Mom knew *exactly* what she was doing. But the worst part is that Mom did it all for... me."

Ally tilted her head. "What do you mean... you?"

"She was pregnant with me at the time. And... she thought she would lose the baby. That's why she did it, Ally. I'm alive, so... I guess it worked."

Ally nodded slowly. "That makes sense."

"What makes sense?"

"The stuff I found in the apartment today, mixed in with Dad's old stuff—used occult objects. Dad kept them, except they belonged to Mom. Dad kept everything, like he knew about what happened at the quarry too."

Nora's heart sank. "So it's true."

"It seems so," Ally said. "Except I know Mom never completed her end of the bargain. She refused the sacrifice, and now the demon wants payment."

"I wish she hadn't done it," Nora said softly.

"Don't say that."

"It's true. I wish more than anything that she'd let me survive or die on my own. Lucy's gone through hell. What did she ever do? She's innocent. I should be down there wrestling with that thing instead of her."

"Somehow, we're going to make this right." Ally reached into her backpack and pulled out a stack of old papers. "Before we start, I wanted to show you some of Mom's things I found there. Dad never threw anything of hers out—not the important stuff. I thought he didn't believe any of this, but he kept everything she brought home from the quarry. There are also a few letters from Tess, and some notes from Mom's college years. He hid all of this from us."

"What do they say?" Nora glanced over the items. It was shocking to see what her father had kept, but even more shocking that he had kept silent about it all those years. Flipping through the papers, she couldn't read them fast enough. She pointed at different pages, scanning for anything familiar.

"Just that Mom and Tess opened it, like Father Tony said. They made a covenant, but they didn't finish the offering. It's still open. That's why it wants Lucy. It's claiming a vessel."

"A vessel," Nora repeated softly.

Ally's fingertips brushed across the rosary's beads. "She was desperate, I suppose, and misinformed."

"Mom thought she could get away with it," Nora said. "I could tell by the way she was talking with Father Tony on the recording that she had no intention of sacrificing anything to complete it. She thought she could just walk away."

"And she did," Ally added, "because of what Father Tony did at the quarry. After discovering their plans and interrupting their ritual, he performed his own rite. One that held the demon in place that night, like a cage."

"So what broke it open?" Nora asked.

"Gabriel's death? That must have weakened it. Maybe the failed sacrifice with his dogs triggered something? And then Tess's ritual at the quarry with Lucy—that further weakened it. And then, I'm guessing when Father Tony died, that was the final blow. No more protection. When he was gone, that's when things... That's when Lucy—"

"He was the anchor holding it in place." Nora nodded.

"When he was gone, it came to collect on the debt. It came for Lucy."

Ally nodded. "But she's not possessed yet. Not completely. She's tethered to the demon in some way—like an umbilical cord. It's connected, but it doesn't live in her. Not yet. We need to sever it, Nora. Before it possesses her completely."

"Then we'll need to sever it," Nora said. "Can we do that?"

Ally nodded slowly, but there was doubt in her eyes. "Yes, but it would require us to..."

"To what?"

Ally met Nora's gaze. "To complete the ritual."

Nora paused and stared at her sister. Had she *really* said that? Finally, she shook her head. "Are you crazy? We're not sacrificing anything. Not an animal, and certainly not a person."

"No," Ally interrupted. "That's not what I'm talking about. That was their mistake. They thought sacrifice was the only way to fulfill it, but that only works if you're making a pact." She turned to a different page. "If you're *breaking* one, you can offer a replacement."

Nora stared into her sister's eyes. "What do you mean, replacement?"

Ally's gaze softened. "The person whose line was marked in the first place—yours."

Nora swallowed hard. "So what you're saying is, I should cut myself open and hope that works, right?"

"No." Ally smiled nervously. "I mean—yes. We'll need a little blood. But it's the intention that matters. The rite Father Tony wrote about—the one he messed up—it's the unbinding. You don't feed the demon or give it what it wants. Instead, we need to claim the bloodline, accept it, and then sever it. That's all."

"That's all," Nora scoffed.

"It will work," Ally insisted. "Mom refused to fulfill the covenant, and Father Tony's rite only delayed the inevitable. Instead of running from it or fighting it, we're going to go through with it. Once the debt belongs to you, we can sever it.

We can control it. Everything that's inside Lucy gets forced out. It dies in her, because it will belong to you."

"What happens to Lucy after the demon gets forced out?" Nora asked.

"It won't have power over her anymore," Ally said. "It can't take her."

Nora stared down at the papers, scanning the handwritten diagrams and Latin annotations. It made sense, but it terrified her at the same time. Ally was the expert on all things occult, but so many things had already gone wrong.

"What happens to me?" Nora asked. "Wouldn't *I* become possessed then?"

Ally's expression turned somber. "Yes, it would occupy you for a short time... until I sever it."

"Can't we just sever it from Lucy?"

Ally shook her head. "That time has passed. And if we force it to leave, the trauma might kill her. Breaking the covenant by force would strengthen the entity. Breaking it through law will destroy the claim."

"Yes," Nora said softly. "Of course, I'll do anything to save Lucy. But if this is what Father Tony wrote, then why didn't he do it?"

"He couldn't," Ally replied. "Only the bloodline can sever the claim. Only you. I'm sure he never thought it would be necessary. He thought he had solved it decades ago. And it lay dormant for all those years—until Gabriel weakened it. That's why he never did anything else. He thought it was over."

Nora's stomach churned. "So... after I bind it to me—accept it—how do we sever it? What's the process?"

"It's all here." Ally gestured to the papers. "And I've got all Mom's items in my backpack. I gathered everything before coming over. The ritual's complete instructions are right here."

She pulled them out one by one: candles, salt, iron nails, a shallow bowl, a burnt rosary. She placed them all beside the crucifix Father Tony's secretary had given her on the way out of his office.

Nora picked up the crucifix and turned it over in her hand.

Ally gestured to it. "We won't need that."

Nora didn't let go. "I'll keep it just in case."

Ally nodded, glanced toward the basement door, and touched Nora's hand. "We should start now. Don't worry. I know exactly what to do."

"What if she wakes up?" Nora asked. "She might... try to get away again."

"We'll need to restrain her during the process. What are you thinking?"

Nora didn't want to think about it. The thought of strapping her daughter down in any way, restraining her like an animal, sickened her. "She has some heavy blankets down there. We can wrap her in them. That should be enough."

Ally nodded. "I can do the ritual while you hold her down. Unfortunately, there's no time for you to practice the words. You'll need to repeat everything I say *exactly*. There's no Latin this time, thank God, and I've already got all the text. Mom wrote everything down in her notebook. The same words she used during her ritual at the quarry. Maybe she thought she might need them again, or maybe she was just documenting it."

"I'll say them," Nora said. "Perfectly."

Ally glanced at the floor. "We should start."

Gathering everything in a cloth grocery tote bag, they descended the stairs together. The air seemed to grow colder as they went down. Blanco stayed near the top of the stairs, watching them, his tail curled tightly against his side. He gave a small meow, as if to say, *Good luck.*

They approached Lucy cautiously, stepping over to where they had left her on the mattress earlier. She was still in the same spot—curled up in a ball, one arm over her face to block out the overhead light that glared down on her.

Nora walked over and began carefully wrapping Lucy with

one of the heavy blankets they'd brought down earlier to keep her warm. She tucked it under her daughter's body lovingly—then under her arms, around her legs—tightening a little more as she went.

Through it all, Lucy never woke up. Or at least... she never fought Nora's efforts.

Once finished, Nora sat on the mattress beside Lucy. She placed her hands gently on each of her daughter's arms as a ball of anxiety tightened in the pit of her stomach. "Ready."

Ally nodded. "Then let's begin."

28

Nora sat behind Lucy with her arms around the girl's shoulders. She held her the way she did when Lucy couldn't sleep. The girl hadn't yet fully awakened, but her body was trembling. She was breathing in and out a little too fast, but her eyes were still closed.

"It's okay, sweetheart," Nora whispered into her ear. "I've got you."

Lucy didn't respond. She'd turned to face the furnace with wide eyes. It wasn't fear, but something else—attention. Her eyes had snapped open when the flame had ignited. The blue gas flame was visible through the small opening on the side of the furnace, and she stared attentively at it.

Ally created a salt circle several feet wide just beyond the mattress. She had prepared everything. The bowl was there, along with the burnt rosary and the crucifix. It was just comforting to have it there, despite their doubts that it would do much good against the demon, especially after everything they had seen. But it was a piece of Father Tony, a connection to him. And... she felt his presence through it, in a way.

When Ally was done, she met Nora's gaze. She stared into

Lucy's face and cleared her throat. "Okay. We'll do this in order, just like we planned."

Nora nodded.

Lucy's fingers twitched within Nora's grasp. She wasn't fighting to escape, but she was flexing and relaxing them again and again. Was she preparing for something?

Ally stood. She took the knife she'd brought down—just an ordinary kitchen knife—but Ally had promised it would do. She stepped over to Nora with the bowl and rosary and then kneeled beside them.

Releasing one of Lucy's hands, Nora extended her own toward her sister, offering her finger up while glancing away and cringing. "I hope this works."

"It will." Ally took one of Nora's fingers and held it over the bowl that contained the rosary. With a small thrust, Ally sliced her palm. The pain was sharp, and a few drops of blood fell onto the rosary.

Nothing happened.

More drops fell.

Then Lucy gasped. Her body arched against Nora's arms. Nora pressed her forehead to the back of Lucy's head. The blanket around her tightened. Lucy started squirming, her mouth stretched open wide. Instead of screaming, she gasped for air, coughed it out, and choked it back in again.

Nora flinched but pulled her daughter in closer. "Hang in there, honey. We're almost done."

After cleaning the wound with disinfectant, Ally rushed to wrap it with a bandage. When she was done, Nora grabbed Lucy's arm again.

Ally kept going. She grabbed a piece of paper and took the bowl and the bloody rosary with her back inside the circle. Settling back into place, she sat with it in her lap and unfolded the page.

Nora recognized their mother's handwriting immediately. The perfect cursive, the slant of the text. Her voice trembled as she prepared to read from the paper that Ally had set in front of her.

~

"I WILL NOT GIVE MY CHILD.
*   I will give my blood in place of blood.*
*   What was opened by fear will not be finished by it..."*

~

LUCY CRIED OUT THIS TIME. HER HEAD JERKED BACKWARD, knocking against Nora's chest. Her eyes rolled into her head then locked on the furnace again. It rattled wildly. Something pounded against the metal walls from the inside.

Nora kept reading:

~

"MY LIFE IS MINE TO OFFER.
*   My silence is mine to keep.*
*   This debt ends with me."*

~

ALLY MET NORA'S GAZE AND NODDED ONCE. "YOU DID IT."

Lucy screamed. It was an emotional cry, full of pain and fear, and it pierced the air. She folded forward into Nora's arms and started shaking uncontrollably.

Something cracked. A loud, sharp crack, like a firecracker going off.

Ally stared down at the bowl in her lap. "It's working."

Nora followed her sister's gaze to the bowl and the rosary inside. One bead had split in half. Another exploded a moment later. And then... Lucy slumped forward.

Her chest heaved as she gasped for breath. She tightened her hand into a fist and then relaxed it before falling silent.

Nora caught her before her head hit the mattress. "Lucy? Lucy?"

The girl was silent for several seconds before her eyes fluttered open again. When she looked up, something was different now. They were beautiful, brown—and clear.

Lucy stared into Nora's eyes and whispered, "Mommy?"

Lucy was back. It was her.

Nora embraced her daughter completely, squeezing against her without fear for the first time in days.

Even before Ally said it, before she confirmed the ritual had succeeded, Nora was already removing the blanket they had wrapped around Lucy. It wasn't necessary anymore.

Her girl had returned.

"It worked." A warm smile spread across Ally's face.

"I know," Nora whispered. She squeezed her daughter against her chest.

Fully unwrapped, Lucy backed away for a moment and stared into her mother's eyes. "Why are you crying, Mommy?"

Nora couldn't answer. Her joy had taken her breath away.

Blanco came down the stairs at the same time and jumped onto the mattress beside them. Instead of hissing or keeping a safe distance, he walked over and pushed his face against Lucy's arm.

The girl broke into a wide smile and stroked his fur. "Where did you go, Blanco? I missed you."

He allowed it for a few seconds, cuddling up beside her without objection—until he stiffened again. This time, not at Lucy. His gaze jumped toward the furnace.

A sharp *whoomp* filled the air behind them as a wave of heat burst out. The furnace had fired up again. But this time, not just the starter flame. Flames erupted through the cracks in the metal panels.

Blanco hissed and jumped off the mattress. He stopped in a

darkened corner a few feet away and stared back at them with wide eyes.

"Do you smell that?" Ally stared at the furnace.

Nora did.

Smoke. But not coming from upstairs this time.

Lucy broke from Nora's grasp and rushed toward the stairs. Stopping at the bottom, she glanced back. Her expression had changed again. Her little eyes hadn't just darkened again. They were gone. Empty sockets. Her grin stretched wider, and she stood taller with confidence.

Both Nora and Ally struggled to get to her before she rushed up the stairs. But within seconds, it was too late. Lucy made it to the top and shut the door.

Nora hurried up the stairs and slammed into the door, landing on her shoulder. "Lucy, open the door!"

On the other side, the latch clicked shut.

She'd locked it.

Nora shook the door handle, pounding it with her fist. "Lucy, what are you doing? Open the door!"

Only silence.

"No." Nora shook the handle and pounded her fist again. The smoke coming from the furnace had filled the stairway. It entered her lungs, and she coughed. Crouching, she took a deep breath, leaned back, and then hurled herself forward again.

Something cracked, but it didn't open. She had no leverage on the stairs. The smoke around her thickened.

"Lucy," she said, softer now. "I know you can hear me. Please. Fight the thing inside of you with everything you've got."

A few seconds later, footsteps rumbled through the house, and the front door slammed shut.

She was gone.

❧ 29 ❧

Nora turned back. Ally was already sprinting toward the nearest basement window. Within seconds, she climbed over a pile of boxes to reach it and started clawing at the frame.

"Don't bother!" Nora cried out.

"What?" Ally asked as she continued to push and pull at the frame, shaking it with both hands.

"There are cinder blocks behind all of them," Nora said. "I put them there."

Ally froze for a moment, but then grabbed a metal T-ball baseball bat from nearby—one that Daniel had used the previous summer to teach Lucy how to play baseball—and slammed the butt of it through the glass. The bat cracked against the cinder block, and it shifted... but the wrong way. She hit it again and again with growing frustration. "Dammit! It won't move!"

"Wait!" Nora cried out. "Not like that. You'll make it worse!"

Ally leaned back and lowered the bat. "What do you mean?"

"I wedged them into the dirt, and then under the lip of the window well. Pushing out just jams it in there."

"Damn."

Nora rushed over to the bottom of the stairs again and glanced back at the furnace. The flames were bursting from the sides, while thick black smoke poured into the air. They were running out of time. The fire wouldn't get them, but the smoke would. The noxious fumes made her gag and cough with every step. Her eyes burned and watered.

Ally climbed back down, gestured to the top of the stairs, and coughed while staring at Nora with wide eyes. "Won't it open?"

Nora shook her head. "Lucy locked it, and there's a deadbolt."

The panic swelled on Ally's face, and then she crouched.

Nora did the same, grabbing a towel from nearby—one that she'd brought down earlier that morning to clean up a mess Lucy had made beside the mattress. Ripping the towel in half, she covered her mouth and handed Ally the other half.

Turning toward the furnace, Nora followed the pipes through the smoky haze. She'd watched Daniel working back there so many times. He'd mentioned something about a shut-off valve. One of the pipes had a red valve. Was that it?

Jumping toward it, she stepped into the heart of the smoke and turned it. Almost immediately, the flames inside the furnace died down, but something deeper within the furnace—parts not meant to burn—still raged.

At the same time, Nora spotted a collection of Lucy's drawings taped against one of the large ducts near the furnace. There were layers and layers of her drawings hastily taped to it, some of them backward and upside down. It caught her off guard for a moment until she realized what was behind them.

The furnace intake.

Lucy had intentionally blocked it with her drawings before they'd arrived.

Starved of fresh air, the furnace had overheated and caught fire. Nothing would put the thing out without serious intervention from outside.

Nora's heart raced, although she forced herself to stay calm. Without catching a full breath, she wouldn't last long.

Frantically hurrying back to Ally's side, her sister grabbed the metal baseball bat she'd used earlier on the window. Wielding it like an axe, she gestured toward the door at the top of the stairs.

Coughing and gasping for air, the two of them charged up the stairs with Ally leading the way. She sped up near the top and hit the door like a raging bull, throwing her whole body against it while simultaneously slamming the end of the bat into the wood. The door cracked under her weight, but it held.

Backing away and nursing her injured arm, she yelled, "Damn!"

A moment later, she wound up again and thrust herself forward. The end of the bat cracked against the wood, closer to the lock this time. The wood fractured, splitting apart a few inches. Nora could see through the opening to the other side. A wave of relief swept through her.

Only a little more, and they would get through.

Ally poked her arm through the gap. She fumbled with the lock for a few seconds before the latch clicked. When the door finally opened, the two of them tumbled forward onto the hardwood floor.

Blanco's stare met them from across the room. He sat frozen near the kitchen table, observing them with wide eyes, as if caught between curiosity and fear.

While Ally struggled to stand, Nora turned back and closed the door behind them to keep the smoke from rising. Pausing a moment, she took her first clean breath in several minutes.

Ally glanced around. "Where's Lucy?"

Nora turned to face the front door. It was closed, but it had slammed shut earlier.

Scrambling to her feet, Nora hurried outside. Ally followed her.

Lucy was out there, crawling away from them at the edge of the yard. She was struggling forward, scraping her arms and legs against the grass in erratic motions, as if they didn't work right. Luckily, she hadn't gotten far.

Rushing to catch up with her, they came up on either side of her and dropped. Each of them grabbed an arm and held her in place.

"Lucy!" Nora cried. "Are you okay?"

She didn't answer. Instead, Lucy fought to break free. The same low, guttural cry rose from her throat. "You can't keep what is mine. I will have the girl."

Lucy struggled to break away, pushing and clawing at their skin. She grabbed Ally's hair at one point, yanking it down until Ally's ear met Lucy's mouth. The girl hissed something in her ear, but Nora only caught the last of it. "Always like your mother... Clutching at hope where there is none."

It took both of them another minute to pin her to the ground. The demon fought against them, but it slowed toward the end. It was getting tired.

Glancing around the yard, Nora hoped nobody had seen them. Would someone call the police if they saw them wrestling Lucy to the ground? Probably. And she wouldn't blame them if they did.

The sun was setting in an orange glow—it was getting dark fast. Usually around that time, the sidewalks were full of dog walkers and neighbors casually strolling by. They'd gotten lucky so far, but she didn't want to push it.

Ally glanced back at the house. "We can't bring her back inside."

"Take her," Nora said.

Ally met her gaze. "Where?"

"Anywhere," Nora answered. "To the parlor. To your apartment. Just don't let her out of your sight until this blows over."

Ally glanced back toward her car. "Help me put her in the back seat."

Together they lifted Lucy, even as she kicked and cried out again with renewed strength. Still in pajamas, her bare feet slammed against Nora's chest and arms a few times along the way. She couldn't help thinking of Daniel's broken arm and what he must have endured.

"Honey," Nora said, "I know you're still in there. Try to resist."

Lucy laughed. "Your daughter is gone. And before the end of the night, she will burn in hell."

Her words took Nora's breath away, but she continued without stopping.

Those were the demon's words, not her own.

Still, they cut deep, and Nora's heart ached as they struggled to get Lucy into the back seat of Ally's car.

They had completed the ritual in the basement, but it hadn't worked. The demon still possessed Lucy, at least on some level. So what had gone wrong? If the covenant's claim had passed to Nora, like Ally had said, then shouldn't *she* have felt something? But she hadn't felt a thing.

Pushing aside her thoughts, they strapped Lucy into her seat. As soon as the belt buckle clicked shut, she seemed to surrender, and her body went limp, as if she'd fallen asleep again.

Had the demon put her to sleep, or had Lucy fought and won the battle, even for just a brief time? At least, the moment of peace gave them a moment to gather their thoughts, to calm down, and to plan their next step.

"I'll be right back." Ally dashed away and ran into the house. She came back only a moment later with Blanco's carrier. He was inside, but he'd pushed himself back into the corner.

Jumping into the driver's seat, she placed Blanco's carrier on the passenger seat, started the car, and rolled down her window. "I'll call you."

Nora caught sight of Lucy's angelic face in the backseat. It seemed impossible that she had anything to do with what had just happened. "Where are you taking her?"

"Somewhere safe," Ally said.

❧ 30 ❧

Moments after Ally drove away, Nora called 911. The trucks arrived a short time later, their blaring sirens and flashing lights filling the air as they approached. She waited for them by the front door, with her arms crossed over her chest. She wasn't cold, but the events had rattled her nerves. The house had filled with smoke, but the fire hadn't spread—at least, as far as she could tell.

When the firefighters arrived, one of them checked to make sure she was all right. He asked if anyone else was inside the house.

"No," she said. "Nobody else."

Thank God, nobody else.

The smell of smoke still filled her nostrils. There was no clearing it out—no amount of coughing or spitting could get rid of the toxic taste in her mouth.

He stayed with her while another group rushed into the house, dragging along a water hose they'd attached to the fire hydrant near the street. They went straight down to the basement and came back up several minutes later with curious expressions. She waited for their reaction, but they'd avoided her gaze for a long time.

After talking with the others in private for another few minutes, the man returned, took off his gloves, and narrowed his eyes. His voice was low, calm, and firm, and his questions centered around the furnace and the objects around it.

"Any idea how it started?" he asked.

"I don't." Lucy's drawings flashed through her mind. They had found them covering the furnace intake. He must have spotted them too, but she didn't want to admit it. It was better to let them share what they'd discovered and leave it at that.

He nodded slowly, watching her face for a reaction. "There were some odd things down there on the floor. Some candles. Chalk markings. Some religious items."

She forced herself to meet his gaze. "My sister's things." It wasn't a lie—just not the whole truth. "She's into that kind of thing."

"I see." He seemed to study her face for a long, awkward moment before nodding again and stepping away. "All right."

They went back to work. Nora never left her spot beside the front door, waiting nervously for the air to clear and to receive news of the damage. Firefighters moved throughout the house in bursts. Their heavy footsteps shook the floor and walls. At one point, a framed picture beside the staircase rattled loose and fell. The glass exploded across the floor. Nora didn't flinch. They could do whatever they wanted in there—none of that mattered right now. Her thoughts were on Daniel and Lucy.

It could have been a lot worse—not just for the house, but for all of them. Daniel was in the hospital, and she debated whether or not to call him right away or to wait. He was undoubtedly struggling to recover from his broken arm. He didn't need the added stress in his life right then, although she knew he wouldn't blame them for anything—not anymore. After his latest encounter with Lucy, it was clear he understood now.

Lucy's pale face flashed through her mind. She couldn't stop thinking about her—the way the girl had kicked, thrashed, and fought them in the yard. She'd intended to crawl away into the darkness, but where might she have ended up if Ally hadn't stopped her? She'd almost gotten away.

Thank God, Ally had arrived at that exact moment. In a few minutes, Lucy would have...

Nora swallowed and pushed away the disturbing mental images. It wouldn't have ended well.

But they *had* stopped her, and Ally had taken Lucy to safety. Still, things could have ended *so* much different.

Why had the ritual in the basement failed? The flames had strained through the cracks in the furnace metal as though they were fingers trying to claw their way out. The tendrils had seemed to come alive in some areas, reaching toward them, but they hadn't spread beyond that. Shouldn't the flames have climbed up the walls and the ceiling in no time? A gas furnace should have eaten the house from the inside out.

But it hadn't.

It had stopped.

The ritual had failed. Or at least, it had seemed to fail. So why hadn't it consumed them all?

"Nora," a firefighter called out and startled her.

Glancing up, he stepped through the basement doorway, holding out something in his gloved hand. "We found these near the furnace. Didn't seem right to leave them down there."

The crucifix and the rosary.

He dropped them into her palm. They were stained with ash, still warm, but they hadn't burned either.

"Thank you." Nora cupped them in her hands.

He gestured for her to follow him. "Let me show you something."

She followed him inside and down to the basement. The firefighters had opened the basement windows. The smoke had cleared, and taking a breath came easy now.

"Let me show you what we think happened." He walked her over to the furnace and gestured to where the mattress had sat.

They'd tipped it on its side and leaned it against the wall. "Has someone been sleeping down here lately?"

Nora's heart beat faster. "My daughter likes to play down here sometimes."

He nodded. "I understand. But it's not safe to keep that so close to the furnace. Fire hazard."

Nora nodded but kept silent.

"And let me show you something else." He walked her around to the side of the furnace. The metal panels were charred, and smoke had left a layer of soot along the ceiling. Other than that, the unit was intact.

He gestured toward the furnace intake. It was clear now. Lucy's drawings were gone. They hadn't burned—not the paper—despite their proximity to the furnace. The firefighters had stacked the pages into a neat pile on the floor. He pointed at them. "We found those blocking the furnace intake. The air must have sucked them into the air, and they got stuck. You have to keep it open at all times. Nothing can block it. I advise you to keep your daughter out of this area. You're lucky we got here in time."

"I'm so sorry," Nora said.

His gaze jumped to the circle on the basement floor. He stared at it while speaking to them. "Unfortunately, you'll need a new HVAC system. A small price to pay considering what could have happened. At least the weather is nice. If this had happened in December, you might have been stuck using electric heaters for a while."

The firefighter continued talking. Something about taking precautions in an old house like theirs. But her thoughts kept drifting back to the ritual, Daniel... and Lucy. The flames hadn't touched anything inside the circle. Nothing had breached it. Despite their possessions covered in soot—boxes, the mattress, the walls, the ceiling—the ritual had worked, at least on some level. And it hadn't spread much beyond that.

She nodded. "Thank you so much."

He finally turned back to her. "Good thing you were home in this case. Glad nobody was hurt."

...nobody was hurt.

She pictured Daniel's broken arm and the scratches across his face and neck.

Maybe their efforts hadn't failed after all. The demon hadn't left Lucy—no—but it hadn't completed its possession of her, either. They had interrupted its plans, bound it for a time, although not banished it.

Why not?

What had they done to stop it? As far as she could tell, nothing had shifted. The claim hadn't changed hands. Nothing had severed.

But... nothing had gotten worse, either.

Taking out her phone, she snapped a few pictures of the area to show Ally. Her sister should see this. Ally had been so sure about the ritual's outcome, but it hadn't quite gone right. Something was still off. Something was missing.

But what?

The firefighter continued to stare at the markings on the floor. "Be careful. With the candles. Maybe keep your child away from them. It's easy to knock them over."

"Thank you." Nora put away her phone and led him across the basement.

He scratched his head and followed her.

At the bottom of the stairs, she caught him glancing back over his shoulder at the circle again.

He opened his mouth but then shut it again, and they went upstairs.

Ally stopped at the red light and glanced into the rearview mirror. Lucy was still curled up in the back seat, her mouth hanging open. She was asleep. Hibernating? Or contemplating her next explosive move. The girl hadn't moved since they'd lifted her into the car, but at least she had calmed down. She was breathing slowly now, with her eyes fluttering every few seconds. Besides that, she hadn't moved an inch.

Blanco was on the passenger seat in his carrier. She couldn't see his face, but she guessed he must have sensed that something was wrong because he was pacing back and forth.

When the light turned green, Ally focused on the road again, but her mind kept jumping back to the ritual they had performed earlier in the basement. They'd done everything right, hadn't they? The words, the actions—all of it had gone flawlessly, but something still seemed... off.

Why hadn't the claim transferred to Nora as planned? Instead, Lucy had remained unchanged, and the girl had even charged up the basement stairs with renewed strength, leaving them trapped down there.

Throughout their ritual, Lucy must have been planning her

steps. The girl had waited patiently for them to fail and then had taken advantage of it.

So why hadn't they gotten through to her? What had they done wrong?

Nothing.

That's what made no sense. They had done *nothing* wrong.

It was possible the process just required more time. Maybe the claim didn't transfer all at once. Maybe at some point, the demon would slip out of Lucy and enter Nora—later that night, or maybe while they slept.

Was that how it worked? She was treading in unfamiliar waters. She'd studied the occult in college—excelled at it on paper—but nothing could have prepared her for dealing with *this*. Not in real life. She knew just enough to be dangerous—just enough to let the solution slip through her fingers.

Something in the rearview mirror caught Ally's attention.

Glancing back, Lucy's eyes were wide open.

She was awake.

Ally's heart raced, and her foot jerked against the accelerator before she could stop herself. The engine surged and then settled.

Lucy didn't blink. Instead, she lay still on her side, staring forward, her lips parted slightly—as if she were about to say something but holding back.

"Lucy?" Ally asked nervously. "Hey, kiddo, you awake?"

Lucy met Nora's gaze in the rearview mirror. It was dark, but even with the faint light coming through the windows, Ally could see the hint of a grin curling at the corners of Lucy's mouth.

"You were wrong," Lucy said in a low voice.

Ally swallowed. "About what, sweetheart?"

"The covenant." Lucy's grin spread a little more. "Your little game... didn't work."

Ally forced herself to keep her breath steady, even as her pulse thudded in her ears. "What do you mean by that?"

Lucy shifted as if she might sit up—but she didn't. "You made it worse. Much, much worse."

Ally tapped her fingers nervously on the steering wheel. The girl's voice was all wrong. It sounded nothing like Lucy. This wasn't a conversation with her nine-year-old niece anymore... but with that thing inside her. "No. You're wrong. It just takes more time than I thought."

Lucy giggled. "You have no idea what you're doing. It doesn't enjoy waiting. But it likes you."

A chill crawled up Ally's spine. "All right, that's enough."

"I want to talk." Lucy sat up sharply, but not all the way—just high enough to be seen in the mirror. "You can't stop it, you know."

"We'll see about that," Ally shot back.

"The flames of hell will consume her. Tonight. You'll do it yourself."

"No. I absolutely won't be doing that."

"Oh yes, you will," Lucy said in a sing-song voice. She giggled wildly and then continued. "You're thinking about the circle in the basement, aren't you? About how all the pieces came together perfectly, but then nothing fit. You're thinking about what you did wrong. Well... let me tell you what you did wrong. You were born."

Ally didn't answer, but the girl's words stung. Instead, she sped up slightly and tried to push everything away. She had buckled Lucy into the back seat, but there wasn't much to stop her from lashing out, from grabbing Ally from behind and forcing them both off the road. If Lucy could break Daniel's arm under its influence, she could do far worse.

Stopping at a red light, Ally gripped the steering wheel tighter. The light seemed to take forever to change. Her heart raced, and the hairs along the back of her neck bristled. Even without turning around, she *knew* Lucy was staring at her. The girl hadn't attacked her for a reason, although Ally could only guess what that was. Lucy was plotting something again, waiting for the right moment to strike.

The parlor wasn't much farther up the road, but what would she do with Lucy once they arrived? Where would she put her? She hadn't thought that far ahead. The priority had been to get her out of the house, away from danger. But now it was just the two of them. Alone.

Ally had locked the doors, but Lucy knew how to open them. What was stopping the girl from jumping out of the car and running off into the night?

Lucy's voice broke the silence. "I won't run."

Ally met Lucy's gaze in the rearview mirror again. "Run where?"

"Home."

They stared at each other for a long moment. "Where's your home?"

Lucy giggled. "I think you know. I'll be going there soon enough. And I plan to take you all with me."

"You won't be taking any of us."

"Oh yes I will," Lucy repeated coldly.

The light turned green, and Ally drove a little faster.

"You can't have Lucy." Ally forced herself to keep her eyes on the road. "Or any of us."

This seemed to agitate the demon inside Lucy. "I have her soul. It's too late. All of you will burn, burn, burn. And we'll dance together in the flames of hell. Isn't that fun?"

Ally pushed her lips together to keep from responding. It was better to keep silent for now.

She made a right turn at the next street and spotted the parlor only a short distance ahead. They'd be inside within minutes, but not out of danger. Maybe her mother had left something behind? Something buried within all of her father's belongings that Ally had missed. Something she could use to stop it from taking over Lucy.

"What are you going to do with me?" Lucy asked.

"I don't know yet."

"You're not going to put me in a cage, are you?"

"I don't have a cage," Ally replied.

"Would you put me in one if you had one?"

Ally turned into the parlor's parking lot and avoided the girl's gaze. "No."

"You're lying."

"I'm not. I would never put Lucy in a cage, but I would cage a demon."

Lucy's voice shifted to her sweet, soft tone. "But I'm Lucy, Aunt Ally, remember?"

"Not right now, you're not." Ally parked the car. "Lucy's still in there. You've just pushed her aside for now. She'll be back."

"No, she won't. Moloch has already claimed her, and he will enjoy watching her burn."

"You can't have her," Ally said through clenched teeth.

"You're too late."

Ally shut off the engine and paused a moment to think. How would she get Lucy out of the car without making a scene? There were pedestrians walking on the street. Plenty of witnesses if Lucy started kicking, screaming, or tried to run off like she had done at Nora's house.

And then what would she do with Lucy after getting her inside?

She imagined every possibility. Most rooms had windows, and every room had a weakness. None of them were completely secure. The only space without windows was the old séance storage room. There was plenty of clutter in there, but it was clean and safe—no way out except through the door. It had a lock. Maybe it was enough—for now. It was that or tie Lucy up, but that seemed cruel. She would go to that extreme only if Lucy tried to harm herself.

Stepping out of the car, Ally went around and opened the back door. Lucy crawled out slowly. Ally held the girl's hand, then grabbed her by the arm. Lucy didn't try to escape, but Ally still held her with both hands and kicked the door shut behind them.

She left Blanco sitting in his carrier on the front passenger seat. It wasn't possible to bring him inside yet, but she would come back. Maybe on some level, he understood the danger she was facing. She couldn't let Lucy out of her sight, even for a moment.

Leading Lucy into the parlor, as soon as the door clicked shut behind them, Ally let out a sigh of relief.

Lucy laughed. "What are you so afraid of?"

"I'm not afraid."

"Liar," Lucy whispered. "I can smell the stench of your fear."

"That's enough." Ally ushered the girl through the parlor and into the storage room. It was just as she'd imagined it—plenty of room for the girl to move around, but nowhere to hide or escape.

And Lucy seemed complacent to follow along, stepping inside without a fight.

Before leaving the girl alone, Lucy turned to face Ally and lifted her hands to her eyes. She touched her fingernails to her eyelids. "What's stopping me from taking out the girl's eyes? It would please my master."

The thought sent a chill through Ally. "You won't."

Lucy giggled with a sheepish grin and lowered her hands. "You're right. I won't do it... for now."

❧ 32 ❧

Nora's heart beat faster as the parlor came into view. She'd left as soon as possible after the firefighters had cleared her house, but it had taken longer than she'd hoped. Ally had been alone with Lucy for *hours* now. The thought of what might have happened during that time churned her stomach. If the girl had awakened during that time—if she'd done *anything*...

Pushing the thought out of her mind, she pulled into the parking lot and clung to the fragile hope that Lucy was still sound asleep. Maybe, by some minor miracle, nothing had changed.

Parking her car next to Ally's, she climbed out and hurried toward the front door. Her head was still spinning from the ordeal at her house. Daniel would find out everything when she returned to the hospital, but there were more important things to deal with now, and he had enough on his plate. He needed rest, and it was better for everyone to focus on Lucy.

Rushing into the parlor, she called out, "Ally?"

A moment later, Ally appeared from around the corner carrying a handful of folders. She placed them on the front desk and held her index finger up to her puckered lips. "Shhh. She's in the old séance storage room. She's safe. I gave her some water, but she refused to eat."

Nora glanced down the hallway toward the back area. "Did anything else happen?"

Ally shook her head. "She said some things in the car—strange things—but she didn't try to get away again."

"That's good."

Blanco's carrier in the corner caught Nora's attention. The door was open, but Blanco hadn't come out. He was crouched inside, staring up at her with a look of anticipation. Nora whispered to him, "You know what's going on, don't you?"

Ally followed her gaze. "He won't come out. Maybe it's better that way."

"You're probably right." Nora held out the crucifix and rosary. "The firefighters found this on the basement floor."

Ally glanced at the objects with a curious expression but didn't reach for them. "They look the same."

"Exactly," she said in a quiet voice. "They didn't burn. Not even the cord. The fire burned around the circle."

Ally exhaled slowly through her nose. She didn't look surprised but seemed to realize the significance even without saying anything.

"I didn't feel anything," Nora said, "when we did the ritual, when you said the words. I don't feel any different now, either. The floor around it was scorched—everything else was worse. But inside the circle where we stood... it was untouched."

"At least we know *something* worked—the circle held. Now we just need to complete the claim. I'll figure it out. I promise." Ally opened the folder she'd brought out. It was stuffed with hand-written notes and old photos.

Nora gestured to them. "What's all this?"

"Everything Dad was hiding," Ally said. "Most of it belonged to Mom. It's all the stuff I told you about."

"What do you suppose went wrong?" Nora asked.

Ally stared at the top paper and scanned the text. "That's the problem. I know just enough about this stuff to make it work... just not to make it work *perfectly*. Maybe Mom and I aren't so different, after all, just like Dad feared." She went silent for a moment, flipping to the next page. "I think that's why he hated it when I left for college. He was afraid of what I'd learn there, that I'd use that knowledge to make all the same mistakes Mom did. He was just trying to prevent me from going down the same road she did. I understand now. He knew it was better to leave that stuff alone."

Nora considered her words and then nodded. "So what are we going to do? I feel like we're on the right track."

"I *know* we are," Ally said. "But there's an element of this we haven't considered yet. The ritual didn't fail—it did *exactly* what it was allowed to do."

"Allowed by whom?" Nora asked.

Ally didn't answer right away. She picked up the rosary and let the beads slide slowly through her fingers. "Not who—*where*. The house was just a convenient place for us to do the ritual. We always tried to keep Lucy from getting out. We were afraid she'd escape, and we'd lose her. After I thought about it for a while, the basement... it never made sense. It wasn't the source. It never was."

"Lucy always talked of fire," Nora said.

Ally nodded. "That's why she liked sleeping beside the furnace. If she stays here... the same thing might happen to the parlor, because of what's inside her."

"We can put her inside the circle this time," Nora offered.

Ally shook her head. "It's not strong enough to hold something so powerful. She would get out. And maybe that's what she's planning—to wait for just the right opportunity, to wait for us to put our guard down and then trap us again. We can keep doing it like this, trying one thing after another, until we realize —too late—that she set us up for failure the whole time. We need a place to work where things don't burn. Remember what

Father Tony said about the items he found at Gabriel's house—the box and the statue?"

The answer flashed through Nora's mind. It all became clear at once. "They didn't burn."

Ally nodded. "It took holy water to destroy them because they were connected to the quarry."

Nora's dream of her mother flashed through her mind. She remembered her mother's face as she called up to Nora from the bottom of the pit, beckoning her to descend into it. Daniel had gone down there and found the cross, but maybe that wasn't what her mother had intended her to find. Maybe there was something else.

"Not the quarry," Nora whispered. "We can't go back there. That's what it wants."

Ally shook her head. "No. It *wants* us to think that's what it wants. Lucy keeps trying to go back there, so we fight like hell to keep her away, but it's messing with our minds. That's where it all started—that's where it can't win."

Nora's chest tightened. "No. We can't take her back there. We can't."

"We have to. It's the only place that works. The stone with the screaming veins, the incinerator, the ground itself. It wants us to fail—to die here—but we have to go back to the source."

"You don't know that."

"I do." Ally stared into her eyes. "I've never been more sure of anything."

The certainty in Ally's voice was unshakable. It was just like all the other times she had confidently led a ritual or an action. But this was different. She wasn't trying to convince Nora of anything. She wasn't trying to prove herself. There was no ego in her voice or face. It was just pure truth.

But the thought of going back there... of bringing Lucy back... it was terrifying. It was where Lucy had nearly died before. Nobody in their right mind would even consider taking

Lucy back to that place. "No. She's already been through enough. We'll find another way."

Ally glanced back down the hallway toward the séance storage room. "There isn't another way."

Silence fell between them. The faint sound of a car passing on the street filled the air. The windows rattled faintly—it reminded Nora of when the front window's glass had shattered under the weight of the blackbirds just after Gabriel had died in his grisly ritual. She'd thought everything had started with him, that he'd been the source of all their problems, but that wasn't true. They couldn't have known it back then, but their lives had already changed decades before Gabriel had arrived. Even before they were born, they'd been destined to face the problem their mother had created... out of love.

"I don't want to lose her," Nora said in a weak voice. Her throat tightened, and her eyes watered.

"We'll lose more than just Lucy if we don't go back. It will destroy you, me... Daniel. We have no choice."

Ally's words hung in the air. She wasn't suggesting or begging. She was just giving the answer.

Nora slumped forward. "Alright—"

Before Nora could finish her sentence, a noise came from the storage room.

Someone was pounding on the door, over and over.

Then, a wailing sound filled the air.

Lucy's voice. It was mixed with the dark, guttural tone Nora recognized as that of the demon. The sound came through in waves that seemed to reverberate through the walls. It sent a chill down Nora's spine.

They could wait—for now—and keep trying every ritual over and over to save Lucy. *Something* had to work... didn't it? Their mother had left notes. There were other priests at the church who might help them. But in the meantime, the thing inside Lucy would break them all down. It would eat away at their souls until Lucy withered away to nothing, finally consumed by the horror that their mother had refused to face decades earlier.

They could wait. But the outcome had only one solution. It was clear now.

Ally was right. They had to go back and do the ritual at the quarry.

Nora lifted herself and nodded. "Let's take care of this. Now."

Nora stepped toward the hallway but stopped. Lucy's small voice came echoing through the house. She was singing a melodic tune in a soft voice. The words weren't clear, but they sent waves of joy surging through Nora's heart. That wasn't the demon. That was Lucy's voice. Her sweet, precious, *normal* voice.

Yet it chilled her.

Was she really back? Was it really *her*?

What if the demon had now completely taken control of Lucy, and it was just playing with them?

The thought hung in her mind for a long moment. Maybe it was true, but she followed the sound back to the séance storage room anyway. Ally went with her, and together they paused outside the door.

Lucy's sweet song filled the air. It was the same song Nora had sung to her so many times as an infant during bedtime. Was the demon manipulating Lucy to lure Nora inside? There was no way to know for sure, but her heart said no. Not this time.

Nora reached out to open the door but hesitated.

Ally seemed to sense her fear. "I think she's okay... for now."

Bracing for the worst, Nora opened the door slowly. Her pulse thumped in her ears.

Lucy came into view a moment later. She was sitting motion-less against the wall with her face down and her knees pulled in against her chest. She looked up when Nora came in, and the hint of a smile crept over the girl's face. Not a malicious smile. A sweet smile. Her eyes were bloodshot, but at least she was awake. It was her little girl again.

"Lucy?" Nora hesitated near the door. It took all her strength to keep from rushing forward to embrace her.

"Mommy?" Lucy whispered. "I'm hungry."

"I know you are. We'll get you some food soon. But Ally said you refused to eat anything."

"I'm starving, but I can't eat." She touched her stomach. "It makes me sick."

"We'll keep trying."

Lucy sighed. "I'm tired of trying."

"We're all tired, honey."

Lucy pushed her eyes closed. "I know what you want to do. He told me."

Nora swallowed. "What did he tell you, honey?"

"That we're going somewhere."

"We are." Nora stepped inside and shut the door behind her. "But first, I want to talk with you."

Lucy opened her eyes again. Nothing had changed. "Okay, Mommy."

Nora sat on the floor facing Lucy. She didn't quite drop to Lucy's level. The demon was still inside her somewhere, and Nora feared it might rear its ugly head at any moment. It was better to stay near the door.

"Who am I speaking to right now?" Nora asked.

Lucy broke into a small smile and rolled her eyes. "It's me, Mommy."

Nora laughed nervously and nodded slowly. Nothing in the girl's appearance showed signs of deception. "Let me know if you feel anything... change."

Lucy was still there. Somehow, she'd come back, at least

temporarily. But there was no telling how long they had before that thing came back. They needed to take advantage of this moment. It might be their last chance.

Nora reached out and gently took Lucy's hands in hers. The girl's skin was cool and damp with sweat, and a few stray hairs clung to the side of her face. If the demon was trying to lure Nora closer, then she was vulnerable. It could attack her now, like it had with Daniel. It could rise and end her life. But it didn't. Lucy's eyes were steady—clear—with no changes.

"Do you know where we're going?" Nora asked.

Lucy nodded once. "The quarry."

"Did he tell you that?"

"Yes." Lucy brushed the loose hairs away from her face. "It keeps telling me about the hollow earth. The freezing darkness and the stones. Why are we going back there, Mommy?"

"It's important that we go back there to stop it. To stop what's been happening to you."

Lucy shivered. "I don't want to go back there."

"Why not?"

"It will hurt."

"No, honey. I won't let it hurt you."

"It keeps telling me to do mean things."

Nora wanted to ask her what kind of mean things... but decided against it. "Push it away, honey. Push those thoughts as far away as you can."

"It wants to kill me."

"I know," Nora said. "But we won't let you die. Not for anything."

Lucy's eyes watered. "I'm scared."

"Don't be scared." Nora couldn't hold back any longer. She jumped forward and embraced her daughter against her chest.

Lucy's skin was ice cold and damp with sweat. Her body was limp, and she wheezed in and out with every breath.

Emotions surged through Nora's chest. "We're going to fix this, honey. I promise. I won't let anything happen to you."

"Please don't take me back there, Mommy."

"I'm sorry, honey. I won't let anything happen to you. I promise."

Lucy glanced toward the door. "Where's Blanco?"

Nora forced a smile. "He's with Ally."

"He's scared of me." She frowned. "Everyone is scared of me."

"Trust me, honey, we're not scared of you. We're scared of what's gotten inside you. It's difficult to explain, but we know you're not to blame for doing all those bad things. We know the real reason."

Lucy showed a brave face. "A demon?"

Nora hesitated. Occult symbols and texts had surrounded the girl for years, but somehow it seemed wrong now to tell her the truth. Still, Lucy deserved to know. "Yes, honey. A demon. It keeps trying to come out, but we won't let that happen. All of this will be over soon, I promise. We'll get this fixed."

"Sometimes, I can't breathe."

"Keep breathing. Whatever you do."

Lucy took a shuddering breath. "I'll try."

"We should get you out to the car now. Before it comes back."

Lucy nodded.

Nora stood and held her hand while helping her to stand. The girl wobbled and stumbled forward. At least she wasn't resisting their efforts.

Stepping out into the hallway, Ally rushed forward and grabbed one of Lucy's arms. "Oh, thank God. She came back."

"For now," Nora said.

Ally crouched in front of her. "Lucy, we're going to fix this. Tonight."

Lucy nodded but stayed silent.

As they passed Blanco's carrier in the hallway, Lucy stopped and dropped to her knees in front of it. Instead of pressing his face against the bars to let Lucy stroke his fur, Blanco backed away.

"You see?" Lucy said. "He's afraid of me."

"It's not you he's afraid of," Ally answered.

Lucy stared at him for a moment with sad eyes. "Is he coming with?"

"Not this time," Nora said. "You can see him when you get back."

"I'll miss you, Blanco." She tried to stroke his fur, but he backed away even further into his carrier.

"He'll be right there when you get back." Ally gave a sympathetic smile and then rushed to stuff a backpack with supplies before leaving the parlor. "I grabbed everything I could think of. At least, everything that would fit."

"I'm sure it's enough," Nora said.

Walking Lucy out to the car, they carefully loaded her into the back seat and shut the door, this time strapping her in while she was still cooperating.

Ally sat in the passenger seat with her backpack while Nora climbed into the driver's side.

Just before pulling out onto the street, Nora glanced back at Lucy.

She was grinning now.

Her eyes had gone dark again.

❧ 34 ❧

Nora parked the car near the quarry where she and Daniel had parked days earlier. She shut off the engine but hesitated to open her door. Lucy had started acting up again, kicking and thrashing in the back seat. Ally had sat beside her on the way over, and she was doing her best to restrain her, speaking in a calm voice, but the girl wouldn't cooperate anymore.

They'd managed to buckle her seatbelt earlier, and she hadn't said a word the whole way over—until now.

"You're going to kill me," Lucy said. "Is that what you want?"

Her words stabbed at Nora's heart, but Lucy said them not in her own voice, but the demon's. The two contrasting tones were clear. When Lucy spoke, it always came from the heart—unstrained. But the demon came through forced and low.

Ignoring Lucy's emotional cries, Nora climbed out of the car and hurried around to the backseat. Ally stepped out at the same time, slipped on her backpack, and together, they guided Lucy to her feet, gripping her arms in case she tried to get away. The girl was still barefoot and wearing her pajamas, but at least it wasn't cold at that time of year. Still, the mosquitoes were out in full force, buzzing around their heads, into their ears and faces.

"This way." Nora switched her phone into flashlight mode

and led them into the brush, toward the spot where she and Daniel had slipped into the quarry.

She followed the chain-link fence for several yards and found the opening again near the ground. Weeds had already begun to mask the spot. Dropping to her knees, Nora lifted the bottom of the fence while grasping Lucy's leg with the other.

Ally released Lucy, dropped to the ground, and slipped under the fence. Within seconds, she turned back and grabbed hold of Lucy's other leg as she and Nora worked together to get her through the opening. Lucy struggled to escape a few times.

"Stay with us, Lucy," Nora said each time. "Fight it."

A dark groan filled her throat, followed by a soft chuckle. "I don't love you anymore, Mommy. Do you know that? You're going to kill me."

"That's not true, honey."

They descended the slope toward the river until the sound of bubbling water filled the air. The smell of old machinery came with it.

The quarry was close.

Pushing through a wall of trees, they emerged into a clearing and paused. Everything was there exactly as Nora remembered it: the incinerator, the slab, the utility shed. Except now, it was silent and pitch-black in the darkness. Despite the stillness, the moonlight lit the incinerator's gaping mouth, and it seemed to grin at them.

Turning her phone's screen toward the slab, Nora caught sight of the bloodstains on the ground where Tess had failed to complete her ritual. Despite the recent rain, the water hadn't washed the stains away.

Lucy squirmed a little more with every step.

Nora gripped her daughter's arm tighter and nudged her forward. "We're almost there, sweetheart."

"Are you planning to burn me alive? Toss me headfirst into the incinerator like Tess?" Lucy giggled. "Or maybe drown me in the river?"

Ally seemed to take the comments in stride. Those weren't Lucy's words. "We won't let anything happen to you. I promise."

Lucy didn't seem to hear. She tugged a little harder against their grasp, letting out a low growl as they continued forward.

"It won't take long," Ally said to Nora. "Once we get to the bottom—"

"You're wasting your time," Lucy said sharply. "The girl is already mine." She collapsed, and they paused. Lifting her face toward Nora, her voice changed—thinly veiled sarcasm. "Don't hurt me, Mommy. Please take me home. I don't want to die. Are you really going to kill me? You must enjoy killing children to drag me back here. You're a shitty mommy, do you know that? I hate you."

"Don't listen to her," Ally snapped.

Nora nodded, but her daughter's words still hurt. They sounded *so much* like Lucy—close enough to ring true. The demon knew *exactly* what to say, and the emotional impact was devastating.

Taking a deep breath, Nora cleared her mind. The nightmare would end soon. They wouldn't leave until it did.

The pit was up ahead. The cement barrier's cracked opening loomed like jagged teeth, and the rope Daniel had used to descend to the bottom was still hanging through the opening. Everything was in place.

A chill went up her spine. "Are we really going down there?"

"We won't be long." Ally slowed but didn't stop. "And it's the only way."

A wave of déjà vu swept over Nora. This was exactly how it had gone in her dream, when she'd seen her mother standing at the bottom of the pit, shadowed and calm, one hand beckoning her like an invitation to come down. And then that dark, shadowed thing had climbed out of the pit toward her.

Lucy dragged her feet along the way to the edge of the pit, but finally, they arrived.

Ally continued without a pause. After making sure Nora had

a firm grasp on Lucy, she stepped forward and grabbed the rope. Staring down into the opening, she too used her phone to illuminate the darkness below. "It's the only way." She said it softer this time, as if trying to convince herself it was true.

Nora followed her gaze. The darkness seemed to descend forever. "Father Tony said someone in Mom's group had dove to the bottom to retrieve an object for their ritual. Water must have filled this at one time. It must have drained away, but... to where?"

"It's still there," Ally replied softly. "Just not where you can see it."

Nora extended her phone over the hole and lit the walls of the pit, but the light didn't reach the bottom.

"It's deeper than it looks," Lucy said in a mischievous voice. "I know where it goes."

Nora watched her daughter's face for a moment, trying to decide whether or not to take the girl's bait. "Where does it go?"

"Straight to hell," Lucy said. "Back to my father."

Nora shook her head. "Your father's in the hospital."

Lucy laughed in a shrill, almost piercing voice and pointed into the hole. "My father's down there, waiting for all of us."

A chill swept through Nora, and she turned back to Ally. "Can't we do the ritual from up here? She won't get away."

"Yes, I won't get away," Lucy mocked.

"We have to go down," Ally said. "To the bottom. The stone acts as a conduit. The further down we go, the closer we get to the stones with the screaming veins. That's where everything stems from. The closer we get to the bottom, the stronger the connection."

Lucy struggled with more strength against their grasp. She bared her teeth and then opened them toward Ally, as if she might bite her way out of there.

Before she could do anything, Ally dragged Lucy toward the rope. "You're going down first."

"I'm not," Lucy growled.

"Yes, you are." Ally guided Lucy's hands to the rope. "I know you won't try to escape, either. You don't want the girl to fall, do you? You want her alive until the possession is complete. That's your plan. I know you won't risk injuring your prize, so get down there."

Instead of obeying, Lucy released the rope and clutched Ally's neck, digging her little fingernails into her throat. Nora tugged her away, but not before it had cut off Ally's breath.

Ally stepped back with wide eyes, gasping and coughing. Lucy's nails had left a string of small cuts etched into her throat.

"Do you see?" Lucy laughed. "I can do it. It would be so easy."

"But you won't," Ally said through another gasping breath. "She's not yours."

"Not yet." Lucy's arms relaxed—just enough so Nora could force her hands onto the rope again. Turning her face back to Nora, Lucy stared up at her with pleading eyes. "I'll fall, Mommy."

Ally shook her head. "She won't."

Lucy's expression changed sharply again. She laughed. "You're right! I won't fall. I'll hang you both with this rope on the way out."

The words sliced through Nora's heart like a red-hot fire poker. The demon was getting stronger. Had they made a mistake by bringing Lucy there? Nora wanted to believe that Ally had everything under control, but doubt crept in. There was still time to back out.

"Isn't there another way?" Nora cried.

Ally moved forward again and shook her head. "No other way."

Lucy seemed to surrender and started climbing down the rope.

"Lucy," Nora called gently. "Hang on."

Lucy glanced up, and just for a moment her daughter's genuine expression came through. Terror. Nora wilted within her daughter's gaze. But then it was back again. The demon took over, and Lucy's fear turned to joy. Her grin stretched from ear to ear.

A sound bellowed from the pit—like the groan of a sleeping giant. The vibration rumbled through their bodies and shook the ground.

"It knows we're here," Ally said.

Lucy slipped down the rope, a little at a time, until her face disappeared below the opening and sank into the darkness. Nora circled the edge, staring down with her heart racing. She aimed her phone's flashlight into the pit.

Ally followed right behind her. A few minutes later, the sound of their feet hitting the stone floor echoed through the cavern.

"We made it," Ally called.

Nora went next. She left her phone in flashlight mode, slipping it into her back pocket and leaving the top half sticking out to light her way. Still, it wasn't enough. The shadows moved and shifted around her as she climbed down.

After touching the bottom, she glanced up at the only exit above them. How would they ever climb back out? The rope was dry—but would they have enough strength when the ritual was done? And Daniel couldn't help them.

Checking the signal bars on her phone, she saw that the signal had dropped to nothing.

Nobody could help them.

Turning her attention back to Lucy, instead of attacking them or trying to escape back up the rope, the girl had scurried away to a corner. She sat crouched against the damp wall, her head lowered, and she was crying. At least, it *sounded* authentic, but there was an absence of emotion in her voice. No, she wasn't crying but laughing.

Nora joined Ally's side, and they both stood together facing Lucy.

Ally broke away a moment later and removed her backpack.

She set it on the ground beside them in the dirt. Turning away from them, she scanned the walls with her phone. Her light stopped at the opening that Daniel had also pointed out when he'd gone down there.

Staring through the opening, Nora was reminded of what Lucy had said while staring into the darkness of the bathroom drain.

It's deeper than it looks.

It *had* seemed to go on forever, just like the gaping black mouth in front of them.

"We shouldn't wait," Ally said.

Nora clenched her teeth and nodded. "I'm ready."

35

Nora shivered at the bottom of the pit, embracing Lucy while Ally prepared everything. A steady flow of icy air drifted up from the opening near their feet, driven by a source somewhere far below. It blew around them, circling like a flock of birds preparing to dive.

Ally unloaded her backpack, pulling everything out and placing it on a blanket she'd stuffed inside at the last minute. As soon as she laid it on the ground, the damp surface began to seep through the cloth.

Nora gestured to the broken terrain beneath them. "Is this going to work? There's not much space down here."

"There's no need to draw a circle in chalk," Ally answered, keeping her gaze on the task at hand. "The pit itself is the ritual space. No perfect geometry to follow down here."

Nora pulled Lucy a little closer, if only to keep her warm. The poor girl was barely moving but trembling, and her skin was cold and pale. She hadn't eaten much of anything for at least a couple of days. How long could she survive like that? It had taken a great deal of effort to drag Lucy away from the walls and move her toward the center, where they could keep an eye on her. She seemed to gravitate toward the darkened corners, and only after coaxing her forward with a bit of force had they gotten her to cooperate. She stood now, hunched forward with her face down, mumbling something under her breath. The words came out broken and sharp.

"This is all your fault, Mommy." Lucy struggled within her grasp. Her strength was returning in a fresh wave of resistance. "I'm going to die because of you."

Nora stopped listening. "How much longer?"

Lucy was struggling within her grasp again, building a fresh wave of resistance.

"Almost there." Ally placed the last items on the blanket and stepped back.

She positioned Nora on one side of the blanket and Lucy on the other so that they faced each other, with Ally standing in the middle.

With a grand gesture of her arms, she began. "The energy in this place binds us together. My body is the living boundary between the two of you. I'll facilitate the transfer, and then we can begin the process of satisfying the debt that our mother created."

Ally stared at Lucy for a long moment, then leaned forward and spoke down to her. "You were never meant to bear the burden of this claim. Tonight, it transfers from you to Nora."

Lucy finally turned her face up and met Ally's gaze with burning eyes. According to Ally, the demon hadn't yet possessed Lucy, but if that was true, then it was almost there. Her little eyes gleamed with something dark and dangerous.

Gripping Lucy's hand, Ally directed them to sit on the blanket. Lucy didn't resist. Instead, her gaze fixed on the dark opening nearby as she lowered herself to the ground and sat obediently facing Ally.

When they were all seated, Ally took Nora's hand and began calling out to the air around them. Her voice echoed through the small chamber. "I call on my mother's covenant—the one she made in blood to save my sister Nora's life before she was born."

The pit answered—not with sound, but with pressure. Nora felt it in her ears, behind her eyes. The air had changed, and the energy seemed to ripple across her skin. There was a presence with them in that place, something unseen but palpable, and it was watching them.

Ally squeezed Nora's hand and tugged her a little closer. She whispered, "I'll try to make this as painless as possible."

"I'm not afraid of pain," Nora said. "I just want my Lucy back."

"I won't fail." Ally held her hand for a long moment.

In the pause, something shifted in Nora's pocket, sliding down against her leg as she leaned toward her sister.

The pendant.

Nora dug it out, and then offered it to Ally. "We might need this."

Ally stared at it, nodded solemnly, and then accepted it. "Mom's pendant."

"Where it all started."

"And where it'll end." Ally held it up and called out to the darkness, "My mother dropped this into the pit on the night of the covenant. Tonight, I will use it to transfer the debt from Lucy to Nora. The bloodline isn't broken, but it moves from one to the other. The claim is not broken. Instead, it becomes fulfilled in my sister." She turned to Lucy and spoke in a soft voice. "Lucy, I promise you will leave here free of this debt."

Lucy's grin widened, and her throat erupted in a dark voice. "You can try."

Ally ignored her and turned back to Nora. Extending the pendant, she turned Nora's palm up and placed it in her hand. Closing Nora's fingers around it, she cupped Nora's hands within hers. "We're going to end this—now."

Ally grabbed the knife beside her backpack. It wasn't an ordinary kitchen knife. This one had an ivory handle, and the blade was etched with grooves where someone had clearly sharpened it by hand. It lacked the flare of the dagger Tess had used on Eve—and almost Lucy—in the woman's ritual near the incinerator.

"I found this among Mom's things." Ally held it up. "Maybe it's the same one she used to bind the bloodline to this place that night."

Nora swallowed. Would the ritual truly work this time? And then what would happen to her after it did? Would she lash out at Ally and Lucy once it was complete? A flood of disturbing images filled her mind, and she shivered.

Ally ran her fingertips across Nora's palm, gazing at the lines.

"What are you looking for?" Nora asked.

"The Life Line. It's unnecessary, I suppose, to draw the blood from any particular spot, but my palmistry knowledge might help elicit the right symbolism in this case. Connections are important." She followed one line down to the base of Nora's thumb, paused, then glanced up with a sympathetic smile. "Sorry."

Nora nodded with a stoic stare. "I can handle it."

Ally carefully pressed the knife to Nora's palm. The tip sliced the exact spot where Ally's fingertips had stopped a moment earlier.

Nora barely felt it at first, but then the cool pain flashed through her mind, and she winced. The cut was mercifully quick, but the blood flowed freely down her wrist and dripped onto the blanket beneath them.

Ally grabbed their mother's pendant next and pressed it into the blood. The two smeared together until Ally folded Nora's fingers around the bloody object while holding Nora's hands. "Sorry," Ally said again.

"It's okay."

Returning the knife to the backpack after wiping away the blood, Ally picked up a folder she'd placed under her foot. Opening it, she began reading lines of handwritten text. She read the words slowly, enunciating every syllable with great care. Nora caught a glimpse of the handwriting. It was her mother's.

She spoke of debt passing hands, a promise made in fear and sealed in silence. She spoke of a covenant tied to their bloodline, not broken, but fulfilled.

As she progressed through the lines, Lucy's behavior changed. The girl had watched everything with wide eyes, but now she tried to pull away. Instead of letting her go, Ally tightened her grip on the girl's wrist and continued without a pause.

Lucy writhed in place. "You seem to know what you're doing, except you're doing it all wrong."

"I'm not," Ally replied.

She repeated the phrases over and over, with Lucy becoming increasingly agitated.

"Let me go, you bitch!" Lucy cried out in a dark tone. "The girl is mine. You're too late—she's already dead. And you will soon join her."

"No." Ally spoke the words louder with an escalating intensity until a burst of icy air spiraled through the opening and surrounded them.

The cold air didn't just chill them to the bone. It also seemed to invigorate Lucy. The girl rose to her knees and lurched toward Ally, clawing at her skin and hair like a wild animal. Ally tumbled backwards, and Lucy pounced on her, tearing at her clothes and skin.

"I'll kill you," Lucy cried. "I won't wait a minute longer. She's mine!"

"No, Lucy!" Ally threw up her arms in defense, but the girl relentlessly clawed her way toward Ally's face and neck.

In the struggle, Ally reached for her backpack and pulled out the knife she'd just used on Nora's palm. She lifted it but paused.

Nora held her breath. Would she really use it on Lucy, even in self-defense? The thought sent a shiver down her spine, but Ally released her grip on it a moment later. The knife fell, clanking against the rocks beneath their feet.

Nora jumped forward a moment later and grabbed Lucy's wrists, trying to force her way between them. "Lucy! Stop!"

At the same time, Lucy stopped moving. Convulsions shuddered through the girl's little body. Her mouth dropped open, and her eyes rolled back into her head.

Nora glanced down. Lucy's wrist was bloody—not with her own blood, but with Nora's. It had come from the cut on Nora's palm. She'd pressed the bloody pendant against the girl's skin during the struggle to restrain her. Had that interaction broken the demon's hold on her?

A bristling energy filled the air, and it sent a wave of terror sweeping through Nora's body.

A thick black substance ejected from Lucy's gaping mouth. Instead of splashing across the ground, it streamed into the air above them and floated like a living, inky black cloud.

When it left her, Lucy collapsed into Nora's arms.

Nora scooped her up and cradled her while pleading to the darkness, "Oh, Lucy, please don't die!"

The shadow form coalesced into something almost solid and stood upright in front of them. Instead of returning to Lucy, the demon hovered in front of Nora.

"Take me!" Nora screamed. "What are you waiting for? Just end this!" Nora rocked Lucy in her arms, trying to wake the girl without success. She whispered into the girl's ear, "Lucy, honey, please wake up. Please wake up."

Ally recovered slowly, and her hands shook as she picked up the crucifix and held it in front of them. "I offer the blood of the covenant to be transferred to Nora now, in this place. She fulfills the claim of our mother, Claire Vale."

Nora stared into her daughter's soft face, knowing it might be the last time she laid eyes on her.

Throughout it all, the demon didn't move. It didn't take her. What was it waiting for? Instead, it backed away and cowered silently in the shadows.

For a long moment, it seemed as if time had stopped. The air paused. Nothing moved. Until another looming figure emerged from the edge of the pit. It came through the opening and took shape beside them like the other one. But this one was different. It was larger, with horns that curled back into the darkness and hollow pits for eyes. Its putrid skin folded and twisted into place over a thick, black cloud.

Nora couldn't look away. It commanded her attention. The ground shook beneath the weight of its desolation. A warm stench came with it, filling the air with the sickening smell of rotting flesh and sulfur. Fire followed the dark figure, but the flames stopped near the cavern's opening. The tendrils seemed to rise and lash out toward her, as if daring her to cross the threshold.

This was Moloch. The demonic figure Lucy had drawn in crayon so many times. The one she had envisioned as surrounded by a sea of flames. Ezeran had done his job, delivering the sacrifice as promised, and now its master would have his way.

Nora gently lowered Lucy to the ground, moved away from her, and cried out, "End it!"

It didn't react. Instead, it stared back at Nora with judgment and hate. Its empty sockets held a burning glow that radiated from somewhere within its infinite void. Staring deeper, the source of the glow became clear—a river of molten souls. The sockets whistled like the pit itself. No, not whistles—endless screams of the damned.

Without warning, a churning cloud of darkness pierced Nora's mouth like a dagger, filling her throat, her lungs, and spreading through every cell of her being. Her skin, her nerves, the air she breathed—everything was on fire as it seemed to consume her with a raging intensity.

The air fell silent, and then soon filled with the endless screams of the damned. Their torment was deafening.

She fought to keep her eyes open, if only to get one last look at her daughter before it took her life. The demon wouldn't allow it. It held her in place, binding her very soul to the stones around them. They were one, and her flesh was no match for

Moloch's nightmarish intentions. It could do whatever it wanted with her—and it would. She was sure of that.

Darkness filled her vision, but gasping in a breath, she cried out, "Take me now."

It did.

The force knocked Nora back, and Lucy rolled out of her grasp. Nora's head landed on a pile of rubble. Pain flared through her mind.

The darkness took hold of her arms and lifted her into the air, carrying her high above her sister and daughter.

"Nora!" Ally called out.

But there was nothing anyone could do. At least Lucy was safe.

Smoky tendrils slipped around her throat and tightened. Her air cut off, and the pain swelled. The threat of eternal darkness seemed inevitable now. The transfer had worked.

She could only think of her mother and the desperation she must have felt to go this far to save Nora's life in the womb. Her mother had acted out of love, but without consent or choice. She'd failed to consider the consequences of her actions. It was doomed from the start.

Tess had made the same mistake, trying to forcefully sacrifice Lucy to save Eve. The offering had to be made voluntarily.

Nora had gotten it right—a willing sacrifice out of love for Lucy.

That made all the difference.

And now, it was over.

Until the demon's voice boomed in her face. "I reject."

It dropped her.

She landed on the floor of the pit, but her body kept rolling, pushed by some unseen force toward the opening in the corner. Every muscle burned with pain. The darkened hole appeared like the gaping mouth of a giant now, its jagged edges becoming teeth ready to devour her. She was powerless to stop herself from sliding forward. The force propelled her through the opening and swallowed her up before she could even let out a scream. She hit her head on the stones as she passed through, and stars filled her vision. Gasping for breath, she tumbled and fell for what seemed an eternity.

Darkness filled her vision, and a loud ringing sound filled her ears. She flailed within the chaos, trying to grasp something—anything—on her way down. The demon, the quarry, Ally and Lucy—it all faded away.

When she stopped moving, she found herself lying in near-total darkness on a stone surface. The only bit of light came from somewhere far above her, and the cool air flowed around her. Judging by the sound of rocks and dirt crashing against a surface far below, she hadn't reached the bottom—she'd landed on the edge of the abyss.

Pain flared in her right leg. She'd landed on it in the fall, but nothing had snapped. Maybe she hadn't broken it, but something had twisted sharply. It throbbed when she moved it, so she kept it straight.

Through it all, she had somehow still held on to her mother's pendant. A vision flashed through her mind as she squeezed it in her bloody palm: a woman screaming in a hospital bed, a whispered prayer over a swollen belly, fingers clutching a stone slab as she stood before the incinerator's flames. And then her mother's voice echoing in a desperate plea.

"Please save my unborn child. I'll give anything."

❧ 36 ❧

Ally gasped at the sight of her sister tumbling away into the darkness. Every muscle in her body stiffened, and she lurched forward to stop the inevitable, but it happened too fast.

She was too late.

The demon had moved too quickly, and Ally had failed to calculate its response. How could she have known it would reject Nora? Why would it refuse? It made no sense. Nora was a willing sacrifice, born of their mother's bloodline, and she had offered herself without fear. The questions tore at her heart and mind. She'd made a terrible mistake, and now Nora was paying for it.

The plan had always been to coax the demon out of Lucy and turn its attention toward someone else—Nora. She was stronger than Lucy, willing and able to bear the agonizing process long enough for Ally to close the covenant another way. The possession *should* have taken more time.

So what had gone wrong?

Staring into the opening at the edge of the pit where her sister had disappeared, she froze. She couldn't breathe. Nora was gone.

The hulking mass of shadows churned with delight. He

seemed pleased with her reaction, relishing it in some twisted way. "Do you understand now? I will take what I want."

Gasping in a broken breath, she let out an agonized cry—all her emotions, fear, and pain were knotted up in that one burst of air. It was all she could do to hold herself together.

The thing turned its attention back to Lucy.

Ally snapped back to reality, forcing herself to move, to jump forward and get between them. Her mind raced to remember the lines of the ritual that might stop it—anything to slow its progress.

"No!" she cried. "Nora is a willing sacrifice within the bloodline. You can't reject her."

The twisted form laughed. Its voice rumbled through her, through the air, through her body.

"You dare to tell me what I can accept?"

"The covenant—it's complete with Nora. The bloodline flows from mother to daughter. Lucy isn't next in line. Nora is."

"A life for a life. One for another. They are never the same."

Its words echoed through Ally's mind. That's what she had gotten wrong—Nora was the beneficiary of her mother's covenant. She couldn't also be the sacrifice.

The thing continued toward her, toward Lucy. She braced herself for the worst. She had seen what it could do and scrambled to block its view of Lucy. On the way, her foot hit the side of her backpack. She nearly stumbled over it but knocked the contents across the blanket. The knife rolled out. Her phone's light reflected off its glistening blade.

Ally instinctively scooped it up, held it up defensively, and screamed again. "If you won't take Nora, then you must accept me. I claim the covenant—fully."

It stopped. Its shifting form hovered silently in front of her. The bristling energy scratched at her skin like a million tiny fingernails. It could have overwhelmed her in that moment. It could have done anything it wanted. At least she had delayed it a bit. That would give her time to think. But for how long?

The thing seemed to contemplate her now.

Ally continued, "You can't reject me like you did Nora. I'm a willing vessel, and my blood—"

Ally slashed the knife across her palm. The blood came swiftly, dripping down over her wrist as she held out her palm toward the demon.

"My blood. It runs freely, just as it did for my mother decades ago when she made the covenant. I've sealed the claim. It's over. Now you have no choice."

"We will see."

The demon thrust forward, pressing its face against hers. A tendril burst from its mouth like a spear and sank down her throat. It took her breath away. Gasping for air, she gagged and choked, powerless to stop its intrusion. Her mouth, lungs, and nostrils filled with the stench of sulfur and ash. Hellish heat came with it, burning her alive from the inside as it made its way down her throat and into her stomach.

Ally resisted, desperately trying to lead the demon away from Lucy, knowing what she had done was irreversible. She had given herself willingly. This had been her decision, but the will to protect Lucy pushed her forward.

A million thoughts and sensations flooded her mind—not her own. Twisted images of unforgiving hate, burning rage, selfishness, greed... evil. The demon's dark essence consumed her mind all at once. It was anchoring itself into her like it had with Lucy, except this time, there would be no one to stop it.

No one to save her.

Stumbling backward, she forced herself to stay upright only inches from Lucy. The thing continued its push forward toward the girl. Maybe it still had plans for the girl, in some twisted way. To possess them both?

Its voice echoed through her mind. *I will take what I want.*

Her arms and legs still worked, but barely. Within moments, it would debilitate her. Dark clouds filled her vision. The world as she knew it shifted and fell away. She could still see her surroundings, but everything was wrong. She saw what it saw and held its perspective. Its nightmarish thoughts became her own. Little by little, she was slipping away.

She didn't have long. It would complete the possession within minutes at that rate. And after it was done, it would play with her, torture her, and use her to kill the others.

Lucy. Nora.

It planned to burn them alive in the quarry's incinerator before forcing Ally to launch herself headfirst into the mouth of the beast like Tess had done.

They would all burn. This was the price to pay for their mother's transgressions. No bargaining, no forgiveness, no mercy. Their bodies turned to ash. Forever.

The images Lucy had drawn with crayons months earlier flashed through her mind—the towering demon surrounded by smoke and fire, while a young girl knelt adoringly before it.

This was her future—events that would come to pass. Their mother had opened the door, but the demon would close it—not Ally. It had planned everything. And there was no escape.

Ally fought to move away from Lucy. The greater the distance between them, the better. She trudged several feet before stumbling again, catching herself just before losing her balance. If she toppled over, she wouldn't have the energy to get back up.

All she could do now was stand against it. Resist. Defy its will.

"It's hopeless," it grumbled without emotion.

Its thoughts pierced her mind clearly. She knew them intimately—and it sickened her. *Terrified* her. The gates of Hell had opened wide in her mind, and something evil was pushing her toward them.

"Accept your fate," it ordered. "There is no hope."

Taking another step away from Lucy, Ally caught sight of her sister's face. For a moment, joy swept through her, but the demon swallowed it as quickly as it surfaced. Nora was crawling out of the opening, inches at a time, clawing at the stones with her fingertips. Blood flowed down her face from a source somewhere along her hairline. She was gasping for breath as she struggled to glance up.

Her eyes reflected horror as she met Ally's gaze.

"Ally!" Nora screamed. "No! Oh, God! What have you done?!"

Ally grinned.

She couldn't help it. Her expression wasn't her own. That thing inside her stretched her mouth impossibly wide with perverse satisfaction.

The demon let out a guttural moan. "You've returned for more." The sickening sound shook every cell in Ally's body.

Nora's eyes welled up with tears. Dragging herself forward, she collapsed at the edge of the opening. She was crying, but she had survived. If she could just grab Lucy and get the girl up the rope somehow... But how long could Ally resist the demon's possession? The last spark of her will was nearly extinguished.

Glancing back, Ally stared into Lucy's solemn face—perhaps for the last time. Her face was pale, and she lay unconscious on the ground near the blanket they'd laid out for the ritual. At least she was still breathing.

Moloch had latched itself onto her soul, burrowing itself deeper with every passing second. It delighted in her pain, but it hadn't consumed her yet. Was she embracing a ray of hope?

The demon shouted in her mind. *No, none of you will survive.*

"Run," Ally cried through a strained, cracking voice that was no longer hers. "Take Lucy and run!"

Nora lifted her head and shook it. The tears had left trails down her cheeks. "I can't."

"You have to. I can't hold it..."

Nora wobbled and struggled to rise, but her legs... The blood —the damage—was worse than Ally had imagined. As she moved forward a few more inches, Ally noticed Nora's ankle—it was twisted at the wrong angle. Broken.

How would she climb the rope? Lucy couldn't do it by

herself. Nora collapsed again, only a few feet from where she had emerged from the hole.

The demon's thoughts flooded her awareness. It wouldn't be long now. Ally's dreams, emotions, and personality faded into the background. The damp stone walls of the pit around her caught her attention. This place had become their tomb, like so many victims before them.

She wasn't the first. The demon's history became her own. They'd almost merged into one. This was how it had always been. The demon thrived there. Its history flashed in front of her, all laid out like a movie—thousands of lives lost over thousands of years. Death and decay had passed through here countless times. Sacrifices. Rituals. Tragedies. The stone had drawn the curious and desperate for generations. All of them had suffered the same fate—betrayal.

Their voices cried out from below—up through the opening. She stared into the darkness. Their cries filled her ears—agonized screams, pain like nothing she'd ever heard.

It invigorated the demon.

It drove it to ecstasy.

And it broke her heart.

That's what it wanted. Her broken heart. Her surrender.

But it hadn't fully possessed her. Not yet.

That was it.

Sacrifice.

The way out. Maybe not for her, but for Nora and Lucy. She could end her mother's covenant in only one way. Something the demon couldn't control—couldn't possess.

Self-sacrifice.

Love.

Her mother's love had created it, and only through sacrificial love would it end.

She could still maneuver, guide her body to some extent. The light was fading. Her mind was dropping away. Despite the relentless, inevitable possession overtaking her, she stumbled toward the opening. There were only a few moments left.

"This vessel is yours," she cried. "The covenant is closed. But you won't have my heart. My soul. You can't break it. So let's send you back home."

With the last of her strength, she pushed forward to the edge of the pit and wavered before the opening. An icy wind rushed out like a breath trying to push her back.

Through the demon's vision, she could see the maze of ancient caverns below. The earth sloped just below the opening and jutted out a bit, forming a ledge. Nora must have landed there. It had saved her, but beyond that... just an endless void. Nothing to stop her fall.

A moment of clarity flashed through her mind. With the demon bound to her, it couldn't escape. It couldn't crawl free into another body or abandon her at will. She'd become its vessel, and they were bound by the covenant until it consumed her one way or another.

Struggling to maintain control of her body and her thoughts for just a moment longer, she realized that the pit wasn't simply a place where the demons lived, but a conduit leading back to the source of something much darker. If she fell into the abyss, she could drag the thing in with her, cutting it off from the world forever. This was how she could end it.

From somewhere behind her, Nora let out an impassioned plea. "Ally, no!"

Ally glanced over at her sister one last time and forced a smile. It was the best she could do.

Nora looked so terrified in that moment. So heartbroken.

But it was the only way.

She gathered every ounce of strength and charged forward. Moloch fought back, flooding her senses with agonizing pain, as if every muscle and bone had burst into flames. Its rage surged through her veins as it tried to shut her down. It wasn't done with her yet. It wanted more—much more—but she had robbed it of its prize.

And Ezeran erupted as the binding unraveled. He couldn't flee this time—couldn't escape to another vessel. Instead, he was bound to follow his master back to the gates of hell.

With the last spark of her identity fading away, she launched herself over the edge, plummeting into the void. Her heart raced with fear at first, then joy.

The covenant was sealed.

❧ 37 ❧

For a long time, nothing happened.

Nora had dragged herself back up the piles of stone and earth to reach the opening. She'd pushed herself as far as she could go, climbing toward Lucy with every bit of her strength, moving away from the edge of the abyss behind her. Her elbows and chest scraped the ground until they throbbed with pain.

Only her left leg worked properly. Her injured right leg had gone numb. Every muscle burned, and her head throbbed. The darkness seemed the greatest obstacle. It pressed down on her from all sides as she lay exhausted on the rubble, while the damp air filled her lungs.

Despite all the pain, she couldn't shake her last memory of Ally. It flashed through her mind over and over. Her sister had intentionally thrown herself through the opening, charging head-first into the darkness while clearly wrestling to fend off the demon's control in the last throes of her life.

Nora's heart shattered.

Ally was gone.

The thing hadn't taken over Ally completely at the end. Her sister's eyes were still clear when she'd glanced over in that last moment before hurling herself through the opening. The last spark of her sister had come shining through in the end. She'd known what she was doing.

She'd sacrificed herself for them.

And then a rush of air had trailed her through the opening. An icy wind had sucked the dark energy in that place down to the bottom of the cavern. She'd taken it with her.

A silence had filled the air for just a moment until a crash had echoed up through the opening. She'd hit the bottom. And then again... silence.

Nora had shuddered in that moment. The sound had reverberated through her soul. Curled forward, she'd cried for a long time. The mental images and emotions were crippling. It would take years to process it all.

But within the heartbreaking shock of Ally's absence, the silence and solitude had given her time to recover physically and refocus her attention on the present.

Lucy still needed her.

With renewed strength, Nora moved forward.

Until Lucy's sweet voice pierced the darkness.

The girl was mumbling something and crying. The words were slurred, but it was *her*. In her normal voice.

The phone's screen still illuminated the area in flashlight mode, but it was angled away from them. Still, it provided enough light for Nora to get a glimpse of her daughter. The girl's eyes were open, and she was wiping away tears, sniffing every few seconds. The sight of Lucy doing anything normal sent joy flooding through her heart.

Clutching at the rocks around her, Nora dragged herself closer to Lucy. The stones cut into the underside of her chest and arms, but she inched forward, a little at a time. Her leg throbbed, sending waves of pain surging through her brain every few seconds.

But it didn't matter. They were safe. She could feel it in the air. That thing was gone. Lucy had returned.

Somehow, Ally had defeated it.

"Lucy," Nora said in a raspy voice, the sound barely louder than her breath.

Lucy turned and met her gaze. "Mom?"

Just hearing Lucy's natural voice again sent another wave of joy surging through Nora.

"I'm here," Nora whispered.

Lucy rose to her feet slowly. Her gaze darted around the area. She was clearly shaken and confused, standing in the damp stillness for a few seconds before lumbering over and dropping beside Nora with a sigh.

"Mommy," Lucy said, "my head hurts."

Nora managed to lift her arm and wipe the hair out of Lucy's face. "We'll get out of here, honey... somehow. Can you please grab my phone?"

Lucy nodded, reached down, and grabbed it. The beaming screen's flashlight mode flooded Lucy's face with light. Color had returned to the girl's skin. Her eyes were clear but red with tears.

Accepting it, Nora switched it back into normal mode to check the signal again. Still no bars.

Her stomach dropped. How would they call for help? In their rush to save Lucy, they had failed to plan a way to get back to the surface. Going down the rope was easy. Ally had done most of the heavy lifting. Like Daniel, she had done some climbing over the years. But getting back up...

Nora followed the rope up to the opening above them. A few stars were visible through the small opening. The twinkling lights seemed almost magical, a refreshing connection to the outside world. Their exit wasn't that far away, but neither she nor Lucy could make that climb alone. The nauseous sinking feeling in her stomach expanded to fill her body.

What were they going to do now?

Lucy's eyes widened. "What's wrong, Mommy?"

Nora struggled to calm the rising panic in her mind. "We have to find a way out, honey."

Lucy cuddled up beside Nora and turned her attention to the

pit's only exit above them. "How did we get down here? I don't remember coming down here."

"We climbed," Nora answered. "You were... asleep."

"Asleep," Lucy repeated. "That's weird. Why would I come down *here*? It stinks."

"We came to finish something important, honey," Nora said gently while stroking Lucy's back. "We'll find a way out, I promise."

Sinking further into Nora's embrace, Lucy rubbed her eyes. "I remember Aunt Ally was here." She glanced around. "She's not here anymore."

"She had to leave," Nora said softly.

Lucy frowned, and a wave of deep emotional pain flashed across the girl's face. The tears welled up again in her eyes. Within seconds, they started flowing down her cheeks. "Did she die?"

Nora nodded. "She saved us."

She pulled Lucy closer, embracing the girl against the side of her body. Despite the chilly air, Lucy's skin was damp but warm.

Lucy wiped away the tears with the back of her hand and shook her head. "I never want to come back here."

"We won't," Nora said. "I promise. We'll never come back. Not in a million years."

The phone's screen went dark, plunging them into darkness. Lucy shuddered and tensed until Nora returned the phone to flashlight mode. The battery had drained down to twenty-three percent. How long would that last? They had to get out of there, but... how? Someone would find the car parked up there—eventually—but that might take days. Daniel would still be in the hospital. She hadn't told him their plans to save him the added stress. Now, she regretted that decision.

Was this the demon's plan all along? To trap them down there forever with all the other poor souls entombed in that place?

Lucy's voice broke Nora out of her thoughts. "I felt it go. It was pulling me... everything—my insides... out. And then it stopped. It hurt, Mommy."

Nora squeezed her daughter. There was no amount of comfort she could offer to erase the trauma Lucy had endured. All they could do now was to work through the pain and wait for it to fade away with time. "I'm sorry, honey. You won't ever have to go through that again."

The papers that Ally had brought along lay scattered across the ground. The wind had stirred them in every direction, although now, nothing moved.

Just as the pit seemed to have taken its last breath, a sound came from above. Nora looked up. A figure stood silhouetted in the opening. She couldn't make out the face, but judging by the silhouette, it was someone with a cast on their arm.

Daniel.

"Nora?" he called out. "Are you okay?"

Another figure came up beside him, and then another. The sound of police radios grew louder and echoed through the pit. Flashlights beamed down at them. Powerful flashlights. He'd brought help.

"We're fine," Nora called out. But "fine" seemed wrong in that moment with Ally gone. She burst into tears. She couldn't help it.

He let out a relieved laugh. "I thought I'd find you here. We'll get you out."

More rescuers arrived. They were preparing to take action, to lower someone down.

Daniel stayed near the opening and continued, "Do you know, I tried to call and text you for hours? After you didn't answer, I knew your phone was dead, or the signal had dropped. Not too many places you could go where that happens."

Nora laughed and wiped away tears of joy. "You know me so well."

Daniel finally stepped out of sight when a rescuer started lowering himself into the pit. Nora grabbed Lucy's attention and gestured to the loose papers on the ground, along with the other items sitting on the blanket Ally had laid out. "Lucy, honey, can you do me a favor? Can you pick everything up before they arrive? I'd rather not have them see this."

Lucy nodded and began to gather the papers, although it didn't really make much difference. The police would probably search their backpacks. They'd trespassed on private property, after all, and the police would have a ton of questions. *Why was she there? Why had she brought along her daughter? Was she on drugs? Why had she brought along ritualistic objects?* And the question she dreaded: *How had her sister fallen into the cavern below?* That question would haunt her until the day she died.

She didn't fall, Officer. She voluntarily threw herself off the edge. To end our mother's covenant with the demonic forces that exist here.

She couldn't tell the truth. Not even a little. A simple explanation would have to do.

She slipped.

Lucy stuffed the papers she'd found into Ally's backpack and then presented an object she'd found on the ground near them. "What's this, Mommy?"

The pendant.

Nora hadn't let go of it throughout her struggle to get back to the surface, but she'd dropped it soon after that. Why hadn't she left it behind? She stared at it for a moment, then accepted it into the same palm Ally had cut earlier with the knife while attempting to transfer the claim.

This is what her mother had left behind during the covenant's ritual to save Nora's life, whether intentional or by accident. It looked so insignificant now compared to what they'd lost in exchange for it.

Ally's life.

Her mother had saved Nora from dying in the womb, but the demon had claimed Ally in return.

"Was it worth it, Mom?" Nora whispered.

Letting the pendant slip from her fingers, it hit the stone

floor with a soft clink. Lucy watched it fall and then stared up into Nora's eyes. "What is it, Mommy? Don't you want it?"

Nora shook her head. "It belongs here."

Lucy pushed up against Nora again and shivered. "It's cold. I want to go home."

"We will, honey. It won't be long now. Help is on the way."

Squeezing Lucy's hand, Nora whispered into her ear, "I will never, ever let you go again in my life."

Lucy squeezed back and smiled. "I like that."

38

Despite their injuries, Nora, Daniel, and Lucy had attended Father Tony's funeral service. He was laid to rest in the small cemetery behind his church, not far from where they'd gathered with him beneath an oak tree months earlier to bury the stone statue. They hadn't stayed long, but Nora had wanted to honor him in some way. Just being present in that moment warmed her heart, watching his parishioners grieve and pay tribute to a man who had made a difference in their lives too. Maybe they understood, like she did, the value of his devout service, even though his most important work had gone unnoticed.

Ally's memorial happened only two days later. It was quieter, but no less devastating. There was no body to bury, just the memories spoken aloud and a sadness that settled over the handful of attendees. A few of Ally's college classmates had stopped by, along with some cousins Nora hadn't seen since she was a child. It was a comfort to see her extended family, and their emotional support helped.

Lucy had clutched Nora's hand through it all, but the girl stood tall and seemed to draw strength from the love Ally had left behind.

Nobody had walked out with dry eyes. Father Tony and Ally had been their anchors. With both of them gone, they had lost their guidance and protection—and a piece of their hearts—but Nora was sure that none of them would ever forget their sacrifice.

The day after Ally's memorial service, Nora found herself in Ally's old apartment—the apartment they now called their home —going through some of her sister's possessions. The process of sorting through everything she'd left behind was painful but necessary.

She opened a box marked simply "Books," and inside found a pile of Ally's notebooks. Not the ritual ones, but the ones she'd used in college. Ally had kept everything from her classes—notes on demons, covenants, and that sort of thing. Everything she had studied, archived in her meticulous way. Just like their father, Ally had kept things for no reason at all.

It had taken everything out of them to adjust after losing Ally. They had moved into the apartment because they had nowhere else to go. The house hadn't burned down completely, as Nora had initially feared. No collapsed roof, no total loss—but it wasn't livable, at least until the repairs were finished using insurance money. There had been extensive smoke damage, waterlogged walls, and the contractors had said it would take months to restore.

Until then, they would stay at the parlor and make do.

They had grabbed the essentials from the house, but they didn't need much. Ally had plenty of necessities stocked in the apartment—enough to get them by.

Moving back into the apartment was bittersweet. The place where Nora had grown up had now become a time capsule of her sister and parents' old lives. The smell of their father's menthol cigarettes sometimes drifted through the air, reminding Nora of her family's past. Ally had done wonders to clear it away during her stay there, but the smell seemed to live behind every wall. At least, the place wouldn't be their permanent home.

Some things they'd stumbled across, she'd rather not think about again. But she was here for at least a few months, and it would take time to clean it all out—the things they no longer needed, the things that no longer mattered.

Going through Ally's belongings was heartbreaking. She had saved all her birthday cards Nora and her parents had given her over the years. Every single one of them was there in a box labeled simply "Cards," all mixed in with souvenirs and mementos from family excursions.

They needed space, so the spare bedroom would become Lucy's room as soon as they cleared it out. Everything had to go, either into storage or into the parlor's back room, at least until they figured things out. But some things Nora couldn't just stuff away in a closet. Some boxes she found were treasure troves of memories. And those she refused to part with.

Nora closed the box containing Ally's old notebooks and taped it shut before moving on to the next one. She would keep it for now and reevaluate its worth later. There was simply too much to keep everything. The decisions would be difficult, but she couldn't do it now.

Crossing the room, Nora paused in front of a narrow bookcase beside Ally's old bedroom door. Her sister had always kept her things thoughtfully arranged, even when the rest of her life was in chaos. One book stood out among the others—a journal. Nora opened it and flipped through the pages. Her sister had kept a diary for the last few years, just as her mother had. Nora hadn't even known about it.

She stopped at one entry.

Nora called today. I always sleep better when she calls.

Nora stopped reading. She would start crying if she read another word. Maybe she could skim through it again later.

Placing the diary back on the shelf, she stepped into what used to be Ally's bedroom—now it would belong to her and Daniel. They had already brought in a fresh mattress. Sleeping on Ally's old mattress just felt... wrong. They'd cleared out most of Ally's old items—her clothes and any photos that had no connection to their family.

Sitting on the edge of the bed, Nora glanced around at the empty walls. They hadn't brought over any of their framed photos yet from the house. It wasn't necessary—not if they were just going to move out again in a few months—but they would need to fill the space with something meaningful. New photos? Just something to distract from all the painful memories that echoed from every wall and corner. Every little thing in that place reminded her of Ally, of their father, of their mother.

It was too painful to stay in the long run. She could handle a few months—but she could never live there again. That much was certain.

Daniel came in a moment later and stood in the doorway. He glanced around before asking quietly, "How are you doing?"

Judging from his tone, she knew what he meant. *How are you really doing—dealing with the loss of your sister?*

"It's not easy," she said.

"I'm sure it isn't," he replied. "I know she meant a lot to you. I won't force you to get rid of anything, you know. We can keep it all if you want. We can even keep the parlor running, keep the business going—"

"No," Nora cut in, shaking her head. "My family's business needs to end. I've been thinking about it a lot. We should sell the parlor when the house is repaired. And when we leave here, we leave for good."

He didn't respond at first. He was digesting her words, glancing at the floor and nodding slowly.

"I need to go back to school," she continued. "Like I always said I would. You said it was about time, anyway."

"We don't need to make any decisions right now," he said gently.

"It's okay. I think it's the right thing to do. The right time."

He nodded once. "We'll move in that direction then. But if

you change your mind, I won't object. I know this place means a lot to you."

"It does," she said. "But I'm just not sure I want to do this anymore."

He nodded slowly again. "We can think about it some more later."

Just then, Lucy came in cradling Blanco in her arms. She stepped around Daniel and moved gracefully toward the bed with Blanco purring.

"Blanco is my best friend." She squeezed him gently, brushing her cheek against his fur.

Nora smiled. "I'm sure you have plenty of friends at school."

"I have some," she said, "but he's my best."

She sat on the bed beside Nora and stroked Blanco's fur, gently scratching him behind the ears. He purred and soaked up the attention like a spoiled child.

"I know what you're thinking." Lucy glanced up.

Nora met her gaze. "What am I thinking?"

"That Aunt Ally might be a ghost now... that we might see her sometimes if we stay here."

Ironically, Nora *had* considered that, though she hadn't mentioned it to anyone. Maybe there was a little psychic in the girl after all.

Nora answered calmly, "No. I wasn't thinking that at all. Your Aunt Ally is in a better place now. She won't come back. She won't haunt us."

"I hope she does," Lucy said. "I'd like to say goodbye."

Nora swept her arm around her daughter, and Daniel stepped forward too, sitting opposite Lucy on the bed. The three of them crowded in against Lucy, snuggling her in their arms while she continued to pamper Blanco in her lap.

"We don't always get the chance to say goodbye," Daniel said. "We should try to say everything now, if it's important—before they're gone. But I'm sure your mother is right about Ally. She's in a better place. And we'll all get to see her again someday... on the other side."

"I know we will," Lucy said quietly, "but I still miss her."

"I miss her too," Nora said. "But we won't bother Aunt Ally anymore—in the afterlife. We should focus on what we have now. On those around us... and our future."

As Nora spoke, something caught her attention in the doorway. She glanced over and froze.

There, just for a moment, stood Ally.

She was smiling softly, not trying to speak or catch Nora's attention. She looked peaceful, just the way she used to before everything went wrong. Her hair was loose, her face relaxed, her eyes clear. She wasn't hurt or sad, or afraid.

Nora looked away, glancing down at Lucy—whose gaze had also stopped at the doorway.

When Nora looked back up, Ally was gone.

Maybe Ally had heard them on some level, felt them talking about her, and had come to let them know everything was all right, that things were okay between them now.

Nora closed her eyes and leaned into her daughter again. Daniel did the same from his side, squeezing Lucy in the middle until she laughed and wiggled out.

"Okay, okay!" She giggled. "You're going to smush me—I can't take it anymore!"

Daniel stood, kissed Nora's forehead gently, then turned to go.

"Whatever we do," he said from the doorway, "whatever you decide, I'll support you."

Nora smiled. "That's all I ever wanted."

He walked out of the room, leaving Lucy standing in front of Nora. The girl held a curious expression.

"Is something wrong?" Nora asked.

Lucy glanced at the doorway again, then turned back to her mother. "Did you see her too, Mommy?"

Nora hesitated—but then nodded. "Yes. I think she wanted to say goodbye."

"I think she just did," Lucy said with a bright smile. "Goodbye, Aunt Ally!"

Blanco darted out of the room, and Lucy ran after him, laughing.

CONTINUE THE THRILLS WITH A PSYCHIC HAUNTED MURDER mystery series, starting with Hanging House Book 1! Available now!

Read more from Dean Rasmussen on Amazon.com!

PLUS, get a **FREE** short story at my website!

www.deanrasmussen.com

★★★★★
Please review my book!

If you liked this book and have a moment to spare, I would greatly appreciate a short review on the page where you bought it. Your help in spreading the word is *immensely* appreciated and reviews make a huge difference in helping new readers find my novels.

The Last Séance: Dark Covenant Series Book 1
The Last Medium: Dark Covenant Series Book 2
The Last Demon: Dark Covenant Series Book 3

Shine House: An Emmie Rose Haunted Mystery Book 0
Hanging House: An Emmie Rose Haunted Mystery Book 1
Caine House: An Emmie Rose Haunted Mystery Book 2
Hyde House: An Emmie Rose Haunted Mystery Book 3
Whisper House: An Emmie Rose Haunted Mystery Book 4
Temper House: An Emmie Rose Haunted Mystery Book 5
Raven House: An Emmie Rose Haunted Mystery Book 6
Amber House: An Emmie Rose Haunted Mystery Book 7

Dreadful Dark Tales of Horror Book 1
Dreadful Dark Tales of Horror Book 2
Dreadful Dark Tales of Horror Book 3
Dreadful Dark Tales of Horror Book 4
Dreadful Dark Tales of Horror Book 5
Dreadful Dark Tales of Horror Book 6
Dreadful Dark Tales of Horror Complete Series

Stone Hill: Shadows Rising (Book 1)
Stone Hill: Phantoms Reborn (Book 2)
Stone Hill: Leviathan Wakes (Book 3)

ABOUT THE AUTHOR

Dean Rasmussen grew up in a small Minnesota town and began writing stories at the age of ten, driven by his fascination with the Star Wars hero's journey. He continued writing short stories and attempted a few novels through his early twenties until he stopped to focus on his computer animation ambitions. He studied English at a Minnesota college during that time.

He learned the art of computer animation and went on to work on twenty feature films, a television show, and a AAA video game as a visual effects artist over thirteen years.

Dean currently teaches animation for visual effects in Orlando, Florida. Inspired by his favorite authors, Stephen King, Ray Bradbury, and H. P. Lovecraft, Dean began writing novels and short stories again in 2018 to thrill and delight a new generation of horror fans.

ACKNOWLEDGMENTS

Thank you to my wife and family who supported me, and who continue to do so, through many long hours of writing.

Thank you to my friends and relatives, some of whom have passed away, who inspired me and supported my crazy ideas. Thank you for putting up with me!

Thank you to everyone who worked with me to get this book out on time!

Thank you to all my supporters!

www.ingramcontent.com/pod-product-compliance
Lightning Source LLC
Chambersburg PA
CBHW021127190726
48288CB00008B/2531